ROAD TO HARM

An absolutely gripping British crime thriller full of twists

JUDITH CUTLER

Fran Harman Mysteries Book 6

Originally published as *Green and Pleasant Land*

JOFFE BOOKS

Revised edition 2024
Joffe Books, London
www.joffebooks.com

First published as *Green and Pleasant Land* by Severn House Publishers Ltd in Great Britain in 2014

This paperback edition was first published in Great Britain in 2024

Cover art by Nebojša Zorić

ISBN: 978-1-83526-696-0

For John and Marion Bench, with love, and to West Bromwich Albion, a team which delights and frustrates in equal measure its army of loyal and dedicated fans.

PROLOGUE

I was driving from Cleobury Mortimer to Bewdley. The twenty-first of January. Any other day I'd have taken the main road — yes, the A road. The A41. But there were a lot of road works where it joins the Tenbury Road, so I thought I'd risk the B roads, although they're much slower, aren't they? But you couldn't go fast anyway, not with all the fog. Although it was supposedly still daylight — about three o'clock in the afternoon — you could hardly see your hand in front of your face, and I kept thinking I ought to turn back. But my aunt — she was nearly eighty — would have been really worried if I didn't go, not when I'd promised. And I'd got a dozen fresh eggs for her.

Anyway, I was picking my way through the forest, and wishing I'd started earlier, because now the light was going too; if I put my head-lights on it didn't really help. So I tried putting them on main beam; that made it far worse. And then I saw this car — one of those big ones, like a young tank — pulled up at the side of the road just past Buttonoak, although there are double white lines down the middle and it's quite dangerous to overtake . . . The forest clears a bit then it thickens up again. It'd be about a mile in — just before the Hawkbatch Valley car park — and I wondered why whoever it was hadn't pressed on another hundred yards. Or, come to that, stopped a few yards back on the other side of the road — Withybed, I think that one's called. Anyway, this big car was parked, and it had its emergency flashers going. I wasn't going to take any notice — I'd actually driven past — but when I looked in the mirror I realized a door was open on the passenger side. The rear one. Don't ask me why I didn't notice before; I suppose I was too busy worrying about pulling on to the wrong side of the road. No, I'd not long passed my test — never needed to drive till my husband died. First husband, that is — he never liked my being independent. I thought how odd it was. And I stopped. I got out and — it was so still and quiet. Everything. As if someone had switched off the sound.

I went round to the driver's side to see if I could help. No one in the driver's seat. But in the back there was a baby strapped into a child seat. I'll swear I knew straight away there was something wrong with it, poor little mite. Something strange about its head. And its poor face. I tried to open the door, but it was locked. So I went round the other side (where the door was open, remember) and peered in. What a mess! There was a sea of toys and crisp packets and goodness knows what else, with another child seat in the middle. I had to put my hand on it to lean across to the baby; it was still just warm. The seat, I mean. And the baby — that was still warm too, but not warm enough. It was as floppy as a rag doll. I'd once been taught CPR, but I couldn't find any pulse. And — yes, I was reluctant to interfere . . . to bring so damaged a child back . . . In any case, it wouldn't have been any good, or that's what they told me later.

So what should I do? I didn't have a mobile or anything, not in those days. Half of me wanted to stay with the baby, for all it was dead. The other half wanted to go for help. But then someone on a Forestry Commission tractor came along, and he'd got a radio and called for help. We just stood there waiting. Neither of us could think of anything to say. So we just stood side by side looking into the woods. That was when I noticed the footprints in the grass.

CHAPTER ONE

'So this is Hindlip Hall,' Mark Turner said, passing between impressive modern walls announcing the fact — the corporate equivalents of gatehouses, but with no gates directly attached to them. 'It's somewhat grander than where we worked in Kent.'

Fran pointed through the streaming passenger door window. 'Did you see that notice? Telling folk they enter at their own risk?'

'What? *Abandon hope all ye who enter here?*'

'Almost. Should we chicken out now? Hey, didn't I read that the place was supposed to be haunted?'

'That would be this building's predecessor,' Mark said. 'Priest's holes and Catholic plotters and such in the first, which burned down. You don't get ghosts in elegant nineteenth-century gentlemen's residences. Or gentlewomen's, for that matter.'

Fran sniffed to show she was rightly ignoring the equal opportunities dig. In his time as Kent's assistant chief constable, Mark had done more than most to promote and support women. He'd never made it to chief constable, and would probably have hated such a managerial position even more than he'd hated being ACC. At least in that post he'd managed to make enough time to be reasonably hands-on in dealing with people and crime as opposed to policy and statistics.

'How on earth did something like this become a police headquarters?' she demanded.

He waited for the security barrier to rise. 'More to the point, how on earth, in the current economic climate, have they managed to hang on to it?'

Fran nodded. 'It's great real estate. I'll bet my teeth someone wanted to sell it off when West Mercia Police merged with Warwickshire. It would make a wonderful high-end hotel — extensive grounds, too.'

'I wonder what it'll be like to work in.' He put the car in motion.

'Do you mean that in the literal sense: will they have made proper office space in what's probably a listed building?' Fran asked, as they peered through the driving rain for the signposts to the car park to which they'd been despatched. 'Or the abstract: being parachuted in to solve another force's unsolved crime?' She pointed. 'It's over there, I think.' By now the rain was bouncing so high it was hard to tell.

'We're hardly being parachuted,' Mark objected, parking as neatly as he could, given that it was impossible to see the white lines between bays. 'We're not enemies invading someone's territory. We came because Gerry Barnes invited us.'

'Invited *you*!'

'But you were part of the deal; he might have asked me first, but you were his choice as lead investigator. Something to do with your solving a few crimes,' he added with a grin.

'He'd never have chosen me for my administrative skills, that's for sure. Or my tact and diplomacy.' As for Fran herself, the very mention of her own likely promotion to ACC had made her grab at overdue retirement with both hands. Admittedly, at the time she'd been on sick leave, needing crutches for even the most trivial errand round the house, but while her leg hadn't been working her mind certainly had and she'd not regretted her apparently impulsive decision for a second.

The windscreen was awash the moment he cut the ignition. 'Shall we wait a few more minutes and hope the rain eases or grab a brolly apiece and make a run for it?' he asked.

'And arrive with no dignity and hair in rats' tails?'

He squeezed her hand. 'And when did you ever worry about dignity, Ms Harman? No longer Detective Chief Superintendent Harman, of course,' he added, anxiety creeping into his voice. Though why should he worry about her? She had natural authority by the bucket-load. 'I've had long enough to get used to being plain Mr Turner, not to mention the times the media called me Mr Harman . . .' With a grin, he squeezed her hand to show he found it amusing, now at least. Back then, however, it had grated. 'But it'll be strange to be civilians in a police world. We'll be neither flesh nor fowl—'

'Nor good red herring,' she concluded for him.

The rain beat more heavily on the car.

'Do you suppose they'll *sir* and *ma'am* us? No, let's be Fran and Mark.'

She squeezed his hand. 'I'd better not call you *sweetheart*.'

'You can call me all the other things in private, though,' he reminded her, with a deep chuckle. 'Look, we could sit here all day waiting for the rain to ease. Let's make a dash for it.' He reached for and passed her an umbrella and her bag before retrieving his own.

'I'll race you!' She was already halfway out of the car.

'In your dreams!'

So no dignity there, and he'd swear she'd cheated. But it was more or less a dead heat, and if anything he was too busy being relieved that her leg had recovered from its injury to make more than a token complaint. Dignity or not, it was time for a quick hug.

Fran and Mark had had a wonderful spring and summer. She'd forced herself to toil through endless physiotherapy sessions and exercise plans so that she could walk up the aisle at their wedding — heavens, she'd even broken into a very swift canter as Mark turned to greet her at the altar. Thereafter they'd had a magic honeymoon in springtime Crete; could you have a honeymoon after living together for so long? You bet your life you could. Then there'd been a summer filled with tennis and gardening and the delights of Mark's grandchildren (hers too now, and she couldn't have loved them more dearly had they had a blood relationship). With the children back in school, autumn had brought more travel.

But she'd sensed in Mark, once the garden was tidied up in readiness for the winter, a restlessness that even building a wonderful 00 railway layout in the loft hadn't been able to assuage. Once she'd detected it in him, she had to admit to herself that perhaps she too lacked an intellectual challenge; certainly she'd missed the team she'd worked with for so many years. She still saw many of them as friends, of course, when they had the time. They cracked the old jokes, referred to her half-puns on her name when she'd reminded them as youngsters to do no harm, or to take care even when putting themselves in harm's way. All good fun. But somehow reliving team fun wasn't the same reliving as team work.

Which now awaited her and Mark.

New year, new challenge.

Having wet hair and soaking clothes was one thing, but she suspected it was quite another to leave wet and muddy footprints on the carpet of the grand entrance hall. Mark dumped their brollies in a bucket already occupied by several others. Then, as one, they headed for the big reception desk, where they were greeted by a laughing woman with a strong Midlands accent. Iris Day, her badge said. 'I've got your IDs here.' She burrowed in a drawer, her face puckering in defeat. 'I've got one for Mr Turner and one for Mrs Turner, but nothing for a Mrs Harman.'

'No problem, Iris: I'd best be Mrs Turner for a bit, hadn't I? But since legally my name's still Harman, maybe you could arrange another one for me? Sorry to put you to extra trouble.'

'It's no trouble at all.' She made a note. Looking up, she added archly, 'So are you really Mrs Turner or are you living in sin?'

Fran responded to the twinkle in the woman's eye rather than the abrupt and old-fashioned question. 'We're living in *Kent*! I'm sort of Mrs Turner in that we're married. But I've been Harman so long I clean forgot I should sign a different name. So now I'll be Fran Harman for the rest of my life.'

'Not a bad name,' Mark added.

The woman put her head on one side. 'So you'll be a Ms on the ID, not a Mrs, won't you? No problem. Unless in these modern times you should be Ms Harperson? Now, if you don't mind my saying, you've still got rain dripping off your hair and on to your nose and your mascara's running riot. There's a ladies' loo just down there — and a gents', Mr Turner. Quite nice but not as Downton Abbey as the rest of this place. Then I'll get someone to take you along to see Mr Webster.'

'Mr Webster?' Mark prompted. 'We were expecting to see Mr Barnes.'

Iris leaned confidentially towards them. 'Not here today. Redundancy, I reckon. With this merger, there'll be a lot of to-ing and fro-ing, you'll see. Anyway, it's Mr Webster, the new assistant chief constable (Crime), who's expecting you. The chief constable's busy.' Even she grimaced at an official faux pas, if not a snub.

Mark nodded: no problem. At least he hoped there wasn't one. Gerry Barnes had brimmed with enthusiasm for the project, promising both a skilled team of serving officers and unlimited back-room support. Would a replacement deliver the same commitment? Without such back-up, their job would be very difficult — and extremely time-consuming. But if anyone was used to police politics, he was, so he must negotiate the best deal he could. He smiled at Iris. 'Just checking: with all these changes, is the chief constable still Andrew Barwell?'

'Of course. No, not of course. He has been for the last six months, but with things the way they are . . . Do you know him?'

'We might have nodded at each other at a few conferences, but that's all. Fran?'

'Wouldn't know him from Adam,' she declared, as she nipped off to the loo, 'though I suppose he might be better dressed.'

She returned to find Mark still waiting for their escort. There was nothing for it but to look around, as if they'd strayed into a National Trust property.

Surely a room like this — what a fireplace! — ought to have been filled with classical statues, not display cases full of truncheons and other constabulary memorabilia. And look at that grand staircase! For the moment, however, they were not to ascend it. They were to follow a pin-thin young woman whose badge identified her as a senior security officer, along the wide corridor that led — inevitably — to the offices of the higher echelons. She knocked at a mahogany door and silently left them to it.

The door opened to reveal a beautiful airy room that was roughly the size of their living room, with Victorian proportions which to Fran's mind were slightly less elegant than those of their newly restored Georgian rectory. She fell into step beside Mark as they approached the desk of the assistant chief constable. Bowed with an age that was probably nearer fifty than forty, and maybe even a couple of years more, he was so nondescript Fran saw him for a moment as Mole, for some reason ensconced in Toad Hall rather than Mole End. The rather vulgar overweight cherubs in some of the heavy gilt frames would certainly have been more at home in Toad's establishment.

'Colin Webster.' He shook their hands with a surprisingly small, very cold hand, before gesturing to comfortable seats facing a big OT screen. Registering with what appeared to be disapproval how damp they were, he switched on a small but welcome heater, the red elements of which made them all glow orange. His hospitality didn't extend to switching on his coffee machine or offering biscuits from a tin beside it.

'Change of plan,' Webster began, as if begrudging the effort of speaking in complete sentences. 'Teething problems after the merger. I gather Gerry Barnes brought you here.'

They could read the crib-sheet on his desk, outlining their qualifications and experience. They'd packed in a lot of both, between them. He didn't seem pleased; perhaps he felt intimidated. 'How do you propose to divide the work?'

'It depends how it needs to be divided, Colin,' Mark parried. 'After all, we've both been on the Review Officers' National Course, though at different times; we're both fully accredited.' Clearly he wasn't about to be patronized by an equal. Ex-equal.

'Of course. Your room is on the floor above this one, though you don't get quite as nice a view.'

Fran couldn't stop herself looking towards the floor to ceiling windows, currently steamed up and revealing nothing more than a cascade from an overflowing gutter.

'When you've got up to speed on the case, I'll allocate resources. Within reason. We're under pressure at the moment—'

'When is a modern force ever not?' Mark asked.

'Worse: we've got a murder in Warwick and an unrelated one in Tamworth.' Webster's face suggested that they were mere administrative inconveniences. 'Your fee—'

'We agreed with Gerry that we'll donate it to the Police Benevolent Fund,' Fran put in. 'All we're claiming is expenses.'

'Expenses?' Panic filled Webster's eyes. Yes, another senior officer driven by budgets. 'I gather you're renting somewhere; you should have been told that there is accommodation available here.'

Gerry had mentioned that. Single accommodation, food supplied by the canteen which closed at five. 'We like our own roof,' Mark said firmly. 'We found a cottage with the fag-end of a rental period left so we got it dirt cheap. Near Ombersley, so it's very convenient.'

Webster ticked a box. Literally. 'You will of course notify HR of any change of address. And car, of course.'

As for the cottage, they'd not actually seen it yet. Having left home soon after four, they'd meant to check in before they started work. However, the traffic was so bad on the rain-drenched M25 that what was usually a three-hour journey had become six and they'd had to come straight to Hindlip.

Webster checked his script again. 'What I want is a simple review of a misper enquiry. Some twenty years ago a young woman and her child went missing in the northern part of the Wyre Forest.'

'That's the district or the ancient woodland?' asked Mark.

'Woodland. You know the area?' Webster looked surprised.

'I took my grandchildren on the Severn Valley Railway in the summer.'

'Oh. Anyway, Natalie Foreman and her son Hadrian went missing here.' He touched his keypad and a map appeared on the screen. 'No sighting dead or alive since.'

Mark snapped his fingers. 'Wasn't there something about a baby too?'

Fran joined in: 'Left in a car? About the time we had that major manhunt in Sandwich and were all working eighteen-hour days,' she added aside to Mark.

'That's another thing. No overtime unless it's absolutely vital, vital to the point of desperate, and I sign it off myself. Personally. Any questions?'

'One thing we'd certainly like to know,' Mark began reasonably, 'is why this case has taken on a sudden urgency. Is there someone in CID we should be talking to?'

The hunted expression returned. 'It's not their bag — drat!' His phone warbled to announce a text. He checked. 'It's the chief's secretary. I'm late for a meeting.' The clear implication was that it was their fault. As he stood he fished a bubble-pack of tablets from his pocket and popped two. He and a strong smell of Gaviscon ushered them from the room. 'Up the stairs. Turn left. The door should be ajar. This is your key code.' He grabbed a scrap of paper and scribbled barely legible numbers.

* * *

'Takes you back, doesn't it, all that stress?' Fran remarked, pushing open the door of their new domain. To judge from its position and dimensions it had probably once been a bedroom for a less important guest. She headed for the window and threw it up. 'A nice view of some kennels — enough to house an entire force's dogs.' With a face full of rain she closed it again. She turned back towards twin desks pushed together so that the occupants would face each other.

'Feng shui,' Mark mused. 'Which would you prefer — back to the door or back to the view?'

'Just to be contrary, I'd turn them round through ninety degrees, so we can both see who's coming through the door.'

He laughed. 'All the time I was in the force, I never met a cop who liked sitting with their back to a door. Or who didn't try to grab a seat at a restaurant table with their back to a wall. Is it part of the DNA? Let's just move these boxes on to the floor.' He peered inside first one, then another. 'There's not a lot in any of them.' He passed them to her; she stacked them in date order along a wall.

As they heaved the desks into position, there was a knock on the door; they turned simultaneously. 'Come in,' they sang in unison.

It was Iris, carrying another cardboard box, which she put, after some hesitation, on a desk. 'Talk about being caught red-handed. Black-handed rather. Look at the pair of you! But what on earth were they doing, giving you furniture this old? They must have dug it out of some store room. And the cleaners haven't exactly exerted themselves, have they?' Iris produced a couple of tissues from her pocket and wiped both chairs, then, less thoroughly, the desk tops. She held up the tissues, grey with dust, triumphantly. 'That's better. Now, I'm on my coffee break so I haven't got more than a minute, but I bet no one's had time to give you a conducted tour. I haven't myself, to be honest. But there is a canteen — just follow the signs.'

'I'm surprised they've still got one.'

'They've closed them at the other major hubs. How about that for a trendy word? And of course, they've shut down loads of police stations. Such a palaver there's been about saving this place. But there's so many working here it'd be hard to relocate them, that I will admit. Over nine hundred. And I for one am not arguing; I only live just down the road. Anyway, I found you a spare kettle and some mugs. There's tea and coffee and little pots of milk here too.' She smiled and headed for the door.

'All this is so kind of you,' Mark said, opening it for her. 'Thank you very much.'

Iris returned his smile, and then looked him up and down. 'They say you were an ACC, but you haven't any side. Not that most of the folk working here have, but you should have met some of the people coming on courses.' Her voice changed almost imperceptibly; before his hearing aids he wouldn't have noticed it. 'Now, my husband used to be in the force, and I reckon you might find him useful. He was on this here cold case of yours when it was still hot, if you follow me.' She checked her watch. 'He'll be in the Bull down in Fernhill at about one. Lovely chips. Ask for Ted Day.' She closed the door behind her.

CHAPTER TWO

'I'd like to know more about the case before we talk to Iris's husband,' Fran said. She took the kettle Mark had filled and plugged it in. The only place for it was the floor.

He looked round for a proper home for it and the crockery mugs, which he inspected gloomily before simply putting them on his desk. 'They don't look very clean.'

'Some departing colleagues probably abandoned them, the way climbers leave detritus on the face of Everest.' She looked and sniffed. Someone — Iris, no doubt — had done their best with bleach, but tea stains were still etched deeply into the glaze.

Mark stared at the jar of coffee. 'Is it worth nipping down to the car and getting the emergency supplies we meant for the cottage? On the other hand . . .' They stared at the rain.

'You know what,' Fran confessed, 'I'm already missing the cake young Tom used to bring in.'

'But we never have cake at home. Blood sugar. Cholesterol.'

'And I don't miss it at home. But the moment I step back on to police property I do. Talk about Pavlov's dogs. Could you hear them, by the way?'

He patted his hearing aids and grinned. 'When you opened the window. All I hear now is rain.'

'Me too.'

Armed with Iris's instant coffee, they sat down opposite each other, instantly in work mode. 'OK, why not talk to this guy Ted? One of the original team? He could point us in all sorts of useful directions.' He added plastic milk. Would he get round to drinking the thin brew? He looked round in vain for a thirsty plant.

'I didn't really want anyone, even little grey Colin, to fill us in on what they were hoping we'd find. You know how you get all this medical research proving things they want us to believe anyway? You've often said they've probably been very selective with their statistics.'

'And you're afraid that we too will find what we're looking for, not necessarily the truth. Good point. So you want us to read through this lot before we break our vow of silence?' There was no doubting his disbelief.

She wrinkled her nose. 'If we just identified our predecessor's main line of enquiry . . . Come on, it's not yet midday. Let's divide it between us and speed-read as much as we can. There's not much, after all. We spend a few minutes putting together our ideas, then we can beard this Ted character in his den . . .'

The door opened as they reached for the first box. Colin Webster, carrying a card file and a notebook and pencil. He clearly noticed the changes they'd made, but didn't remark on them.

'I need a heads up of what you'll need other than manpower.'

Mark almost did a double-take: even an ACC as unassuming as he'd been would never have been a self-appointed office boy. But he managed to reply smoothly, 'Phone. Computer. Screen. Electronic display board. Printer.'

'I'm sure there'll be spare equipment in stock.' He sounded less than confident.

Mark added to his list. 'Waste bin. Table for the kettle and coffee maker.'

'Coffee maker?' Clearly disconcerted, Webster looked around.

'Don't worry, we'll get our own. But we'll need somewhere to put it.'

'Of course. And somewhere for your mugs and so on.'

'More important,' said Mark, lest Fran start to giggle, 'we shall need a room nearby for the team we shall no doubt acquire.'

'I'll ask for a few volunteers to join you.'

'Excellent — a mixture of old heads and thrusting youngsters, hopefully. And not too few of either, please.'

Webster looked at his watch and stood up. 'We'll talk over lunch. Twelve thirty in the canteen.'

Mark said, apparently idly, 'I always used to leave the premises at midday — breathe in a bit of fresh air, stretch the old limbs.'

'I think you'll find it's still raining cats and dogs—'

Mark couldn't stop himself: 'Yes, we heard them—'

'If you want exercise, there's a gym available for staff use, and a regular lunchtime aerobics session in the sports hall.' Suddenly Webster didn't seem like a mild little animal any more. 'Twelve thirty. Oh, and here's a list of the officers working on the case at the time. With current contact details.' He closed the door with a snap.

'So much for meeting Ted Day,' Mark grumbled. 'Though he's right about the weather, and I wouldn't mind checking out the gym.'

'So much for meeting Ted Day this lunchtime,' Fran corrected him. 'But I have an idea those chips will be calling us quite loudly for supper if Iris tells us Ted drinks there in the evenings too.'

* * *

Over their usual midday salads Mark tried to probe rather than be probed. It was clear that Webster wanted the sort of instant judgement that he and Fran knew was impossible. Thwarted, Webster waved over a number of men who might be wearing plain clothes but who were clearly old-school flat-feet. All would obviously have been nearing retirement even in the normal course of events. These days management had worked out that older people earned more than young, so they were clearly heading for the chop. But not yet. They'd been part of the original missing person case and would be delighted to give the incomers the benefit of their wisdom on what had happened to young Natalie Foreman and her kid.

'Mrs Phil Foreman, of course,' said one, sitting heavily opposite Fran. 'A WAG, for heaven's sake. We all know what WAGs are like, all plastic tits and Gucci bags.'

In one acronym a possibly decent woman, probably a dead woman, had been dismissed as an avaricious airhead. Had one of her own team used such a pejorative term, Fran would have made sure they never did again. Here she confined herself to raising an eyebrow.

It still worked. The miscreant dropped his eyes, chuntering something under his breath. She had a suspicion that he wouldn't clamour to join their team.

Mark's voice was super-calm as he said, 'Fran and I are still working through all the files. We really need your help, but I'd hate to waste your time by asking silly pointless questions. Can you help us another lunchtime when we're better prepared?' He looked at his watch. He flashed a glance at Fran, who produced one of her least favourite clichés, and one of her most duplicitous smiles.

'Tomorrow we want to hit the ground running, so we need to spend every minute getting up to speed.' Least favourite cliché number two. Cue for her and Mark to rise as one, even if it meant missing out on coffee. Fran's ears, still sharper than Mark's, caught the C word, but couldn't tell if it applied to her or Natalie. Since the ACC didn't rebuke the user, she could hardly turn round to do so. But she wouldn't forget.

Mark bought a couple of bottles of water on the way out. Webster, who'd caught up with them and might have been about to speak, stopped abruptly as a man and a woman approached.

Mark had more residual respect for hierarchies than Fran had ever possessed in the whole of her career. It was clearly all he could do not to stand stiffly to attention and salute as Webster did when the chief constable, in full uniform, swept past him. Accompanying him was a short woman, very elegant, with a very expensive hairdo, who managed a good stride despite her viciously high heels. Fran nodded, equal to equal. She got a gracious smile in response. Nothing from the chief, who, come to think of it, looked as drained as Webster. Sending Mark on ahead, she nipped down to speak to Iris.

It seemed that the woman was not a local MP — in Fran's experience they could be relied on to reduce even the most braided and macho officer to jelly — but someone even more powerful, the police and crime commissioner, someone elected to oversee policing in his or her area. The idea had been met with pretty universal dismay amongst serving officers, not least because their hundred-thousand-a-year salaries would each have paid five constables' wages. Fran had been as hostile as anyone, but had to concede that while wild rumours flared round many appointments, some commissioners appeared to be earning their salt. This one, Iris told her, was called Sandra Dundy. If anyone could have given her the local view of Dundy it was Iris, of course, but an influx of visitors prevented Fran questioning her.

Mark rolled his eyes when Fran reported back. 'The commissioner? She looked like — OK, what did you make of her?'

'At first glance? She could be just a small woman trying to stand up for herself in a world of tall testosterone-fuelled men. Or equally, a Thatcher-like power-freak making up in ruthless efficiency what she lacks in inches. Let's reserve judgement.'

'Iris's take?'

'She didn't have a chance to tell me. Anyway commissioners aren't our problem. Not like those case papers.'

As Fran had remarked, there'd been remarkably little in the bulky boxes. Surely there was paperwork missing? Was it just bad record-keeping? Or was there a more sinister explanation: something had been removed? Or was it — and mentally she winced — that she and Mark had been away from the job too long and should have stayed in Kent reviewing the progress of their sprouts and cabbages? In the past she'd always juggled too many cases, had had too little time to reflect. Action plans happened on the hoof, not behind a desk. Somehow she needed to generate some familiar adrenalin.

She got to her feet. 'Let's forget everything we've read and heard, and pretend we were on duty when the call came in. It'd be nice to have at least a white board to jot everything on, but in the absence of anything else at least we've got our iPad and our brains.'

Mark laughed. 'You mean literally thinking on our feet? Why not? You lead. I'll type.'

For a moment she put her hands to her temples, as if that would help her visualize what happened, then she touched the notes she'd made to try to bring them to life. 'To the person taking the nine-nine-nine call — a middle-aged woman called Joanne Aitken — it's clearly a report of one, perhaps two, missing persons. She despatches the nearest rapid response team. Or is it as simple as that? She hears there's a dead baby involved. She picks out what she can from the deluge of information and wonders if perhaps it's a suspicious death. So, having called an ambulance just in case there's any hope for the baby, she now sends CID in the form of a DI and a DC out on blues and twos. Well done, Joanne. She's someone I'd like to talk to. She'd add atmosphere to start the narrative, as it were.'

'Just a despatcher? Would you bother in a live case?'

'I suppose not. No, forget that.'

'So if the police vehicles beat the ambulance to it, theoretically the scene should be preserved from the outset.' He checked his own notes and pulled a face. 'The first officers arrive rather later than current target response-time guidelines would require. CID are really very slow. They get there several minutes after the ambulance. But they all have to deal with thick fog. Everyone makes that point. The woman who called in the incident is definite that visibility is very bad indeed. Marion Roberts. Another one to talk to.'

'This is her witness statement: it's written down by an officer, of course, but she's had a go at it herself, correcting spelling and punctuation.' She waved it at him. 'She's adamant the baby was dead when she made her call. She also said that it wasn't just a normal healthy baby. She could tell that from outside the car. There were problems with its hands — she's very specific about that — and its face was deformed. The paramedics confirmed all that and agreed that there was nothing they could do. One of the paramedics suggested the child was suffering from some obscure syndrome. Have you come across the PM reports yet?'

'Nope. Now, I've got the report from CID here: Mrs Roberts insists that the child seat beside the baby's was warm when she arrived. The Forestry Commission worker she flagged down says the Range Rover engine was still warm too, and that the key was still in the ignition.'

'Did they try calling out: *Hello, anyone there?* That sort of thing?'

Mark frowned. 'They must have done, surely. Except that fog does funny things to you, doesn't it? Like making you drive faster and faster because you're desperate to be able to see again — at least that's what some psychologists say. Perhaps they tried. There's nothing in Mrs Roberts's statement?'

'Nothing. But it's all written in our dearly beloved flat anonymous wordy police-ese. Come on, of course you'd yell. You might even try to look for them — maybe not a woman dressed for visiting someone, but an estate worker? Surely you'd crash around shouting, making a huge amount of noise. Unless this Mrs Roberts was busy having hysterics — again it's not recorded. What do the notebooks of the officers on the scene say?'

‘That they started to search. Except they use the passive voice, not the active. *A search was duly undertaken and—*’

‘Pedant!’

Mark sniffed. ‘No one can fault them on the search. A lot of volunteers, including Forestry Commission workers, and those dogs, of course.’ He jerked a thumb in the direction of the window. ‘But after less than an hour, things went badly wrong. The fog cleared — momentarily. Then the weather really came in. Torrential rain turning to sleet and then to snow. And the snow didn’t stop for twenty-four hours. And it lay for six weeks.’ He shuffled papers. ‘It’s all here, meticulously logged. You can tell how frustrated the officer in charge was when the snow started — he knew that as every minute passed there was less chance of finding anyone alive. Chief Inspector Blount. Another on our “to interview” list.’

‘And by now, I presume, they had a name for the driver and the missing child? We know she’s Natalie Foreman, WAG or otherwise. The child’s Hadrian. That’s right. Hadrian, not Adrian. And the poor dead baby was Julius, God help it. Who in their right mind calls a child Hadrian?’ she demanded.

‘Someone who drives the poshest Range Rover you could buy? A man called Philip Foreman. Foreman plays for a Midlands side, West Bromwich Albion, it says here. He’s their striker.’

‘The striker’s the one who scores goals, right?’ Fran asked deadpan.

‘Right,’ he agreed ironically. ‘He played for England at one time, I think. But I follow football like you follow greyhounds, so this is one area we may need to pick someone’s brains.’

‘Is there at least a photo of him?’

‘I couldn’t find one in any of the boxes, but then, he wasn’t a suspect. But there must be one of him in here.’ He patted the iPad. ‘Shall we look? OK.’ It didn’t take him long to bring up an image of a young man in action, both feet off the ground, one muscular leg outstretched as he kicked a ball.

‘A fine-looking lad,’ Fran said. ‘Is there an image where we can see his face, rather than his quads?’

'Only some team photos where he looks as wooden as you'd expect.'

'But quite attractive. Really nice thighs, Mark.'

'You and your thighs fixation . . . Anyway, Foreman's baby son is dead, and his wife and other son missing. A high-profile case if ever there was one. And, because of the weather, it's pretty well stalled after sixteen hours. The volunteer searchers either drift home or are sent home because the weather's so awful and the forecast even worse. The press cover the weather and probably other crises like our own in Sandwich. And no one ever sees Natalie or Hadrian again. Or,' he adds pensively, 'anything that could be their remains.' He looked at the sky again. 'Any other day I'd say we should go and look at the scene. But I honestly don't think we'd see anything helpful.'

Fran nodded. 'The trouble is, we don't even have a map here. Do you think Mr Mole would let us borrow his technology for a bit?' She waved a pen like a magician's wand, as if she could conjure up visual display screens with their clever electronics. The wall remained predictably blank. No miracle for them, technological or otherwise. 'OK, let's see what the iPad will do.' That was sufficiently miraculous anyway.

Mark leaned over, wrapping his arm round her shoulders. 'It's not a huge area,' he said, tracing the green patch with his forefinger. 'Surely someone as determined as that guy Blount seems to have been would have made sure it was thoroughly searched. Come to that, couldn't Natalie have found her own way out?'

Fran had found another screen. 'According to Wikipedia there's more than ten square miles of it. And it sounds even bigger if you go metric — nearly twenty-six square kilometres. And although there are lots of paths — they are paths, aren't they, not roads? — there are hardly any houses. Apart from that village about a mile from here, Buttonoak, human activity's mostly to the south, the other side of the A456. So what do you do if you get lost? In rain like this, let alone thick fog, it'd be hard to know if you were going in a straight line, unless you managed to come across a path. You'd have to set off on a path, wouldn't you?'

'I'd have thought so. Now, she's got a toddler. Here he is.' He picked up a photo from the file: curly blond hair, chubby cheeks, chubby limbs — Hadrian might have been a model for the cherubs in Webster's room. 'He'd dawdle if you made him walk and if you had to carry him he'd be heavy. Rain, then snow . . .'

Fran drew her hand across her throat. 'Wouldn't take long, hypothermia. Is that any consolation?'

'But with his mother protecting him? And there'd be snow to keep them hydrated.'

'But you don't necessarily drive in warm, bulky clothes. Not if your car's got a good heater. Did you find a picture of her?'

He held one out — a head and shoulders view of a woman barely out of girlhood, with large blue eyes dominating a fine-featured face. 'Looks like a puff of wind would blow her over.'

'Is there a mention of outer clothing for either of them?'

'None. Though with this sort of record-keeping that doesn't mean much. But even if they were wrapped up to the ears, would they survive in weather like this — and worse?'

CHAPTER THREE

'We ought to unpack and settle in,' Mark said without enthusiasm. 'Snowdrop Cottage. Hmph. No wonder the Satnav didn't want to bring us here.' They'd made several passes up and down the road before they'd spotted a tight turn into their lane, narrow and sodden.

'Well, we're here now. And there's nothing wrong with the place. Not really. When the sun shines it'll be perfect — a picture-book cottage!' She tried another tack. 'I know the other bedroom's prettier, but—'

'But we need to be able to stand up in it. I know you think it's all fairy-tale and romantic but I draw the line at sleeping in a room with a ceiling so low that neither of us can walk around except in the dead centre.'

'So we'll use this one. Come on, by the time the central heating's done its job it'll be fine. And as Webster implied, the sooner we've done the job the better — and we can just head for home.'

'What do you reckon the smell is?' he asked with a suspicious sniff.

'Damp,' she said briskly. 'I used to get it in my cottage if it had been unoccupied for a week. That fan heater will help. I'd throw open the window except the rain's driving straight at it.'

'OK. We'll put the central heating on and light the fire.'

'I'll tackle the fire, shall I? Assuming there's some kindling and some dry wood.' She led the way downstairs, careful to miss a low beam. 'Mind your head!'

Mark didn't.

Neither could he work out how to make the central heating work. Technically he knew he was pressing the right buttons on the control panel. In practice, nothing happened. He was just about to suggest Fran take over when she emerged from the living room, slamming the door behind her and looking anxiously at the smoke alarm. There were no firelighters and both kindling and wood were so damp the fire wouldn't draw. All she'd achieved was billows of smoke so thick she'd had to open the windows, and bother the rain.

'Time to call the letting agent,' Mark said through gritted teeth. He was even less happy when he found the only place with a mobile signal was the bathroom, which opened off the kitchen. 'Bugger gingerbread houses!'

Meanwhile in the chic little kitchen, Fran tackled the welcome pack, which included a strange mixture of poor basic items and quite recherché luxuries. Thank goodness they'd brought their own essentials. It was better to sort things out in the dry, however, so she ferried the lot from the Audi, parked on the far side of the yard, currently awash with rainwater.

Mark's face as he emerged from the bathroom was blacker than the sky. 'The agent closes at five on Mondays. So I used the emergency number — turns out it's the mobile of the woman who owns the place. And where is she? On holiday in Portugal. She said the likely cause of our problems was a lack of gas. The tank's supposed to be topped up at the end of each letting. She suggests I go and have a look. There's a gauge on the far side of the tank, which is apparently the far side of the yard . . .' In silence they looked at the rain. Fran, who was after all still in her waterproofs, headed out to do the deed . . .

* * *

No one would have placed Ted Day as an ex-cop, unlike those at HQ. He simply merged with his surroundings, in this case the snug of the Bull. The pub embraced them: it was worth the drive just to thaw out. Like their own local in Kent, it was obviously at the heart of what seemed to be a very flourishing community: football matches, quiz nights, charity fund-raisers.

The girl behind the bar pointed him out immediately at a table near the fire.

'You look like two drowned rats. Cold, too,' he added, shaking first Fran's hand and then Mark's. 'No, you two sit that side: I'll watch you steam! What'll you have? No, come on: you don't come to the Midlands and buy your own, not first time round. While you make up your minds, give me those brollies — I'll put them with mine so none of us can forget them. Not that the weather will let us.'

He ordered a bottle of Merlot, but stuck to the pint he was nursing. It didn't take him long to find out the problems of Snowdrop Cottage.

'The trouble is it's heated by LPG. If it was oil, I might find someone willing to deliver a load for cash,' Fran said. 'But I bet the letting agency's tied into some contract.'

'And the gas people will be tied into some delivery route. How about a few nice dry logs?' He knew a guy who would produce a load at eight the next morning. 'As for firelighters, I've got some spares at home you can have if you don't mind leaving here when I do: Iris likes me back for ten so she can lock up.'

'That's more than kind, Ted. Thank you.'

'Heaven knows why you chose the cottage in the first place,' Ted said. 'Why not simply check into a decent hotel?'

'We thought we ought to save West Mercia some money,' Fran explained. 'But no one told us we should have brought our ark.' But she had an idea she'd said the wrong thing. Or that Ted had simply taken a dislike to her.

On the other hand, over their meal — the chips were as good as Iris had promised, so good they vowed to be more strong-minded next time — Ted seemed to enjoy the wide-ranging conversation. He'd taken an OU degree after he'd left the force, and was a volunteer teacher at a local primary school; not bad, he said, for a lad who'd never wanted to do anything at school except scrape the minimum qualifications for joining the police. Once safely recruited, however, he'd got more ambitious. 'Sergeants' exams; inspectors' exams — oh, ah, I was a keenie-beanie all right. Even acting chief inspector before I reached my thirty years and scarpered with my pension.'

An opening if ever there was one. Mark took it. 'So how were you involved in the Natalie Foreman case?'

'Officially only as a constable on the search party. I was attached to Bewdley in those days, before everything had to be rationalized,' he added bitterly. 'First off, I want to make it clear how hard we worked that first evening and night. As soon as word got round a kid was missing, there was no question of being off duty or off sick, not unless you were at death's door. Every bit of that woodland was searched, as best we could. Even in daylight, with all that undergrowth, it was tough — brambles and nettles and such. But it was dark . . .

'When the weather really came in, just torrential rain at that point, anyone not officially on duty was ordered off. The rain turned to a blizzard which unleashed itself about three in the morning. At that point the chief inspector—'

'That's a guy called Blount?' Fran put in.

'Yes. A really sound cop — pulled everyone out of the furthest reaches of the forest and made us concentrate on the most likely areas.'

'Did you know then you were looking for the family of someone in the public eye?'

He stared at her in disbelief. 'Fran, have you ever lived in the country?'

'We still do. So we can safely assume that everyone knew who owned the Range Rover?'

'More than that: for God's sake, people had known Natalie since she was a little girl. Natalie Garbutt she was then. Dad ran the local garage. Mother helped out at a market garden. You probably saw in the files, Natalie'd been visiting her mum in a local village—'

'Buttonbridge,' Mark supplied. 'More of a hamlet.'

'Wrong Button. Buttonoak. OK? She never came back to live once she'd left for university. But she kept in touch with her mum and when the babies came she visited a lot.'

Fran raised a finger. 'But according to the file, Mrs Garbutt denied her daughter had been in Buttonoak that day.'

The temperature dropped several degrees. 'Why else should she be there?'

Did he genuinely believe the police theory or was he just selling them the party line? Mark didn't want to challenge him on anything yet — needed to keep the meeting friendly and with luck productive. It seemed Fran did too.

'She was a footballer's wife: lots of money. A WAG,' Fran said. 'How did local people feel about that?'

Ted sank the last of his pint, but waved away the offer of another. 'She was never a WAG. Never. Not in the media sense. She had a good head on her shoulders, that wench. She passed her A levels, went to uni—'

'Any idea which one?'

'Leeds, I think. Anyway, she got a degree. Languages, as I recall. But for some reason she decided to do a business and accountancy postgrad course — following the money, people said. After a couple of years she started to work for one of the big London football clubs — Arsenal, I think. Which is where she met Phil. Big tough Yorkshire lad, though he spent all his footballing life further south.'

Mark reached for the jug of water, gesturing the rest of the wine to Fran, who responded by screwing the top back on. He said slowly, 'But Arsenal's one of the biggest, richest clubs. Why should a guy playing for a team like that want to move?'

'He'd move because he wasn't playing for Arsenal. Not on a regular basis. So they transferred him. I've no doubt the Albion's admin team would have been glad to have the services of Natalie too, but she was already pregnant with Hadrian.'

'So they moved to West Bromwich?' Fran's voice betrayed her disbelief. 'I mean, it's not exactly—'

'It's part of the Black Country, cradle of the Industrial Revolution,' Ted said sharply. 'OK, it's not the most beautiful part of the world, any more than Sheffield, but since when did footballers have to live over the shop? There's some posh properties in spitting distance, I can tell you.'

'I know there are,' she said humbly, kicking herself again. They might live in the Garden of England but that was no excuse for south of Watford snobbery. 'I'm sorry, Ted. I really am. I seem to have left my brain behind at some motorway service area or other. We've got friends in Little Aston who live near Roman Road, a millionaires' row if ever there was one! That'd be an easy commute, wouldn't it? Or Knowle, or Dorridge?'

'That's the sort of place,' Ted conceded. 'On the other hand, to be fair, the Albion weren't a Premier League club like they are now. They were down in the Second or Third Division. So it would be a definite demotion for the lad.'

She nodded, still anxious not to make further mistakes. 'Can I pick up on one thing you said earlier? At one point you used the word *officially*. Which implies to me that you know stuff unofficially.'

'Or Iris wouldn't have fixed us all up on the blind date, would she?' Mark observed, trying to give Fran a bit of moral support. Although she got on so well with most people, she certainly wasn't hitting it off with Ted, who continued to look at her inimically. 'You're sure you couldn't manage another half, Ted?'

'OK, you've twisted my arm.' As Mark headed to the bar, Ted grinned at Fran, but still not altogether kindly. 'Like I said, you'd have done better to go to a decent hotel. I can't see that even with enough gas and a log fire Snowdrop Cottage is going to be the most comfortable place on earth for high-flyers like you. I'd see you in a modern house, with proper insulation and high ceilings and double glazing and mains drainage and—'

She met his eye. 'I take your point, Ted. I've been talking like an idiot townie, and I'm really sorry. Something to do with our 4 a.m. start, maybe. But we do actually live in the country, near but not in a hamlet that just about sustains a pub and a church. No shop. We haven't got mains gas or mains drainage at home either. Though I'll admit we have nice high ceilings. And the land around us drains well. Snowdrop Cottage lies in a deep hollow, doesn't it? It's bound to be damp . . . Now,' she continued, smiling up at Mark as he put a half on Ted's mat, 'what's all this *unofficial* stuff?'

'I thought you'd never ask.' He raised his glass in a toast, then changed his mind and put it down again, unscrewing the wine bottle and tilting it, first towards Mark's glass, then towards Fran's. 'Only one of you is driving, for goodness' sake.'

'Me,' said Fran. 'My turn. Go on, Mark, it'll help you sleep.' She raised her glass of water in a gesture matching Ted's. 'To unofficial stuff.'

'To my kid brother's baby — with Natalie.'

Fran thought she picked up the irony in Ted's gesture before Mark did. She replaced her glass swiftly and laid a hand on Ted's wrist. 'It's not that straightforward, is it? What happened, Ted?'

'I'm sorry. That was a very tasteless way of breaking someone else's secret. Everyone knew of my family's connection with her — a connection that hadn't ended happily, as it happens. That's why I wasn't involved in the case once the initial search was over. Rob and Natalie Garbutt, as was, were what the media would probably call childhood sweethearts. They were inseparable from the age of about fourteen. Real Romeo and Juliet. As it goes, the families were both quite happy — neighbours, the dads played for the same cricket club, the mums went to the same WI. You can imagine what it was like for Natalie's mum, by the way, when the WI were asked to provide hot drinks and sandwiches for the search party.'

By now Mark had caught up. 'It must have been very painful for you all.'

'I think Rob was over it by then — it was more than ten years later, for goodness' sake, and he had a new partner and a baby on the way. Whatever Natalie did with her life was no skin off my nose. As for the baby, well, to be honest, with hindsight she was probably right to get rid of it, though Rob wasn't happy at the time or for years after. He'd have been delighted to marry her and do his best to help rear it. He'd even have stood by her if she'd wanted to have it adopted. But she was adamant she didn't want to bring a damaged baby into the world. It was her choice, she said, and she was acting on the medics' advice. They called it a non-viable fetus. It was common knowledge in the village.'

Fran took a deep breath: she was appalled that something as deeply personal, as private, should have become generally known. At last, she asked quietly, 'Was there some sort of genetic problem? Because I seem to recall the baby in the car had some sort of health problem that would have shortened its life.'

He looked at her with slightly more approval. 'You can imagine the talk round the village, but Natalie's mum insisted there was no connection. By the way, while I'm sure you'll want to interview Jeanette, you ought to know that her husband's in a bad way. But he's as sharp as a tack, is Brian.'

'Thanks. We'll tread carefully,' Mark said.

Ted's glance at Fran suggested she'd find it hard.

'Do you remember anything about her school-friends?' Mark asked. 'Girls she went about with?'

'They've all married and moved away: it's nobbut a small place,' he said, deliberately thickening his accent.

'And do you recall her bringing back any university friends?'

He shook his head. 'You'd have to ask her mother.'

'Rob: any idea how Rob would react to an interview?'

'Fancy a trip to Australia, do you?'

'In this weather, I'd love one. But I doubt if the budget would run to it.'

'Not now Colin Webster's got his hands on the purse-strings — he's a tightwad if ever there was one. What sort of team has he pulled together for you?'

'He said something about volunteers.'

'Did he indeed? OK, so no trip Down Under for you.'

'Does Rob Skype?' Fran asked.

'He's spending time in the Bush. But even then he was never really in the frame. They questioned him once or twice, but never under caution. All fingers pointed — round here at least — at her husband. But he came up squeaky clean. He could afford to pay for fancy lawyers, of course, but since at the time they went missing he was up in Newcastle preparing for a match he had a cast iron alibi. In any case, he was actually a devoted dad. Had lots of plans for Hadrian's future. I've no idea how he dealt with Julius, poor little bugger. You were right about the health problem. Edwards' syndrome.' He looked at his watch. 'Look, if I'm not back in five minutes flat, you won't get your firelighters — or if you do, they'll be ready-lit and shoved up somewhere you don't want heat . . .'

* * *

Armed with not just firelighters but dry kindling and a black plastic sack full of logs, they picked their way back to the cottage. There was a lot of lying water on the A449; local radio, cutting in uninvited on the Audi sound system, told them that the Severn was already high and that the Avon at Tewkesbury was about to burst its banks. At least their approach to Ombersley was unimpeded, and Snowdrop Cottage was still accessible, although the narrow lane was awash, as was the yard. They took their booty into the living room.

Fran soon had a fire going, banking it up in the hope of keeping it going overnight. At least the bedroom, courtesy of the fan heater they'd left running, was cosiness itself. The feeble wall heater in the chic and elegant bathroom, currently running with condensation, might do some good if they left it on overnight, but their hopes weren't high. Fran almost looked forward to the conversation she planned to have with the letting agent the following morning.

CHAPTER FOUR

Half an hour in the gym; a post-exercise shower; a canteen breakfast — they both felt as though they'd stepped back into their old life with the Kent Police. Their office showed signs of being equipped: a white board was already on the wall, as was an electronic screen. The workman's activities hadn't extended to sweeping up the plaster dust or removing the boxes the kit had come in. A computer was already up and running, the screen-saver the unfamiliar West Mercia design. No coffee maker, of course, but one of them at least was entitled to a lunch break and could nip out and buy one; meanwhile they'd rely on the green tea they'd brought as part of their supplies and which in any case Mark insisted was better for them.

And now they had a new team to work with — Fran firmly suppressed the words *break in*. She was still inclined to beat herself up for her decided failure to impress Ted the previous evening, and had hoped that a good night's sleep would have cleared her head. However, sleep had been no more than fitful: somewhere something had flapped and slapped intermittently in what sounded like a gale, waking her with a jerk every time she dozed off. The letting agent now had a name — Alex Fisher; he'd promised action on that as well as on the gas, but pointed out that the wind might make it too dangerous for anyone to attempt a repair. He agreed, when pressed, that if he couldn't improve things by nightfall he might have to tell the owner that Fran and Mark would decamp, cancelling the rest of their booking and asking for a rebate.

Fran had felt better after that, but already caught herself out yawning. The victory adrenalin had better stay with her, or she might disgrace herself in front of their new team: three of the men to whom they'd been introduced at lunch the previous day and a couple of women young enough to be their daughters. As they entered, however, one of the trio peeled off and disappeared with a casual wave. After a few moments, so did a second with what Fran tried not to think was studied insolence.

'Anyone else want to leave before we settle down to some work?' Mark asked quietly. 'Because if you've got second thoughts about working for this team, now is definitely the time to go. No?' He gave the three remaining officers the smile Fran always reckoned would pull ducks off the water. 'So we've got DC Robyn Marlow, DS Stu Pritchard and DC Paula Llewellyn, right? This is my wife, Fran Harman, and I'm Mark Turner.' Another smile.

They all responded, but with the sort of caution that might indicate they were well aware of the former rank of these two incomers trying to be matey. 'I don't need to tell you that we shall expect the same dedication and hard work you'd show if you were investigating a live case. But there are a few differences, one being that neither of us has powers of arrest. If any collar-feeling has to be done, one of you has to accompany us. The shorter the investigation the better pleased West Mercia's accountants will be. The grapevine's probably already told you that neither of us will be keeping our fee, by the way.'

Stu, in his mid-forties but trim enough to suggest he put in serious hours at some sort of exercise or other, put up a hand. 'Overtime?'

Oh, dear. Fran had hoped that wouldn't be anyone's priority. She shook her head. 'Not unless the ACC — *your* ACC — authorizes it personally. Sorry.'

Mark took over again. 'Now, just in case you don't know, this is the scenario — ah, the keyboard doesn't seem to be talking to the screen . . .'

Paula, the more strongly built of the young women, put her phone down, tossed back pretty blonde hair and stepped forward. It took her about ten seconds to fix it. 'I seem to be your geek,' she said with a self-deprecating smile.

'Is that what you want to be, Paula?' Fran asked.

'My DCI, the one who put me forward for the job, said I should get all the experience I could — but that's a two-way thing, isn't it? So if it's a geek you need . . .'

So Paula had been volunteered into joining them. They'd have to make sure she wanted to stay. Fran smiled. 'Correction, Paula — a geek *we* need. Us. The team. Right?'

'Right. Thanks.' She glanced down at her phone. 'Sorry — I really need to deal with this — won't take a second.' It didn't. She was back in the room looking alert, if stressed, when Mark started his spiel.

He'd hardly finished when there was a tap at the door. Iris slid into the room, handed Fran a new ID and slid out again.

'There, I'm real,' she said, hanging it round her neck. She smiled encouragingly at the other young woman, slender and elegant, with the most beautiful skin. 'Robyn?'

Her gender-free name matched her androgynous appearance. 'I'm always happy doing house to house, that sort of thing, not that there seems to be much call for that in this case.'

True, so why was she here? But there weren't so many gift-horses that you could look any of them in the mouth. 'If you've got people skills, we'll need them, don't worry,' Fran declared. 'And you, Stu?'

'I was on the original team,' he said, as if that explained everything.

'Excellent,' Fran said with a smile, though she was sure Mark's heart fell as swiftly and deeply as hers did. The last thing they needed was someone like the guys in the canteen trotting out the dogma that had driven a failed enquiry. On the other hand, he might just have been the bright-eyed bushy-tailed young officer who'd oozed good ideas which had irritated his complacent superiors. 'So you'll be able to fill us in on all sorts of things that don't seem to have been kept on file.'

Stu didn't look as if he could.

'For instance, without wishing you to be disloyal, there may have been things you felt could or should have been done differently. When you're ready. Anything you say will stay within these four walls.' Mark looked swiftly around the others.

Stu pulled a face. 'I was still wet behind the ears in those days . . . But I remember thinking — no, it's probably just hindsight . . .'

'We all have twenty-twenty vision in that situation. But spill, anyway.'

'I just wondered if — with all the searching proving negative — other avenues might have been explored with a bit more thoroughness. But it was my first year as fully fledged constable, and what did I know about anything?'

Fran smiled. 'Thank you. That could be very useful, you know. Now, is there any particular role you'd like to focus on?'

Stu's eyes glazed.

'How about you take responsibility for evidence?' Mark suggested.

'What evidence?' Stu spread his hands.

Mark spread his, more expansively, before counting off possibilities. 'Stuff left in the car: Natalie's mobile phone; handbag; outdoor clothes; luggage, if any; passports. Hadrian's child seat. Could you lay your hands on them for me so we can decide what needs forensic testing? Of course at this stage you may have to nag people,' he said.

Fran turned to Robyn. 'I couldn't find any copies of Julius's hospital records on file. Or, for that matter, any medical information about Hadrian. I know he was supposed to be just a healthy toddler, but just in case. I dare say his GP won't have kept any records, but could you find out who it was and make a few calls? May be a non-starter — don't fret if it is. Now, we know Julius had Edwards' syndrome.' There was no need to regale them with what she'd found on the Internet. 'It's a terrible thing to afflict the baby and his family, of course. They must have known he was going to die right from the moment he was born. What's the most likely hospital for him to have been having treatment in? Great Ormond Street?'

Robyn caught Paula's eye and raised an eyebrow. Fran froze.

Robyn asked, 'What about Birmingham Children's Hospital? It might have the name Birmingham in front of it but it's a national centre of excellence.'

Why did people here have such passion for a nearby city? 'Sorry. How stupid of me. Birmingham, of course. While you're talking to them, could you ask if it's genetic and if Natalie might have been a carrier?'

'Actually,' Stu said, 'my kid cousin comes from Swindon or somewhere and he got treated at GOSH. So it does happen if you've got something really rare.'

Fran flashed him a smile. She was just about to ask after his cousin when Stu volunteered, 'He died.'

There was a communal sigh of sympathy. Fran flashed a look at Mark: let him build on it.

'It must be awful — beyond awful — to lose a child . . . of that age,' he said quickly. He was completely estranged from his daughter, by her choice, though thank God he had an excellent model-railway-based relationship with his son and was heavily involved with his grandchildren. His voice became gravelly with emotion. 'Imagine what Natalie's parents must have gone through, losing a daughter and both grandsons.'

There was a tiny silence. One at least of the bosses was obviously human: was this a good or a bad thing? Embarrassed by the crack in his armour, Mark hoped it was good.

Meanwhile Paula looked up from her tablet. Fran had been on the verge of bollocking her for using it during a meeting but her grim smile suggested a minor success. She put some pictures on to their screen. Five hardened officers found it hard to look. 'Edwards' syndrome. Usually tests pick it up *in utero*, it says here, and mothers are offered a termination. If Natalie was, she obviously didn't accept. And . . .' she scanned downwards, 'no, there doesn't appear to be any particular familial or genetic link.'

'Or maybe twenty years back the test wasn't available — or wasn't reliable?' Fran hazarded.

'I'll ask when I call the kids' hospital,' Robyn said.

'Thanks, Robyn. That'd be good.'

Perhaps they were forming into a team despite everything. She might just try pushing on another door, even though it had been one that had annoyed Ted. 'Stu, do you recall where Natalie was going when she disappeared? Where she was leaving from, indeed?'

'There was something funny about it . . .'

Mark nodded encouragement. He thought he knew what was coming. Hoped it would show that Stu was more clued up than he'd feared.

'We all assumed she'd been to her mother's and was on her way home to her pad in . . . now where was it? Edgbaston.'

'That's a posh part of Birmingham — right? With the cricket ground?' Fran stopped there. Winning back some Brownie points was one thing, but she didn't want to sound as if she was toadying.

Stu nodded. 'I saw some pics of it; I don't know if they were kept on file, gaffer, but there were some in the papers. Not very big, but sort of stately. Someone said it had been used for shots in a period TV series. Not the sort of OTT Southfork place you expect footballers to have.'

Paula held up a finger: 'We're talking twenty years ago; were players as overpaid then as they are now?'

'In proportion to the rest of us, yes,' Stu declared.

'But he wasn't a top player any more, and I gather West Brom weren't in the top league then,' Mark said.

'Even so, he was way out-earning me,' Stu said conclusively. 'Anyway, her parents said they'd never seen her that day. Insisted.'

'Why should the team assume that in the first place?' Robyn asked.

Stu frowned. 'Because she was on the road from their village, Buttonoak, see, and was heading south towards Bewdley. QED.'

'But they denied it. Robyn, this could be an ideal opportunity for your interviewing skills. We need to talk to Jeanette Garbutt, don't we?' Exactly why had the apparently frank and reliable Ted accepted the premise that it was obvious where Natalie was travelling from and where she was going? 'Tell you what — and this is the longest of shots — see if the hospital has any record at all of Julius being booked in for treatment round the time of his death. Twenty years ago though . . .' She shook her head doubtfully.

Paula broke her apparent vow of silence. 'Hang on: Stu said she was heading towards Bewdley. You don't have to be going to Birmingham if you're heading into Bewdley, do you? You could be heading for Stourport. And if you were heading towards Stourport, you could have been heading to the M5, and all the places that leads to.'

'But if you're going towards Kiddie then Brum's your likely destination,' Stu argued.

'And you know she was heading towards Kiddie? — that's Kidderminster,' Paula said in a possibly helpful aside.

'I'd got that, thanks,' Fran said. 'I do have trouble with some place names round the Midlands. Wednesbury, for instance. First I thought you had to pronounce every syllable and then last time we came down the M5 I swear the Satnav woman called it Wednesday.'

'She did,' Mark corroborated. 'Every single time. Wednesday. In fact it's pronounced Wensbry — right?'

'Right,' Paula agreed, with an incipient twinkle in startlingly blue eyes. 'And you're OK on Worcester and Alcester?'

'I do my best,' Mark assured her solemnly.

Fran added, 'Not to mention Bicester . . . So was she heading to Kiddie or Stourport? Was there any evidence either way, Stu?'

'How could there be?' he asked, prepared to be truculent.

'Quite,' she agreed. 'But the investigators back then must have had some reason for their assumption, though I couldn't see anything in the paperwork the ACC left us.'

'Tell you what, I'll have a word with some of my old mates, not necessarily those based here. And maybe some that didn't work on the case — they often pick up rumours, like.'

'Excellent. First up, before you even start on the evidence, could you have a very quick look at the list of the team working on the case originally. Give me any low-down? Then I'll arrange to talk to them. Robyn will fix a time for us to talk to Natalie's parents. Stu will hunt for the missing evidence. Paula — can you dredge the Internet for anything happening at the time that could possibly have had any bearing on the case?'

'Would you mind if I scanned or keyed some of these documents into the computer first? Then we'll all have access to them.'

'Thanks. That's a much better idea.' It was. Where the hell was her brain? 'And Mark?'

'I'm going to go for every scrap of information on Natalie's husband, first hand for preference. I want to talk to him, his mates and — why has no one mentioned his parents?'

'Parents?'

Stu frowned. 'Were they still alive? I certainly don't recall they were ever interviewed. You'd have thought they'd come and have a look at the spot where their grandson died, wouldn't you? Mind you, I don't recall Phil Foreman himself coming either.'

'What?' It seemed all four reacted the same way.

Paula was the first to speak. 'Talk about weird. It'd be a wonderful media opportunity to appeal for information. So no mini-shrine by the roadside like they tend to have now after accidents?'

'Not that I recall. I mean, six weeks' really bad snow . . . Perhaps folk thought the moment was past.'

'What did the family liaison officer have to say about it?'

Stu clicked his fingers. 'There was something funny about that too. One of them refused to have one, either the Garbutts or Foreman. Maybe both. Weird.'

'Anything else at this stage?'

Stu again, only this time he slapped his forehead. 'There was a nanny. Au pair. Whatever. But she left about a month before. She got a job with someone posh. Real posh, old money. We talked to her but got nothing useful.'

'OK. Was Natalie's life insured, by the way?'

'Nope. Her husband's was, for megabucks. But not hers.'

So why was so little of this on record? Despite his anxiety, Mark had a team to encourage and he beamed. 'Well done. But before we do any of these indoor tasks, I'd like us all to visit the scene. It may bring back useful memories to you, Stu, and the rest of us won't be working blind. I'd particularly like to look at the exact spot she parked up and see what her options would be. Fran and I meant to go out there yesterday but we got here so late and it was raining so hard there didn't seem much point.'

As one, the team's heads turned to the window. A squall battered it with serious intent.

Fran caught Paula's eye. 'Could you bring up a local weather forecast for us?'

Her head went down for a few seconds. She looked up with a disbelieving smile. 'Believe it or not, the rain will ease. Round about one. And — wow! Even the chance of a bright interval later. With showers, of course. But later this afternoon and tomorrow — hell's bells, we'll need canoes, by the look of it.'

'In that case, if it's OK by the rest of you, I suggest we grab a sandwich and meet in the entrance hall at one,' Fran said. 'Then we could head back here and pool our reactions. Is that OK with you all? Mark?' To her relief they all nodded enthusiastically. 'Great. I'll hijack an official car but one of you will probably have to drive it. Insurance, of course.'

'I've got advanced driving skills,' Paula said. Her cheeks flamed, as if she was admitting something shameful. She looked swiftly down again. She must take that damned phone to bed.

'Excellent. Robyn?' she added, responding to a hand half-raised, as if the young woman was still in school.

'Do we know why they've chosen to review this case now, gaffer? With cash being so short and cuts and everything?'

'Wish we knew,' Mark said frankly.

'It'll be to do with clear-up rates,' Stu said. 'This new commissioner's dead keen on improving our image.'

Paula transferred her attention from her phone to her tablet. She looked up. 'I can tell you what her widower is up to now unless you think it would prejudice our enquiry?' Responding to the muted cheers of derision, she waved the tablet. 'Apparently he's running a bar in Cyprus. Which doesn't get us very far.'

Fran narrowed her eyes. 'Cyprus or Northern Cyprus?'

'Kyrenia, it says here.'

'That's in the North. Where that Polly Peck millionaire went AWOL.'

'And where there is,' Mark observed, 'no extradition treaty. Assuming we wanted to extradite him, of course.'

'Which might, assuming we find anything against him, be very suspicious.' Quiet little Robyn punched the air. 'Let's get the bastard!'

Fran would have loved it to be their exit line — she was sure Mark would too. But she had to add, 'Let's get him indeed. If — and it's a huge if — he did have anything to do with Natalie's disappearance. We mustn't jump to conclusions. We're simply investigating a misper, right? Come on, what are we waiting for? If he's innocent it needs to be known. If he's a bastard indeed, let's go get him!'

* * *

'I just wish I could stop putting my foot in it! How many people have I offended so far? I nearly blew the whole team this morning!' Fran collapsed on her new desk, head in hands. 'God, I need a caffeine fix! Even that evil-smelling canteen brew.'

Staring at the rain, Mark said nothing. Though she was exaggerating, he had to admit that she'd put in a performance well below her usual. In the past she'd always fired on all cylinders no matter how little sleep she'd had. Last night had been very bad, of course: it had taken her nearly an hour to get the fire established, though he'd be the first to concede that it had been worth a lot to come down to a warm room. And then there'd been that random banging. It had driven him mad, but at least he'd been able to remove his hearing aids and a combination of a long day and more red wine than usual had sent him off straight away. Which probably, of course, made it even worse for Fran. How much sleep had she had? Two hours at most.

He stretched out a hand. 'Come on, let's brave the canteen. We may even need a sugar rush: those Danish pastries looked good. Even if they are pure evil,' he added over his shoulder, as he opened the door.

Her mobile chose that moment to ring. 'Oh, sod it. Bring one for me,' she mouthed.

He returned with two paper cups, which he set down on his desk alongside a paper bag. He opened it to reveal two large, flat, sickly looking confections.

'That was Alex, the letting agent. Partial result,' Fran declared, coming over to him and tucking her hand into his. 'He's delivering more heaters, which he will leave switched on, and he'll chase the gas delivery company. The only thing that worries him is the flapping noise, but he'll see what he can do when he delivers the heaters.'

'I'd have called that a complete result, especially for someone running on empty.' He passed her a pastry. 'Heavens, the sugar in these is more than we eat in an average week; we'll be doing handsprings any moment now!'

'I shall cartwheel down to Iris to find out how to book a car.'

'Done. I sorted it on my way to the canteen.' He waved a couple of sheets of photocopied paper. 'And got Iris to lay her hands on some waterproof bright-wear for us. All we'll need is our boots. I'll rescue them from the boot at lunchtime when I do the Sainsbury's run; if anyone doesn't like my leaving the premises they must lump it. No, there's no need for you to come with me; you used to be able to doze lying on the floor — time for you to try that again. I need your brain, Fran, I really do.'

'I know. I'm sorry.'

'Now, forget your coffee and pastry. The last thing you need is a sugar rush before a bit of a zizz. Actually, I'll go and do my bit of shopping now. I can check out Phil Foreman later.' He looked up, catching her eye. 'This is even stranger for me than for you, you know. In the past I just had to click my fingers and a minion would do everything for me.'

'A minion like me,' she agreed, sticking her tongue out at him. 'Well, if you can't click your fingers, you can at least click a mouse.'

CHAPTER FIVE

Paula drove them along unfamiliar roads. There was a fifty speed limit much of the way, backed up by warnings of cameras. So they got the chance to look at the scenery they'd only glimpsed through the rain the previous day. The fields, many of which were under water, looked a manageable size. As for houses, they were built in warm red brick, interspersed with thatched timber-framed ones convincingly out of the vertical, genuinely, not just picture-book, old. She'd never considered leaving Kent, but this area might be one to tempt her.

They learned during the half hour drive that Stu had a son and a daughter. Paula had two young sons, both at school; her husband was unemployed. Robyn was in a civil partnership but neither she nor her wife was interested in kids yet.

'Where do you want me to stop, gaffer?' Paula demanded. 'Natalie's Range Rover was actually parked illegally, wasn't it?' Her voice indicated strong disapproval.

'We'll park illegally too,' Fran declared, though the question might have been directed at Mark. 'We've got those nice big plastic warning signs: *Police. Slow.* We've all got hi-vis jackets. Go into the village and find somewhere to turn, would you? We need to see things through Natalie's eyes. And those of the woman who called in the incident. Marion

Roberts. What a nice village — some really pretty properties,' she added as Paula completed her manoeuvre. 'Why on earth didn't Natalie simply turn round and walk back to the village if there was a problem? Get someone to phone her mum? Or phone from here? Though mobile coverage wouldn't have been so good in those days, would it? How did you get on with Natalie's parents, by the way, Robyn? The Garbutts?'

Paula parked and cut the engine, but was obviously waiting for Robyn's reply.

'She sounded taken aback. Really disconcerted. As if I'd caught her while she was concentrating on something else. Anyway, she agreed to talk to us later in the week. Thursday afternoon. Something about a dental appointment tomorrow.'

'She didn't sound as if she was leaping up and down in joy at the prospect of the case being reopened?' Mark asked.

'Not really. But perhaps — after twenty years — you've just got resigned.'

'Not a terribly typical reaction, I'd have thought,' Fran said. 'All the literature says that people with unresolved grief long for closure.'

Paula nodded. 'I can't imagine — don't want to imagine . . .'

Fran touched her arm sympathetically, worried by the emotion she heard. This might be a very hard case for a woman with too much empathy.

Mark said nothing: he couldn't imagine ever being reconciled to the loss of his daughter, but didn't argue. Perhaps his wound was too fresh. Keen not to finger it any more, he opened the car door. The others followed his lead.

Time to pull on boots. Mark and Robyn put out warning signs at the rear. Fran added a couple on the Bewdley side. How long was it since either of them had done that? Paula, unasked, took endless photos. And why not? The scenery was breathtaking, as beautiful as anything they had in Kent, the sunlight through the damp air adding a romantic soft filter effect. Fran could have stood and gazed all day.

'I can't see any reason at all why Natalie should stop just here,' Mark said, returning to the car.

Paula stopped snapping and joined the little knot beside him. 'How old was the older boy? Four? Five? It's obvious.' She jigged up and down. '*I need a wee. Mummy, I need a wee. I need a wee NOW.*' It sounded as if she'd heard it many times before.

Fran almost objected that the photo of Hadrian showed him as scarcely out of babyhood, but didn't want to interrupt the young woman's chain of thought.

Robyn shook her head. 'And she'd stop, just like that? Opposite a double white?'

Ostentatiously Mark looked along the road, first one way and then the other. 'How long have we been here? And how many cars have we seen?'

'Quite. I admit it. You have a child wanting a wee, you stop, white lines notwithstanding. Hazard lights. Get the child out; wait for it to wee; strap it back in again. Two minutes. Bingo. Back on the road.'

'Unless,' said Stu slowly, 'the little bugger takes it into his head to run off. Especially if his mum's busy with his kid brother.'

They digested the implications. It was so quiet they could hear a few stray raindrops bounce off the car.

'So poor Natalie might have had a dreadful choice. To stay with the dying baby or go after her son. My God.' Mark swallowed bile. 'A child could have hidden in a million places.' He gestured at the fallen trees, dense undergrowth, bushes. 'So Natalie plays this gruesome game of hide and seek, and Julius dies without her.'

Stu sounded near to tears. 'But we searched and searched. Honestly, gaffer, our clothes were in shreds from wading through brambles. Nettles, too. And look at those fern things. Bracken,' he corrected himself.

'I know. I know you all did your best.' Mark clapped him, man to man, on the shoulder.

Fran was peering at her map. 'Is there the slightest chance that the kid ran down the road — easier, after all, if you've got short legs — and found a path? Where are the nearest ones? Let's leave the car here and walk for a bit — back towards Buttonoak first. Look, there's one.' She pointed to her right. Encouragingly, the flurry of rain had stopped and the sun broke through again.

'I was on the team that searched that bit,' Stu said. 'Nil returns. There's another on the other side of the road — see that bit of a parking area.' There was a gate, perhaps to deter off-road drivers, but a broad clear path heading west. 'The path turns south after a bit. It leads to a stream and the bed of a disused railway. They were going to drag the stream, but it froze. And when it came into spate after the thaw, everything would have been swept away. Towards Bewdley there's a bigger parking area—'

'That'll be Hawkbatch Valley?' Fran said.

'Right. You've not been there yet? Not had a chance to look round?'

Picking up Stu's enthusiasm, Fran caught Mark's eye. They ought to be back inside, oughtn't they, toiling under artificial lights? But the fresh air called so loudly . . . 'Not yet. But I think it would be really useful, and if the rest of you don't mind . . .'

Did they mind? With the sun warm enough to remind them that it existed, they all thought it would be very useful. And for morale's sake, it certainly was.

The paths were solid underfoot, beaten down by generations of walkers. But in places they were slippery with mud and treacherous with puddles deeper than you'd expect. Onwards and upwards, but none of the gradients was so steep they couldn't talk. For some reason Fran had expected a pine forest, dark and dry. There were plenty of trees, but most were deciduous, bare and elegant against the pale blue afternoon sky. There was far more undergrowth, the rampant brambles and bracken Stuart had mentioned, than she'd somehow expected so far up a hill.

'Over there, to the north, there's a reservoir. Trimpley. And if we turned left here we'd find what looks like a giants' play area but is in fact a pumping station . . . or something to do with water,' Stu added less certainly. 'But — if you've time — just look round now.'

No one would have argued with the love in his voice. He might have been introducing them to one of his children. 'Over there is Cleobury Mortimer. And that, that's Clee Hill. Follow your nose and you're in Wales. There — that's Wenlock Edge.'

'The *blue remembered hills* . . . I suppose we can't see the Wrekin? Further north?' Mark asked. '*His forest fleece the Wrekin heaves* . . . No? What a shame,' he murmured.

'Not a bad line for a bloke from Bromsgrove,' Stuart said tartly and unexpectedly. 'Never knew Shropshire at all, they say. Just liked the place names.' As if embarrassed by his unmanly knowledge of poetry he shrugged. 'Now turn the other way and you're thirty miles or less from Brum.' He gestured up the hillside. 'The thing is, though, that all these paths are really clear, aren't they? — as good as roads nearly. So if you knew where you were going, you'd be OK.'

'But in fog or driving rain, you might find a path but not know whether you'd been on it before,' Robyn said, shoving her hands deep into her pockets and looking to the south-west.

There were clouds coming their way and they looked as if they meant business. It was time to end the idyll.

Fran straightened her shoulders. 'A thorough police search. A popular area for walking: even today, a weekday, we've passed at least twenty, some with nosy-looking dogs. No remains ever found. What other possibilities did your team consider, Stu? After all, it's a truism that many mispers don't want to be found. Maybe Natalie and Hadrian left of their own accord and found a place of safety.'

'It was never considered, not really, as I told you. And it wasn't the favourite line in the canteen at lunchtime. They all said this reinvestigation was a total load of bollocks. Natalie and the kid had obviously been eaten by foxes — though there was the joker who said they'd been kidnapped and fed to the lions in the safari park over there.' He pointed again.

'Shades of Lord Lucan, eh?' Mark put in. 'Anything more positive? No? But Stu, you thought there might be a better explanation, didn't you, or you wouldn't have stayed yesterday when the other blokes walked out?'

'I suppose I did. Like Fran says,' he continued, surprising them again, 'that at least half the folk who become mispers actually want to disappear and start up somewhere else. But seeing it all again, it's just brought back the hopelessness we felt then. I tell you, gaffer, for two pins I'd pull out right now.'

Mark mustn't let him. He prompted him urgently: 'But?'

'But I want . . . When I read my youngest his bedtime story he won't go to sleep till he knows how it ends. And I suppose . . . if I can help find out what happened and why, I shall feel I've finished something I started twenty years back.'

* * *

Back at Hindlip Hall, they gathered in their incident room. Paula's long hair was so wet from the latest squall she excused herself for a few minutes to go and dry it. The others huddled over coffee from Mark's lunchtime acquisition. It might be a bottom of the range machine, but it still produced a brilliant brew. He'd acquired an assortment of pods, sugar, fresh milk and a dozen mugs, on the principle that no one in the middle of an urgent task ever remembered to wash up. A cake just past its sell-by date had completed his shop. It was only as he stowed everything in the boot that he remembered he'd need a knife. A tray to put the mugs on. Tea bags. And apples and bananas. Not very efficient for a man who'd run the house himself during Fran's last few months at work and during her sick leave, of course. At least no one need know.

Fran was reluctant to break the air of camaraderie but she was desperate to build on the momentum their little trip had generated. She caught Mark's eye; the others saw him as the gaffer after all. Nice term, gaffer: it implied for one thing that a grandfather had wisdom, and had earned his place at the head of a team. It also had a Hardy-esque ring, though the Wyre Forest was a long way north from Egdon Heath. In any case, she knew the term was also in use in the far from rural West Midlands Police.

He nodded: message understood. But he didn't call the group to order immediately. The finger he raised almost imperceptibly was to tell Fran to listen. Stu and Robyn were deep in conversation, clearly as passionate about the case as if the life of a child still depended on their deliberations. What he wanted to do — or perhaps even wanted Fran to do, given his hearing — was to pick up one of the suggestions bouncing between them and run with it.

Hypnotism wasn't necessarily the word he'd have expected to hear, but he noticed Fran seized on it too.

'Do you think you'd actually need to hypnotize this woman?' Fran asked. 'Her witness statement suggests she was pretty compos mentis, doesn't it?' It appeared with admirable efficiency on their magic screen. Paula? She must have been scanning the vital documents every minute the team had been apart.

'Well done, Paula,' she said, pointing to the screen as the young woman rejoined them. 'How long did this take you? I hope you had some lunch? No, of course you didn't, did you? Look, I know we all rightly regard Elf and Safety as total bullshit when a living child's gone missing, but people need breaks and they need to eat.' She followed the direction of the young woman's eyes and pushed the rest of the cake in her direction, and then the fruit.

'Let's look at this statement, then,' Mark said. 'Anything obvious?'

Robyn shrugged. 'She's changed things, gaffer — that's all.'

'And why?'

'Because whoever was supposed to be taking it was writing down rubbish,' Paula said through a mouthful of cake. 'She must be like me, a bit of a pedant.'

Stu snorted. 'A *bit*! That'll be the day. This is the wench that complained to the chief constable himself when there was a little mistake in a sign.'

Wench? For Mark the term conjured slatternly Shakespearean servants, but neither of the women turned a hair.

Paula continued, 'A lot of mistakes. Apostrophes. Little things matter, Stu. If you miss little things you miss big ones: that was what my mother always used to say. See — she's changed one there.' She selected a banana and pointed at the screen. 'Look, she's even replaced a dash with a semicolon. Good for her. I know I'm supposed to be the techie, but I'd love to meet Marion. Though she'd probably prefer to be called Mrs Roberts.'

'I wouldn't have a problem with you finding out, Paula. Why not take my place? Why not pair up with Robyn when she goes to interview her? If you don't mind, Robyn? I'm sure Mrs Roberts would approve the notion of two sets of eyes being better than one. Pedant and people skills — a good combo.' Fran felt decidedly noble. Mrs Roberts was one witness she'd have liked to talk to herself.

'It'd be fine by me. But I'm really sorry — maybe I shouldn't have volunteered, but I really wanted to get experience . . . and to work with you. Both of you,' Robyn corrected herself swiftly, battling a painful blush. 'The thing is, I'm due in court tomorrow. Just the one day, probably. Maybe Wednesday as well. I really am so sorry, letting you down, gaffer,' she added, turning to Fran.

'You're doing your job; you don't need to apologize,' Fran replied, delighted to be promoted. All the same, it would be hard to cover so many eventualities with just four of them. 'In any case, Mrs Roberts might not be free tomorrow,'

'One way to find out! I know her phone number's somewhere on the data I inputted earlier, gaffer.'

Mark scrolled down till he found it; grabbing her mobile, Paula left the room. 'All these gaffers,' he said with a grin. 'I suppose we couldn't just be Mark and Fran, could we? Because we don't want to have more chiefs than Indians.'

Stu looked as disconcerted as Robyn. 'But we always call bosses gaffer.'

'And you must be bosses if you're jetted in specially,' Robyn pointed out.

'Or are we magicians pulling rabbits out of hats? Or dowsers looking for hidden springs?'

'We might be made redundant, in that case,' Fran observed, eyeing the rain.

Mark laughed with the others. 'Actually, I'm sure we're only here because of the reshuffles brought about by the merger. We see ourselves as team players. So long as you give Fran the captain's armband,' he said with an affectionate glance.

'Thanks, gaffer,' she responded promptly.

Paula blinked at the gust of laughter which seemed to be directed at her as she returned to the room.

'Just Mark making mock of me,' Fran said quickly. 'And me of him, to be fair. Any joy with Mrs Roberts?'

'Ten prompt tomorrow. You and me, gaffer.' She turned aside as Robyn muttered in her ear, and then spread her hands apologetically. 'It would feel odd to say "you and me, Fran". And I reckon Mrs Roberts would expect me to call you something.'

'Apart from referring to me as ex-detective chief superintendent all the time! OK. *Gaffer* in public. I've had quite enough of being *ma'am*, thank you very much; always makes me feel like the queen.' She produced a parody of the royal wave. 'Now, how long will it take us to get from here to — where does she live? — Cleobury Mortimer?'

'Forty minutes.'

'Let's give ourselves time to plan the interview. Could you pick me up from here at nine? Excellent. Robyn, before you go off to prepare for tomorrow's court appearance, just one thing: you told us about the Garbutts. Did you have time to get through to the hospital?'

'Yes. There's a direct line. Really efficient.' She might have been making a point, mightn't she? 'Unfortunately for us they only keep records for eight years after a patient has died. Department of Health guidelines.' She paused to let the others mutter.

Fran said gently, 'It was a very long shot. It's something we could ask her mother when we talk to her. But thanks for trying.'

'That's OK. Actually, if you don't mind, Fran, preparing for tomorrow would be a good idea for me too. I don't want to let the other team down. We need that result.' She gathered her things and left.

As she shut the door, Mark's phone rang. Raising an apologetic finger, he took the call, looking grimmer by the second. The other three fell silent.

'Very well. If you insist.' He turned to the team. 'The ACC wants to review our progress already. Already! And while he talks to Fran and me he wants you two to return to your usual tasks.'

Stu looked at his watch. 'I guess that means going home. But that doesn't mean I for one won't be here first thing tomorrow.'

CHAPTER SIX

Mark wanted to respond with Pavlovian urgency to the ACC's summons, but Fran slowed down their walk to a manageable pace.

'And what do you make of our team?'

'That's a bit of an optimistic term. Stu's a weird mixture, isn't he? That stuff about Housman. I could kill Paula for her addiction to her phone and her tablet. And I really don't feel I've seen enough of Robyn to make a judgement — except to ask why the hell she's there when she's obviously deeply involved with another case. What about you?'

They were turning into the corridor leading to the ACC's office, so she dropped her voice. 'What worries me about Paula is that her being here was apparently her boss's idea, not her own at all. As for Robyn, all I can say is that she really values her privacy. I didn't think Stu was the sharpest knife in the drawer, but now I'm not so sure.' Coming to a halt, she knocked firmly on the ACC's door.

To their increasing fury, they were kept waiting in the corridor like naughty kids bracing themselves for a bollocking from the head teacher. They could hear raised voices, one of them female. She did not sound happy. Nor did she look it when she emerged to head down the corridor. Sandra

Dundy, still elegantly dressed, still managing to stride despite absurd heels. She turned off into the ladies' loo. Fran pressed Mark's hand and set off too, and was soon peering into the mirror applying lipstick. Perhaps a little more mascara.

Dundy was taking her time in the cubicle, but eventually emerged, stowing her phone in her bag. Texting while using the loo? It didn't seem quite decent. But she washed her hands thoroughly and peered for paper towels as Fran finished brushing her hair.

'My poor hair!' Fran groaned — and actually she should have had it cut before she left Kent. 'The wind — not to mention this rain,' she wailed.

'I've never known it like this, all the time I've lived here,' Dundy said. She abandoned the hunt for towels and applied her own lipstick.

'You're local, are you?' Fran asked. 'In that case — would it be an awful cheek to ask where you have yours done? That's a most beautiful cut.'

It seemed it wasn't. And Dundy even had a card somewhere in her bag. A Gucci bag, too. To go with the shoes. Which she'd got from a darling little shop . . . If she cast a disparaging look at her flatties, Fran ignored it. Until Dundy asked the question Fran had been braced for since she'd first opened her lipstick. 'What brings you up here?'

'I'm just doing a spell of freelance work. No idea how long. Hence the need for a hairdresser. And you? Didn't I see you with the chief constable the other day?'

Dundy glanced at her watch and theatrically discovered she had to be elsewhere. 'It's been nice meeting you, Ms . . . ?'

But perhaps Fran didn't hear the question. 'And you!' She gave a cheery wave to the rapidly closing door.

* * *

The chief constable, in normal uniform this time, left Webster's office several minutes later. He ignored Mark and the newly brushed Fran, though of course he'd not acknowledged them before, either. Fran couldn't imagine any of the chiefs she'd worked with recently not stopping to make the acquaintance of well-turned-out strangers and to pass the time of day; most would have done so out of native courtesy, the most recent out of a sense of paranoia that something might be happening on his patch that he wasn't in control of.

Mark counted to thirty and knocked. Fran would usually have knocked and walked straight in, but held back — no point in doing something that would certainly make Mark feel uncomfortable.

It was some minutes before Webster dragged the door open, closing it behind them with something very close to a slam. 'In a nutshell, your instant response,' Webster demanded, not even waiting for them to sit, though he flung himself into his executive chair.

Fran didn't lie often, but she did this time. 'We've found something very fishy. We'll find Natalie, dead or alive.' Against all her principles, she even added 'sir'. She didn't dare look at Mark. But she'd bet her pension he wouldn't contradict her in public. She sat down, crossing her legs. For good measure she folded her arms across her chest — once she'd finished crossing her fingers behind her back.

Clearly taken aback, Webster almost flinched. Was the pressure he was under financial or something else?

'We'll be able to give you a clearer picture this time tomorrow,' Mark said, positive and keen, but also taking a seat. 'Unfortunately we're hampered by several things. There is only paper- and computer-based evidence. We've seen nothing concrete at all. And after twenty years that could prove difficult.' Seeing Webster about to interrupt, he continued, 'Furthermore, two of our volunteers voted with their feet before we even sat down together. Another — and we appreciate there can be no argument about this — has been summoned to give evidence in court. You've returned the other two to normal duties. Five investigators can't be expected to find in three hours what previously eluded a full search team with their follow-up enquiries for the best part of a year. Two even less, of course.'

'Surely that's what you're here for. Meanwhile, we're wasting a lot of resources.'

'With due respect, minimal resources. If you want us to walk away now, we will. Though we would bill you for the entire week and all the out-of-pocket expenses incurred so far.'

An administrator paying someone to do nothing? Webster almost shuddered. 'I never suggested you should quit now. Absolutely not.'

'Excellent. Because what I'd like permission to do is what is common practice in cases like this: in addition to the small paid team which we'd obviously need, to call in some retired officers to work on an expenses-only basis.'

Fran nodded. 'You'll recall that you gave us contact details of all those who originally worked on the case; as you'll have predicted, we would want to speak to them anyway, but some might like to join us.'

Webster looked unconvinced. 'If they couldn't sort it out then, how could they now?' He looked at their implacably positive faces. 'I suppose it wouldn't do any harm. Reasonable expenses only. Till Friday, shall we say?'

Mark's smile would have sold toothpaste as he wilfully misunderstood. 'For our next meeting? Excellent.' He and Fran were out of the room like rabbits who'd seen a gun. If he'd answered a question that hadn't been asked, that was tough.

* * *

They worked on till well after six phoning the retired officers on Webster's list: Anderson, Mike, through to Thompson, Christine. The investigating days of many were all too clearly over; two or three showed even less interest than their lunchtime Jeremiahs, and several others had prior commitments. They were left with a possible four or five, only one of whom agreed to meet them that evening. Another pub, this time, to their great relief only a mile away in Ombersley, an easy walk. So they parked up at the cottage.

More in hope than expectation Mark checked the gas gauge. Still a big red zero. At least Ted's mate had delivered some logs and even thrown a tarpaulin over them. Win some, lose some, obviously. But any moment now they were going to lose the logs, too. When they'd arrived, the yard had been no more than waterlogged. Now, in the space of four minutes, it had become a stream. Yelling to Fran, Mark reversed the car as close as he dared to the woodpile, hauling on his wellies and slinging Fran hers, and then filling the boot haphazardly. She dumped the remaining logs on the kitchen floor before returning the car to dry land.

'This is clearly a declaration that we're staying here come what may,' she said resignedly, helping him off with his waterlogged coat, which was dripping on the polished kitchen floor.

'So was your announcement to Webster that we'd found something fishy,' he countered, easing off his wellies by pulling the heels against the doorstep, and regretting the absence of welly socks. 'Which by my reckoning means both of us are off our heads. OK, OK, I acted on instinct with those damned logs. I should have let them float away . . . Is it my imagination, by the way, or is the place still cold? Because if it is, logs or not, we're finding a hotel.'

The agent had taken the welcome pack. He'd left a note telling them not to use the bathroom extractor fan in case it undid his temporary repair, and several oil-filled radiators, though he'd apparently forgotten to switch any on. Whatever heat they gave, they'd give it slowly. Fran was fairly sure she didn't want to hang round to discover their eventual thermal output.

'Of course we are. Right now. I'll go and pack. Hang on, what's that?' She peered round the door to see a tanker inching slowly back towards her. 'Bloody hell, it's only the gasman who cometh. What a saint!'

'Maybe it's an omen,' Mark murmured, almost hoping it wasn't, and that they could declare their investigations dead and get back to Kent.

* * *

The gas delivery driver proved a saint indeed, saying that as he was wearing oilskins and had to keep an eye on the tank feed anyway he'd help Mark stow the logs. They went in the proper place this time — a shelter behind the tank. Although she was ready to dash out to help, Fran saw they were deep in conversation, Mark asking questions, apparently, and the driver responding. Should she leave them to it while she brewed coffee for them all? And why not dig out some of those lovely biscuits? Dressed as if for a route march, she carried a tray carefully across their new stream.

The men were talking about football. *Football?* In the circumstances it might just be almost as important as the welcome LPG, so she didn't attempt to join in. The driver left with a smile, which should broaden even more when he found the twenty pound note she had tucked in his cab.

Mark's grin was just as wide. 'Roy Swallow. A saviour in more ways than one. He's given me a better lead than any we've had so far,' he said. 'His dad used to be in the West Midlands force. Joe Swallow. Based in West Bromwich about the time of Natalie's disappearance. He was what was called the match commander — police manager, these days. And Roy there reckons nothing pleases his dad more than having a chinwag with other ex-cops. I'll phone him now . . .'

* * *

The King's Arms in Ombersley was as warm and welcoming as they could have wished, with a menu as interesting as the previous evening's. The place was old, with duck-or-grouse beams and roaring fires. But there was no sign of their contact. A man from a later generation might have spent his time on the Internet hunting information; Mark had a feeling that had he even started to research Phil Foreman Fran would have thrust the iPad down his throat. After forty-five minutes — they never ran out of things to talk about, even after all this time together — they gave her up and ordered. But just as their meals arrived, up surged a newcomer, asking for them by name. Fi Biddlestone had arrived.

She was a strong-boned woman who might have been anything between fifty and seventy, with a crushing handshake. She was probably Fran's age, but apparently didn't care about skin or hair care. Fran resisted the sisterly urge to pass on the details of the commissioner's hairdresser.

'Floods,' Fi declared, sitting heavily. 'I'd have phoned but I couldn't get a signal till I got within half a mile of here. And I've got to fight my way back, so I'm sorry, I can't stay. Not to eat, anyway.' She pushed away the menu, but looked regretfully at Mark's lamb shank.

'Look, have you time to eat this? I can reorder,' he said. 'The evening's our own,' he added briskly, hoping nonetheless that their yard-stream would still be navigable. Not to mention the other lanes.

Fi hesitated but took the offer at face value, getting up to fetch cutlery from a side table. 'Tell me about this volunteer policing,' she said, 'and how you see me fitting in. If you don't mind I'll just eat while you talk . . .'

* * *

'Really you're looking for someone to grass up their colleagues for failing to do their job properly,' she summed up as she pushed her plate back and wiped her mouth.

'Not at all. I'm sorry if I've given that impression,' Mark protested, still awaiting his second supper. 'Few enquiries can work miracles, especially given the circumstances in which this was conducted. But occasionally someone will pursue one line as opposed to another that might, with the benefit of hindsight, have proved more profitable.'

'Archie Blount was one of the best,' Fi declared. 'Have you got him on side yet?'

'The first we asked,' Fran said truthfully. She cast an embarrassed glance at Mark, still waiting though she'd finished her perfect steak. 'But he's baking in a heatwave in New Zealand for the next three weeks, poor man — he must wish he was back home.'

'Oh, yes — being warm and dry must be terrible,' Fi agreed, her irony matching Fran's.

'And by that time we're supposed to have everything tied up.'

'Who did you say brought you in?'

'Gerry Barnes, but—'

'Tall thin guy? Knew a lot about the gee-gees. He's done well, hasn't he?'

'Depends if you think redundancy equals doing well,' Mark said. 'The guy we're answering to now is the ACC (Crime), Colin Webster.'

'Little pen-pusher? Look, if I can get through the flood water, I'll happily look through your files. But Archie did his best, even though we kept on falling over the private detectives swarming round. Paid for by that footballer, I suppose. I didn't get the feeling he wanted her back but according to one of the PIs he had ambitions for that lad of his, I suppose. Hector or something . . .' Absent-mindedly she reached for Mark's glass of red and sank it.

'Private detectives?' he asked, regretting the wine rather less than the lamb, though when a waiter brought the replacement shank over, he might as well order more wine, too. A bottle. 'I don't recall seeing anything about that, do you, Fran?'

'It's not the sort of thing you miss, is it? You wouldn't — I mean, it's twenty years ago — recall a name, would you? The firm's, not any individual investigator's.'

Fi flushed. 'No. Not at all.'

Fran caught Mark's eye and made an infinitesimal movement. He knew at once what she meant — he was to take himself off. Muttering an excuse, and hoping their guest would limit her intake of his wine for her own sake — she'd soon be well over the limit and she'd need all her wits for what she'd said would be a tricky homeward journey — he headed for the gents'.

'It's all right, you know,' Fran said. 'It won't go any further.'

'What won't?' The flush spread into her hair, down her throat.

'You obviously don't want to contact this chap yourself. It all went pear-shaped, did it?'

'OK, OK . . . it turned out he had a wife, and though I probably didn't care two hoots at the time, I find I do now. No, I couldn't face seeing . . . even talking . . . It's not as if it would bring Natalie and the kid back, is it? Just a cold case.'

'But we could talk to him very discreetly — say, as we said to you, that we were trying to contact everyone who had worked on the case,' Fran said in the voice she'd always found useful when trying to cajole people into doing something they'd rather not do. 'Just give me the name. I'll sort it.'

Fi paused while Mark's lamb arrived, and while Fran asked for a bottle of Rioja, which came post-haste, along with a spare glass. Fran poured.

'Desmond,' Fi said at last. She stared into the glass, her eyes softening, and lifted it as if toasting the past. 'Desmond Markwell. You could try googling him, I suppose.'

Fran dug her phone from her bag and did just that. Turning the screen so Fi could see, she asked, 'Is that him?'

There was no need for her to say anything. Fran killed the phone and took the other woman's hand. 'Thanks. If you can get through to Hindlip, we'd love to have you aboard.' Her turn to blush. 'What a stupid thing to say, in the circumstances! As if we were going into an ark!' But she couldn't resist glancing at Mark, over in the corner, wondering if he dared return yet; at least he and she would march in two by two.

* * *

Despite the stream bubbling six feet from the kitchen doorstep, the cottage itself was still dry. If only they had some sandbags. Surely the cottage must have been at risk before, and somehow sandbags didn't seem the sort of things you'd throw away. Leaving Fran to get the fire going properly again, Mark rooted round. No sandbags, but a lot of unopened plastic sacks full of potting compost and bulb fibre. He dragged them to the kitchen step, and heaved them into the nearest he could manage to a makeshift dam.

At last he stepped into the blessed fug of the cottage; it was amazing what the combination of oil-filled radiators and central heating had achieved, not to mention a now roaring fire. Any moment now they'd have to open windows to cool the place down. But Fran had already opened the wine that they'd brought back from the pub, Fi having firmly declined it. And who'd want fresh air if they were going to take advantage of the candles she'd found and the wondrous sheepskin hearthrug?

CHAPTER SEVEN

Local radio made interesting, if worrying, listening the next morning. It was Mark's turn to make their early morning tea in bed; what he saw from the kitchen window made him switch on the iPad as soon as, still in his dressing gown, he snuggled back beside Fran. Sleeping nude was all very well, and the central heating was doing its best, to judge by the bangs and throbs, but the cottage wasn't insulated to the standards of their rectory.

'I'm just checking we can get in to work today,' he told the tip of Fran's nose. 'And when I've done that I thought I might just—'

More of her emerged. 'Email Caffy to see if the rectory's still standing? Thank goodness she offered to house-sit for us. Anyway, this 'ere journey to Hindlip. Any problems?' She peered at the iPad.

'Nothing serious — just reports of standing water. But there's a problem with Bewdley: they've closed the town centre so they can erect their flood defences.'

'Will that mean Paula and I can't get through to Thingbury Whatsit?'

'Cleobury Mortimer. Let's check the route — no, the Bewdley bypass is clear. And so is the A449 — I'm heading off to Wombourne, remember, to talk to Joe Swallow. I've not made up my mind whether to take Stu; I know you want to take Paula—'

'Correction: I want to go with Paula. I'd be more than happy to talk to Mrs Roberts on my own, but it was Robyn's gig, remember, in the first place. Actually with Robyn and Paula out, do you think you should ask Stu to mind the shop? Or would he feel horribly left out, like a male Cinders not allowed to go to the ball?'

'The thing is,' he said, getting up and grabbing clothes, 'we haven't enough bodies, have we? I didn't get a great wave of commitment from Fi — looking over our files isn't the same as working your arse off because you're desperate to find answers. You know what I'm wondering?'

'Whether we should ask Ted Day to join us? Perhaps we ought to discover the circumstances in which he left the force first? Or am I being a supine coward? Hell, we're freelance. We don't have to worry about office politics umpteen years ago. Do we?'

'Let me think about it while I shave . . . Then I suggest, having been in the icebox of a bathroom, a repeat of yesterday: gym, shower, breakfast at Hindlip . . .'

* * *

Having waved off Paula and Fran, Mark turned to Stu. 'Can I ask you something in absolute confidence?'

'Gaffer?'

'Do you know anything about the part Ted Day played in the original search?'

Stu's shrug would have done a Frenchman credit. 'I didn't even know he was part of it. Hardly know the guy. Iris would be the one to ask.'

'And would give full and frank disclosures?'

'Depends on the questions you ask, I suppose.'

Mark laughed. 'You sound like Fran. Which you should take as a compliment.'

'I do. I was a bit worried at first, but now I know her . . . Yeah, it's a compliment.'

'What question would you want to ask? Not that for a moment I'm suggesting you do any prodding; that's my job.'

'Look, I'm no high-flyer. Never have been. Can I think about this, gaffer? I've got stuff swirling round here.' He touched the back of his head. 'You know something, I've got a cousin who teaches in the same school as Ted. I'll have a natter to her. But it may not be today. She never answers her phone when she's at work. Not a good example, she says. And she only picks up texts during her lunch break. Anyway, I think ear to ear's better sometimes, don't you?'

'I do indeed. Now, I'm going to be out for the morning. Wombourne. Do you fancy coming with me?'

'You're all right, thanks, gaffer.' Which Mark suspected meant a negative. 'I want to go through the evidence store and then these files again and check why no evidence was ever collected — as far as I can see, of course.'

* * *

The reading matter in Marion Roberts's sitting room told them she was no ordinary little old lady. The floor to ceiling bookshelves to the left of the chimney breast were full of modern first editions, not entirely surprising given the emendations she'd made to her statement. The other side was crammed with books on geology and the environment. An elegant Edwardian display table, essentially a glass box on fine inlaid legs, contained what Fran presumed must be some choice mineral specimens, each labelled in a tiny and meticulous script.

Pouring tea — she used leaves and a strainer — and handing home-made cake, Mrs Roberts settled back, crossing slender legs elegantly. She must have been pushing eighty, but her shoes, if low-heeled, were chic, and her clothes well cut. The fuchsia polo-neck sweater, almost certainly cashmere, shouted joyously under a charcoal jacket. Her fingernails matched. 'Tell me what you want to know.'

'I sensed,' Fran said carefully, 'that making the witness statement wasn't the height of your literary achievement. That whoever wrote it down—'

'Carefully, with his tongue stuck out!' Mrs Roberts gave a mocking demonstration.

'—wasn't as fluent or accurate as you'd have liked him to be. I've brought a copy—'

Waving it away, Mrs Roberts laughed. 'I have no need of an aide-memoire, I can assure you. I can see the events of — it must be almost exactly twenty years ago — as if they were yesterday. Rather better, in fact.'

'Could you recount them again? So we can record them?'

Mrs Roberts shook her head mockingly. 'No shorthand skills? Dear me. Very well. More cake? Can I refresh your tea? There. Are you sitting comfortably? Then I'll begin . . .'

They let her continue without interruption. The narrative matched almost word for word that in the statement. She did make clear that she and the Forestry Commission worker, whose name she now used — Mike Bridge — had shouted and called, only pausing when they heard the first of the emergency sirens. 'It was then that I noticed the footprints.'

'I beg your pardon?' Fran asked. 'That's not in the original.'

'Isn't it? It should have been. That idiot constable—'

'Can I just pick you up on the footprints?' Fran insisted. 'Pretend that Paula and I are the idiot constable and tell us everything we should know about them. Size, direction—'

'First let us establish that the greensward was soaked by the fog. You know what a lawn looks like when it's covered in morning dew? The grass verge was like that. And just as, if you peg the washing out before the sun burns off the rain, you leave clear footprints—'

'And get soaking wet shoes,' Paula, who'd been disconcertingly quiet, put in.

'Quite,' Mrs Roberts said repressively. But then she smiled. 'In fact, that's a very good point. I can't imagine any mother wanting her child to get its feet wet if they were going to continue their journey, can you? Because although our prints covered some of them, there were definitely two sets of prints: very small ones, at first close together, then further apart. You know how your stride lengthens when you run? Like that. Alongside were adult prints. Both sets continued along the verge for some yards, then veered to the right — on to the road, I presume. Certainly they disappeared. At this point the first police car arrived, and then there were more footprints than you could shake a stick at. When an ambulance arrived too, the scene became chaotic, and no wonder. Not that there was any hope of resuscitating the baby, even if anyone had wanted to try, poor little mite. Because I was concerned, later on I did a little research and found that it was rare for a child as badly handicapped as that to survive birth, let alone a few months — though I couldn't tell exactly how old it was, because none of the usual developmental signs were there. The memory still grieves me. Why should anyone . . . surely there are tests? Why should a mother . . .' She broke off, turning away. 'But then, having nursed the child to that point, imagine leaving it the moment it died in order to chase the other child.'

'Poor woman: what a dilemma. Talk about a judgement of Solomon.' Paula stopped. Fran suspected she couldn't speak.

Mrs Roberts passed a box of tissues from an occasional table. 'I'll make fresh tea,' she murmured, perhaps as an excuse to leave Fran to comfort the younger woman. In fact, as Paula gestured her frantically away, Fran got up and followed their hostess. Witness. But Mrs Roberts was so clearly in control of the situation, it felt more like a social call.

'Paula's a mother of two,' Fran explained tersely. 'I'm just a step-grandma,' she added, in response to Mrs Roberts's questioning eyebrow. 'But I'd be hard put to choose between Phoebe and Marko. Is there anything else we should know? Any observations you'd care to make, entirely in confidence?'

* * *

The terrible road conditions delayed Mark so much that he stopped to phone Joe Swallow to apologize. Swallow's immediate suggestion made sense: that he head straight to the pub where there was already a table booked for them. The Vine. All Mark had to do was follow the road round the village green and take a left when he saw the sign.

And what a village green. A huge green flat open space, with idyllically placed tennis courts — though perhaps a little too public for someone at his level. A cricket pitch too. And there was still some room to spare. In fact if anyone had sat down to design a perfect village, Wombourne might have been the result; he was passing more perfect old houses, a lovely mixture of ages and types. The far side of the green hosted a run of local shops, including a Co-op. A church. A library. Signs to the Leisure Centre.

The Vine was all Joe promised it would be, an authentic village pub. For some reason, the inn sign featured a badger, something none of the friendly bar staff was able to explain. They offered to make phone calls, to email people who might know, but Mark waved away the offers with a laugh: in the great scheme of things, explanations about pub signs came pretty low. Equipped with a half of the guest beer, he settled himself at the table reserved in Joe's name.

He'd hardly had time to scan the paper a waiter handed him when the door was opened by a man his height, broad-shouldered and erect. He shook the worst of the rain from his brolly, leaving it in the bucket provided. Though he used a stick it was with obvious disdain, not surprising since he wouldn't be much more than ten years older than Mark.

'Gammy leg: hip replacement a couple of months back,' the man announced by way of greeting. 'Can't wait to see the back of this damned thing. Makes me feel like Methuselah.' He thrust his spare hand in Mark's direction. 'Joe Swallow. You've brought the rain with you, I see. Shame. And I guess you'll be needing to drive back while the roads are still navigable.'

'It's going to be that bad?'

'Maybe if I were you I'd take the M5 rather than risk the Kidderminster road. But that's for later. Have you had a chance to look at the village?'

'Only as I drove through. It looks like retirement heaven.'

'Oh, it is,' Swallow declared. 'All the shops you need at my age; a choice of pubs; the church — and look at that cricket pitch. OK, it's a bit waterlogged now, but imagine sitting out there — or even at the front window of my flat — and spending your Saturday afternoons watching a mixture of up-and-coming lads and wily old stagers battling it out down there. Birmingham and District Premier League. I used to play for West Bromwich Dartmouth when I was free. Wonderful club. Players like Roly Jenkins in the old days. Sorry, you're not here for a nostalgia trip, are you?'

'I wish I was,' Mark said sincerely. 'But as I told you when I phoned, I'm working on the case of Phil Foreman's wife going walkabout. And I gather from Roy — and what a good lad he is! — that you had a great deal to do with West Brom back then, not just as match commander but socially, too.'

'Oh, ah.' The accent, which had been elusive, became decidedly Black Country. 'Look, we might be best ordering now; we can talk while we eat . . .'

* * *

Marion Roberts looked Fran up and down. 'Tell me, what can be gained by dragging up stuff from twenty years ago? Why not let sleeping cases lie?'

Fleetingly Fran was forty years younger — more! — being quizzed by her headmistress. But she managed a serious smile. 'That's a question I always ask when they find another Nazi war criminal. After sixty years might one assume he's atoned for his evil youth? But my whole training has taught me that all I do, in current or cold cases, is uncover what I believe is the truth. It's up to others to decide what to do with what I've found.'

'You sound like Pilate, absolving himself of blame. Are there any cases you wish you hadn't pursued?'

Fran wandered across to the sink by the window, which looked down the broad, elegant street. 'I can think of one or two I wish I'd pursued with even more fervour, when I knew there was something wrong. But my bosses pulled me off — budget, usually, or a more urgent case — and I always felt someone had got away with something. Often it's rich nasty people who get away with the most. Not always. But I was always appalled that people thought East End villains romantic or amusing. It even shakes me that people admire vicious men way back in time.' She gestured at the town. 'Think of all the power struggles a historic place like this has seen. How much violence.'

'I've always found it a remarkably serene town. John Betjeman for one deeply admired it,' Marion Roberts countered. 'But you're right. Might has long equalled right.'

'Absolutely. Think of William the Conqueror, aka William the Bastard. Think of all the people who didn't like his invasion who got killed most horribly. Sorry, I've been reading too much history since my retirement.'

The older woman was laughing. 'You sound remarkably anti-establishment for an ex-policewoman.'

'I tell you, the Poll Tax Riots, the anti-war marches — they tore me apart. Professionally I had to do my job; personally I'd have been out there protesting. Anyway, back to truth and justice. There may be other people involved in Natalie's disappearance. That's why I want to find out the truth.'

'And if the truth could hurt her?'

'That presupposes she's still alive, doesn't it? Marion, if there's anything you know . . .'

'I know nothing. Nothing. Apart, of course, from what everyone knows, which is that no remains have ever been found. But I was worried when the police assumed that she and her son had disappeared into the woods to the left when I'd seen the footprints towards the road. Nothing I could say would make them think anything else. Not the senior officers. One or two of the younger ones tried to support me, but they were overruled by people with rank and age on their side. They thought I was just a silly old woman. Goodness knows what they'd think of me now.' After making tea and setting the pot on a ready-laid tray, she led the way back into the living room.

'I can't speak for anyone else, but you can count me as one of your fan club. Tell me, what's your background? It's a very eclectic mix of books you're got there.'

* * *

Over his next half, Joe was at last talking about what Mark needed to hear. 'As the man in overall charge of the ground — yes, more important than the referee, only no one would agree with that — I got to meet the chairman after matches for drinks in the directors' lounge. There was more alcohol flowing round in those days than now, I dare say. All very friendly. You'd talk over the match, pick up gossip — and some hard facts.'

'Any gossip about Foreman?'

'And some hard facts. Which would you prefer? Any road up, twenty years back and more, I know the chairman was worried about Foreman's habit of picking up red and yellow cards — had the club doctor talk to him at one point. I never got to hear the outcome of that. Confidential, of course. Well, you don't want a potential buyer to get a whisper that the player might have health issues.'

'Health issues? You mean mental health?'

The older man made a rocking motion with his right hand. 'For whatever reason Phil was soon put on the transfer list. Baggies weren't at their best in those days, but the club he fetched up at was even worse. Which was it? It might have been Millwall. I've an idea he didn't hang about too long there, either.'

'I can check that. And any other clubs he went to.'

Joe nodded sadly. 'There's usually a downward trajectory once a player hits thirty. And if he'd got a bad disciplinary record — I mean, what good's a man to his club if he's constantly being suspended for games? — then it gets steeper and steeper.'

'Any idea what happened to him eventually?'

'No. You'll have to check on that too. I've an idea that the Professional Footballers' Association holds the medical records of all club players. I don't know if they'd let a retired bloke like you see them because they're all confidential, of course. But there must be someone in West Mercia with sufficient clout? Hey up, I must be going soft in the head. I know someone who knows the club inside out. The guy who runs the Supporters' Club. Hang on a bit: I'll give him a bell . . .' One of the old school, he walked stiffly to the door and made his call out in the porch, returning to the room with a satisfied smile. 'Alan'll meet you at the ground on Saturday. He's always there on match days, and other days too. He'll answer any questions you've got and maybe find you a couple of tickets — though they're like gold dust, I have to tell you. As are parking spots, but he's managed to do me a huge favour . . .' He overrode Mark's thanks. 'Look, I see our food is on its way.'

CHAPTER EIGHT

Fran and Paula saw no reason not to stay in Cleobury for lunch, fetching up at the King's Arms — they must have been very royalist in the area during inn-naming times — and tucking into bacon and Brie baguettes.

'All this on our doorstep,' sighed Paula, gesturing at the view from their window seat. 'And we never get here. It's all work for me, and looking for work for Gav, and running the kids hither and thither each and every weekend. And I don't begrudge them, don't think that for a minute, not even a second. But a breather like this — Fran, I could bottle it.'

'I could too. In fact, I might stretch out our breather a little longer and take a peep in that church. Look at that spire: all twisted. It's like the one in Chesterfield, isn't it?'

But Paula was less interested in church architecture than her tablet. 'I might as well take advantage of this free Wi-Fi and check my emails.'

Fran nodded. She needed to look up a number and make a quick call, too.

But she didn't get that far. Paula gasped, grabbing her wrist. 'Sorry, Fran: it looks as if visiting the church will have to keep. Look at this.' She turned the tablet so Fran could see a news headline that trumped everything.

* * *

Mark, ever conscious of cholesterol and all the other things the devil would insist on putting his way, tucked into his salmon with a virtuous salad; Joe, pointing out that he couldn't be bothered with cooking fancy things for one, had opted for the fish pie. They sank their halves in perfect harmony. Ideal for a man who didn't have to work. He bit back the thought that they really could have done everything over the phone.

The reason for his journey came in Joe's next words.

'If you've got half an hour and don't mind a bit of rain,' he said wistfully, 'I could show you summat of the town. There's lovely walks along the cut — that's canal, to you soft southerners.'

For all this was a dream village, Joe might be short of company, at least old cops like himself with whom he could have a decent chinwag. Mark resolved to be patient: it might not be too many years before he wanted the same himself. He even smiled at Joe's next question.

'Tell me, Mark, how on earth do you manage without a proper football side down in Kent? I mean, you're OK for cricket, but Gillingham — well, it's not a team going to challenge Chelsea, is it?'

'A lot of my mates used to play hockey. I didn't have time for anything much to be honest. But I've taken up tennis recently. Andy Murray I'm not, but it clears the head.' His phone warbled. 'Sorry. A text from my wife — do you mind if I just check? Bloody hell! Joe: I'm afraid the canal — the cut — walk must wait. I'd better head south. Now. Police work,' he added, getting to his feet and grasping Joe's hand. 'I can't thank you enough. Meanwhile, watch the local TV news tonight.'

'Keep in touch!' Joe said.

'Of course I will,' Mark promised. How else could he react to that hint of pathos? But it didn't stop him running to his car and driving faster than was strictly sensible.

* * *

'Rubberneckers — remember how we used to hate them at our crime scenes?' Fran said, coming up behind Mark and slipping her arm into his.

'I might have known you wouldn't be far away,' he said with an affectionate kiss. 'Hi, Paula. This is a bit of a turn-up for the books, isn't it? Who'd have thought a bit of rain would bring something this exciting?'

The three of them edged towards some of Paula's uniform colleagues guarding a comparatively minor landslip on the Severn Valley line, just north of Bewdley. It'd be the work of hours rather than days to dig out, were it not for one thing — the fall had exposed what the plastic tent now concealed. Already someone from one of the media had put a helicopter up; no doubt the adjacent field would soon sprout the inverted mushrooms of satellite dishes.

'Not just one skeleton but two,' declared a voice behind them. Stu. 'So this could be the end of our investigation before it really got up and running,' he said sadly. 'The Major Incident team'll be all over this like a rash and it'll be "thank you and goodnight" to you and back to basics for us. Can't win them all.'

Paula sounded equally bitter. 'They'll want every last crumb of what we've found and never a thank you.'

Mark and Fran exchanged a glance: how many of their junior colleagues had been disappointed when the interesting case they'd thought their own had been hijacked by the big boys? How many had hated Fran for marching in and demanding all their research, with the authority of Mark to back her, of course?

'You might find a bit more; doing so won't harm your prospects. Take as many photos as you can, but do it very unobtrusively. It's the crowd you want. People's reactions. OK?' She patted Paula's arm. Whatever photos she got, it was better for her to be doing something to occupy her; she didn't want the poor woman to have a rerun of the morning's emotions.

Almost of their own accord, Fran's feet drifted her away from Stu and Mark. The spurious authority of the ID she'd stuffed in her pocket after their meeting with Marion Roberts might come in useful. She fished it out, hanging it round her neck so that the words on the lanyard would be visible but not the card itself, which would betray her with the magic word VISITOR. She was committing fraud, of course. Worse still, impersonating a police officer. But all she wanted to do was talk to people. Most of all, to listen. On second thoughts, it might be better to hide the whole lot, just in case anyone would prefer to voice their thoughts to Josephine Public, and not someone who might want to take them down and use them in evidence.

A new gust of wind and rain — the two seemed inseparable — slapped her face. Putting up her hood might mean she missed snippets. On the other hand, in this wind, using an umbrella was an act of folly or Mary Poppins bravado. She'd just get wet. Safe in the knowledge that there'd be no trains coming along for a day or two, she plodded along the track, greasy and slippery though it was. That was where little knots of people were gathered, after all.

She tried the cocktail party technique of hovering on the edge of a group until she found herself included. It happened much more quickly than she'd expected.

'You were saying something about a body?' she prompted a woman about her own age, sporting a Severn Valley Railway cap in an attempt to keep her flying coppery hair dry.

'Ah. Two on 'em,' she declared in a ripe Midlands accent. 'But why should anyone want to put a body here? That's what I want to know.'

'You tell me,' said another, much smaller woman, shifting slightly to shelter in the lee of the tall women.

'They're not bodies, they're skeletons,' one of the men in the group said over his shoulder.

The Lizzie Siddal lookalike raised expressive eyebrows: 'You have to be one before you become the other, don't you? Stands to reason.'

'What he's saying,' the smaller woman said, 'is that they've been there some time. But how long? That's what I want to know.'

'Quite,' Fran put in, thinking that something was expected of her. And indeed, it was exactly what she wanted to know too. Suddenly she didn't want to be paid off and sent back to the comforts and pleasures of their Kentish rectory. She wanted the impossible, to be part of the investigative team.

'They had some cottages up there before the line was put in, didn't they?' the oldest man in the group said. Another, even stronger accent, almost like Lenny Henry's, but not quite. 'And no one could have put anyone in that bank as long as the railway's been running, or folk might just have noticed, like,' he added drily.

All of which would no doubt be debated in slightly more formal terms in the MIT incident room this evening. Without her.

'How long do you think the line will have to be closed?' she asked everyone but no one.

'Not as long as last time, please God. That was major. Back in '08, wasn't it?' Small Woman said.

'No. It was in 2007,' Lizzie Siddal insisted. 'I was on duty. Remember that rain like it was yesterday. Well, actually it was like yesterday. And today. And what do we get? More bloody interruptions to service.'

'Well,' began Lenny Henry man portentously, 'since it's winter we're only running a skeleton service anyway. Gerrit?'

They fell about laughing. And why not?

'Was you hoping for a trip, then?' Lizzie Siddal asked Fran.

'My husband brought the grandchildren in the summer — they loved it. He wanted another trip for us grown-ups — with fewer purchases in the shop, maybe.'

'No, you'll have to take them a couple of souvenirs, won't you?' Lizzie Siddal crowed. 'And you'll want summat for yourself, I'm sure. Even if you can't go on the train this time.'

'I'll be back, don't worry,' Fran declared. And meant it.

She drifted away, this time spotting a big bear of an old mate. It was a long time since Hugh Evans and she had got mildly drunk together at a jolly for senior officers and forensic pathologists, and had, indeed, a bit of a moment. He'd married, she'd married, of course, but they'd liked each other enough to keep in touch with Christmas cards and the odd email when an interesting case came up. She flapped a hand, grinning. He shed his police escort and headed over, giving her a hug and double kiss, clearly not the sort of greeting a frustrated train traveller would expect. She hoped none of her new friends was watching.

'A bit far north for you, isn't it, Fran?'

'It is indeed. And I'm not really here at all, not officially: Mark and I are just consultants on a cold case.' She gave the briefest of explanations.

'Brilliant. How's married life suiting you? No need to ask, actually: you're absolutely blooming.'

'Blooming what, that's the question.'

'That's my Fran. OK, we'll do supper tomorrow, the four of us? No, three. Jill's up in Sheffield for some conference. Got your phone? This is my number. Best leave it till tomorrow to fix a place — we don't want to choose somewhere only to find it's under water or about to be.'

'Brilliant.'

'Fine weather to find a pair of damned skeletons. Why doesn't the sun ever shine on these gigs?' He pulled down his naturally comic features into a mask of tragedy.

'Because it would make your investigations a lot smellier. Now go and be an expert!' She waved him off. Having achieved rather more than she'd set out to do she walked quite purposefully back to Mark and the others, who were obviously ready to head dispiritedly back to Hindlip. Tucking her hand into Mark's she whispered in his ear, 'Gold dust!' Which is what a good forensic pathologist always was — especially one as indiscreet as Hugh generally was with his friends.

Before she could explain, however, a familiar face appeared. That of Sandra Dundy. Now what was someone as exalted as a commissioner doing at a crime scene? But she could scarcely nip over and ask, could she? Actually, what she might have asked was why even Dundy's boots had high heels.

* * *

Iris raised her eyes heavenwards as the soaking quartet trudged through the entrance hall. Stu, who'd bummed a lift out to the scene with a CID mate, had returned with Paula; Fran had shared with Mark. This time she'd been able to make the phone call she'd postponed since lunchtime, to Desmond Markwell, Fi's ex-lover. He'd seemed disconcerted at the very least, and disinclined to talk. However, most people succumbed to Fran's persuasion sooner or later, and he agreed to meet her in Birmingham on Friday morning.

The coffee machine was the most popular item in their incident room, bar the radiators, to which they were drawn like iron filings to magnets. A general air of depression mixed with the damp of their waterproofs. Fran caught Mark's eye. It was time to raise morale. Should she speak first?

'Let's put into some order what we've found today. Then at least if the MIT takes over the skeletons, you both have information to take forward as part of your claim to be included in the team.' She'd put money on Mark and her being given their marching orders, of course.

'When do you think they'll let us know?' Stu asked.

'Given we still haven't heard officially about the landslip, I wouldn't even guess the answer to that,' Mark said. 'Come on, let's think positive. Paula and Fran — anything useful?'

Fran gestured: Paula should respond.

'Natalie's abandoned vehicle. We have a witness that there were footprints leading from the car when she discovered it. And the footsteps led to the road, not the undergrowth.'

'That'll be the old bat,' Stu observed doubtfully.

'Old bat? Mrs Roberts'd run rings round you,' Paula jeered. 'And me, actually. I'll get her statement transcribed soon as I can.'

Fran smiled her thanks. 'I sensed very strongly that she'd rather we left things well alone. Marion's clearly convinced that Natalie and Hadrian didn't die in the open that night. If we continue to hunt, we may put in jeopardy what she hopes is their new life.' She looked around. Did they agree with Mrs Roberts? And if they did, did they have the moral right to do as she wished?

'It's just her opinion, not founded on any evidence we've found so far,' Stu observed.

'Is non-evidence evidence?' Fran asked. She had an idea it might be.

Mark said, 'I might just have acquired something useful — though I admit it took me far longer than I like to get it. I had lunch with a one-time West Bromwich superintendent, the match commander, Joe Swallow; he's given me a useful contact. I still haven't had time to put together the complete profile of Foreman I promised. I'm sorry. But I gather he wasn't the most gentlemanly of players.'

'You mean he collected red and yellow cards all the time,' Stu concluded.

'Quite. He sold up his Edgbaston place when he moved to Millwall. He had a relationship with a high-profile model a couple of years after that. They split up. Then there was a girl who did TV voice-overs . . . He never remarried, and interestingly never made any attempt to get Natalie declared dead.'

Stu scratched his head. 'That's quite odd. What about money? Don't you need that to get at her bank account? Her savings?'

'Perhaps they had joint accounts in everything,' Fran said doubtfully.

'Joe pointed me in the direction of the Professional Footballers' Association. Stu, you've got police authority, which I haven't; can you get on to them to see his medical records?'

Stu nodded. 'Right. I wonder if he left his violence on the field? But in the UK he's never even been charged in connection with any incident.'

'Not even road rage?' Paula asked.

'Not even a speeding ticket. I checked and double-checked. Nothing about him on file at all.'

'Well done — and thank you for doing what I promised to do.' Mark caught the expression on Fran's face. 'Go on,' he prompted her.

'A year or so ago I'd have laughed at myself for making such a silly suggestion. But in view of certain Top People's recent activities with their speeding points, I'll ask anyway: any charges against Natalie? Traffic violations, anything like that?'

Stu blinked. 'Ah, you mean like Huhne and Pryce. Yeah, good idea.' He made a note. 'As for evidence, I did look, gaffer, but I didn't find so much as a rusty button. Thing is, we were only looking for corpses, not live motorists, weren't we? And CCTV wasn't sprouting out of every bush like it is nowadays, even if the gaffers then had wanted to look. But I did manage something. I managed to talk to my cousin, the school teacher. About Ted Day. At least, I told her I wanted to talk about him. She said I could buy her a drink on her way home from school tonight. Which isn't as early as it sounds, by the way. I always thought it was a nine-till-three job. Seems she always works till gone six, and later if there's a parents' evening. So I'll see her about six thirty. I'll hang on here, do a bit of sniffing round on the net myself.'

'Thanks. And you can claim for expenses, remember.'

'What's a vodka-tonic between friends? Go on, I can shout for that myself. Don't want to blow our budget, do I?'

The phone rang. As one they froze. Was this the call from the ACC to tell them to disband?

CHAPTER NINE

It was actually Colin Webster's secretary. Mark and Fran were invited to meet the ACC at six thirty to discuss developments. She did not divulge which party was expected to announce developments, even when, extremely casually, Fran asked her.

'Hang on, you're freelance,' Paula objected as Fran, pulling a face, cut the call. 'It's part of our contract to have a flexible working day. But you two? I'd have thought you'd be nine till five.' Then she added, with a grin that made Fran want to hug her, 'Actually, not you two. My first gaffer said she'd never ask us to do anything she wouldn't do herself, and you're like that, aren't you?'

'But there's nothing to stop you leaving at a reasonable time,' Mark said with a smile. 'See a bit of your family.'

She looked at her watch. 'It wouldn't feel right, with the rest of you still here. I'll sort out that transcription — it'll be a good start for tomorrow.'

* * *

At least Colin Webster seemed to have been working late, not just wilfully exerting authority, if the heap of files on his desk was anything to judge by. His office was rich with antacid fumes; he was still chomping when he called them in and invited them to sit.

'We've had some interesting news,' he began, stopping as they exchanged a glance. 'Two skeletons have appeared after a landslip north of Bewdley. It looks as if at last we have evidence. That being the case, I'm assuming your work here is done and we can terminate your contract.'

'Assuming the remains are indeed those of Natalie and Hadrian Foreman, of course we're happy to hand over our findings so far to your MIT. But we would put in a plea for the other members of our little team, DS Stu Pritchard and DC Paula Llewellyn, to join the MIT. They've worked very hard and have a real grasp of the background.'

'Not DC Marlow? I thought she'd volunteered, too?'

So he was more on the ball than he sometimes looked. Impressed, she continued, 'She did. But she spent today in court, and may have more days to come. We've absolutely no complaints about her; we were as disappointed as she was when she had to leave us. We'd have welcomed her back, no doubt about that,' Fran declared, adding with a touch of malice, 'We still would, if the remains prove to belong to other victims.'

'I can't see any likelihood of that — far too much of a coincidence.' But Webster looked furtive — guilty, even. He was clearly dying to ask what Fran knew about the find.

She obliged without forcing him to prompt her. 'I agree, quite a big coincidence. But the people I spoke to at Bewdley seemed to have doubts about the age of the remains.' There was no need to point out that these weren't forensic scientists, just railway enthusiasts with a lot of common sense and local knowledge.

'You've been out to the scene?' He popped another couple of Gaviscon and chewed hard. He also scribbled a note.

'Only as members of the public, of course. We headed over as soon as we picked up the information on the BBC News page,' she said cheerfully. 'I was with DC Llewellyn at the time; I notified Mark, of course. And DS Pritchard joined us, naturally. We were expecting an official summons, to be frank.'

'Didn't you get one? I must have a word.' He jotted, as if it was news to him.

Which, given the sentences with which he'd opened the conversation, it clearly wasn't. But this time they didn't exchange a glance, each entirely sure that the other was thinking the same thoughts.

'What makes you think the remains aren't those of the Foreman family?' he asked quickly. 'Whose opinion is it?'

He wasn't getting an answer to that question. 'Just a process of deduction. The railway cutting has been there for over a hundred and fifty years. The line and the line side must be checked regularly by people who get to know every stone, every blade of grass. They'd notice any unusual activity, like a grave being dug.'

'Natalie disappeared in a blizzard,' Webster objected. 'And snow lay for weeks. Any traces would be covered up.'

'Of course,' Mark agreed smoothly. 'But I bet the members of the railway — all dedicated volunteers — would be out and about anyway. I bet there'd be a lot of photos in their archive. Photographers love snow scenes.'

Fran added, 'I'm sure there are plenty of the big landslide they had back in 2007.' Not that that was relevant, but it would show they'd been doing their research. 'And I'm sure once the forensic teams have finished with the scene this time, the snappers will be recording each stage of the repairs to the line. MIT will have lots of easily accessible evidence,' she concluded as breezily as if she was in charge of the enquiry. To her embarrassment, because she loathed having any sort of meeting interrupted electronically, her phone warbled, as if the arrival of a text gave it android joy.

As if the mobile tone was a cue, Webster's phone rang. Fran took his preoccupation, indeed anxiety, with his call, as a chance to check her message. It was from Hugh Evans: 'You may be here a bit longer. X.' She showed it to Mark, who held the phone at arm's length — he'd left his reading glasses in the incident room, no doubt.

Webster's responses to his interlocutor were terse in the extreme. At last, cutting the call, he turned to them and said, 'We shall have to continue this conversation tomorrow morning. Shall we say eight?'

* * *

He could have suggested any time he liked, and in normal circumstances Fran and Mark would have presented themselves bright-eyed and bushy-tailed as ever. However, even Webster might have found it hard to be enthusiastic about an early start if he spent the evening as Mark and Fran did. The straightforward journey back to Ombersley became a nightmare. Trees were down, fellow motorists were stranded awkwardly at junctions and, as they watched, ditches started overflowing on to the road in front of them. As for the cottage, a quiet evening googling information was clearly off the cards. Despite Mark's improvised dam, the water inside was three inches deep. Even though this wasn't their own home, Fran gasped at the pathos of it — items chosen carefully, even lovingly, now dross. Wordlessly, they worked to save as much as they could, filling the pretty bedrooms with everything they could carry upstairs. The sheepskin rug ended up upside down in the bath, but Mark feared it would never recover.

To do him justice, Alex Fisher, the letting agent, was there in response to their phone call even before the emergency services arrived. A gangly man in his thirties, he emerged with difficulty from his four by four, already wearing not just a sou'wester but also waders over his business suit. In other circumstances the effect might have been laughable. He agreed they should leave as soon as they could. They'd done all they could, after all.

But he didn't stop at sighing over the sodden cottage itself. Armed with a portable floodlight — to call it a torch would have insulted it — he set off upstream. Curious, and knowing Mark would finish packing their belongings at least as well without her, Fran followed him. Her waterproof was already streaming, and she reckoned a little more water wouldn't hurt.

'This is above and beyond the call of duty,' she said with a grin. There was no point in yelling at a man in a suit prepared to go to such lengths. Delivering heaters was one thing; trudging through a torrent was another — even if it was only eight or ten inches deep, not yet threatening Fran's wellies.

'I'm just curious. Nothing like this has ever happened before — and we've had some serious weather over the last few years. There's a culvert up here designed to divert water round the property.'

'Doesn't seem to be doing its job very well! Whoops!'

'Are you all right?' Alex asked, grabbing her as the surge, shallow as it was, threatened to wash her feet from under her. 'Here, take my hand.'

Treading more carefully, his grip on Fran firm if bony, he sheared off to his left. He raised his torch. 'That's interesting.'

It was. The mouth of the culvert was completely blocked — plastic sacks, great lumps of timber, a few bits of scaffolding.

'You'd expect a build-up of debris after all this rain,' he said doubtfully.

'But that looks more organized than debris,' she concluded for him.

'Quite. Could you hold this lamp? I need a few snaps. I'll need to report to the owner — big insurance claim coming, I should think. And a bit of photographic evidence is always useful.'

'The police might find it interesting too,' Fran observed. 'Criminal damage. Come to think of it, we'll take it in turns,' she said grimly. 'I shall need some too.'

By the time they got back to the cottage, Mark had just finished loading the car, now intermittently illuminated by the blue lights of a fire service vehicle. 'Where's the best place to stay round here?' he asked Alex.

‘On a night like this it’s hard to tell which roads’ll be open and which not. Look, my aunt runs a B and B about four miles from here. Usually she’s only open in the summer, but if I have a word . . .’ He paddled away to find a signal. Soon he was back. ‘Would you like her to feed you? It’ll be out of the freezer, but she’s got some soup. OK? I’ll lead you there and then come back here and lock up.’

* * *

If the letters B and B had for a moment brought to Fran’s mind the terror of an unyielding seaside landlady and equally unyielding beds, she thanked heaven that she’d not voiced her doubts. A tall, elegant woman whom they would have placed in her sixties, had not a row of helpful birthday cards declared she was seventy-five, Edwina Lally welcomed them to her solid early Victorian house as if they were old friends. ‘I’ve just had the rooms in the main house redecorated and they smell of paint, so I’ve put you in the extension — there are more mod cons there, and you look as if you could do with a bit of a pamper. On sunny days you can even step right out into the little patio garden — it used to be the walled kitchen garden, I think. But I doubt if you’ll be doing sunbathing for a couple of days.’ Almost unconsciously, they somehow surrendered to her all responsibility for their well-being: boots and wet-weather gear disappeared. Edwina ushered them down a couple of steps, across a passageway with doors at either end and into their new quarters, where she left them to get acclimatized.

Thick towels and bathrobes hung in a bathroom warm enough to grow orchids (several growing on the window sill and vanity unit proved it); and a range of delectable toiletries tempted them to the environmentally incorrect but infinitely desirable power-shower. Fran nursed a suspicion that their self-contained unit might once have been a double garage, but felt it would be beyond churlish to ask their host.

They soon found themselves clutching glasses of Prosecco in front of an open fire and tucking into nibbles;

there was nothing like paddling round in flood water containing goodness knows what to stimulate an appetite. Then they were given the promised home-made soup, not to mention home-made bread, with a local white wine to wash it down. Local cheese to follow. Perhaps after all they'd both drowned and found themselves in the same mansion of heaven.

In that case heaven included electronic media: Fran texted Webster to tell him that for reasons beyond their control — and privately, the prospect of one of Edwina's breakfasts was one of them — they must postpone their meeting till nine.

The ten o'clock TV news programme tarnished their euphoria: it wasn't just the Midlands that were suffering from the vile weather. The Somerset Levels were under more water than ever; Devon coastal towns had been engulfed, with the main railway line literally washed away; and the Thames was rising ominously. Almost tucked away was footage from Kent: Maidstone, always vulnerable, was awash. And Maidstone was their nearest town.

Was their beloved rectory still intact?

Mark texted frantically. Caffy, builder extraordinaire, the woman who'd saved Mark's sanity and now their dear friend and house-sitter, responded immediately: *Matthew 7: 24–5 xxx.*

With a huge smile he showed Fran the message.

Fran blinked. 'And that means?'

'That the house is built on a rock and won't be washed away.'

* * *

'We should have told Edwina we wouldn't want breakfast,' Mark said guiltily at seven thirty the next morning, as the smell of bacon wafted upstairs. 'That meeting with Webster.'

'You may not; I certainly do,' Fran retorted. 'Even if we get in late and have to use the floods as an excuse,' she added blithely.

The breakfast was very good. Edwina was full of apologies that she couldn't offer them supper that evening, but offered to book them into a pub that wasn't cut off.

'We've already got plans, thanks,' Fran assured her.

But Mark was more interested in something else she'd said. 'Cut off?' he repeated.

'It's very bad. They've had to close one of the bridges across the Severn in Worcester itself. Gridlock, they say on the radio. It's a good job you're working this side of the city.'

'This afternoon I'm actually supposed to be working the other side of Bewdley,' Fran said, thinking of her meeting with Natalie's mother.

'If you go the long way round you should be all right,' Edwina said cautiously. 'But in these parts, when it's as bad as this, we tend to phone first before we make a journey. It's one thing the main roads being safe, but quite another with the lanes and side roads. More coffee, now, to warm you before you set out?'

* * *

In fact it was Webster who texted to postpone their meeting from nine till whenever he could get in. Both felt they could deal with the disappointment. 'What I want to know,' Fran said, tucking away her phone, 'is why he asked us in the first place.'

'He didn't,' Mark reminded her. 'Gerry Barnes did. Prompted by some official policy, of course. He couldn't just have plucked the notion from the ether — *Let's give Fran and Mark a bit of a gig up here* — could he?'

'And Gerry gets made redundant just before we arrive. Coincidence?'

'Great swathes of officers have been made redundant everywhere — though of course, we shouldn't call it redundancy. I keep forgetting, it's reminding people they can, and therefore should, retire once they've completed their thirty years' service. Silly me. As for coincidence, who knows? All

I know is that Webster wants to be rid of us the moment he can. Which makes me — and no doubt you — want to stick like a limpet.'

Fran didn't argue.

As they parked, Robyn texted to say she hoped to be in later: the roads were so chaotic in Worcester it looked as if the court couldn't sit.

Always one to play things by the book, Mark let HR know their new contact details, even giving Edwina's land line for good measure, before they headed to the incident room. There was the sound of raised voices. Stuart and Paula were arguing about which type of coffee was better. They seemed keen to involve Mark in the discussion, but Fran caught his eye.

Raising both hands, he declared, '*De gustibus non est disputandum*. The word order, even whether to have the verb *est* in at all, has always been a bit controversial. How about reducing it to *De gustibus*, as they say . . . ? Which means pretty well each to their own. Choose your pod, put it in the machine, press the button and await your own miracle caffeine fix. And then — because I sense we're living on borrowed time — let's get to work. Stu, did you get information last night or just a hangover?'

'Was that Latin, gaffer? Because they're talking about teaching it at my youngest's school. Do you reckon it's any use?'

'Your teacher cousin would be the best to answer that.' Fran sat down in the hope the others would do likewise. 'If you can afford another vodka and tonic, that is?'

'Sorry, gaffer.' He sat down. 'OK. Last night. Sharon was inclined to be what you might call discreet. As you'd expect. But I said what was said in this room stayed in this room. OK? Great.' But he spread his hands. 'In fact, after all that, she didn't have much to say. Ted helps with kids with behavioural or learning difficulties — one to one stuff, reading, IT, that sort of thing. Always accompanies one lad to assemblies and such because he seems constitutionally unable to sit still. Ted's one of the few people to be able to control him. Sheer force of personality, she reckons.'

'All good, then.'

'Not quite. He really doesn't like what he calls faffing around. Paperwork and stuff. He had a stand-up row with the last head, but since this guy was leaving anyway, Ted stayed put. And some of the kids are definitely afraid of him. That said, he gets amazing results.'

'Still good. Sounds as if your drink was in vain.'

'Apart from the fact Sharon's spotted him popping pills — the ones she took when she was depressed after her nipper was born. And sometimes, when they ask him to do something extra, he flatly refuses. No explanation, no apology.'

'Even that's not a hanging offence,' Paula said. 'A man's entitled to a private life — especially if he's a volunteer. Does he go to after-school things? Meetings? Parents' evenings?'

'Not keen on meetings for the sake of meetings. Will talk to parents. But apparently a couple of times when he's said he's got a prior engagement that prevents him from going, he's been spotted at his usual table in the Bull. On his own, as usual.' He looked around challengingly. 'And I'm not the one to ask Iris why.'

'Quite. Originally, remember, we thought of asking him to join the little team. In view of what you've heard, do you think — assuming he was prepared to come — you'd welcome him as a colleague? As our folk memory, if nothing else?'

Paula looked around. 'We're not exactly overwhelmed with support, are we?' But a text claimed her attention.

'Even so,' Stu said. He might not have been the most intuitive of men, poetry apart, but when an officer with his experience had doubts, even those he seemed scarcely aware of, they weren't going to rush into things. His mobile rang. 'Sorry.' He left the room to take the call. 'I'll get on to the PFA in a sec,' he added, over his shoulder.

CHAPTER TEN

Any moment now, he'd snap at the mobile phone users. So with a jerk of the head, Mark silently urged Fran back to their own office. Urging her not to risk driving on her own to see Jeanette Garbutt might be best done in private. But she disconcerted him by suggesting without so much as a prompt that either he or Stu ought to accompany her. She'd have loved to help Paula to develop her interviewing skills. But the young woman had been so distressed when talking to Marion Roberts that Fran feared an even more intense reaction if confronted by a bereaved mother — even one who had coolly preferred a dental appointment to an afternoon reinvestigating her daughter's disappearance.

'So I'd like you or Stu with me. It's crazy to risk a solo drive on strange roads. Whom do I choose? Someone I'd trust to interview the Pope about birth control without causing offence but who knows as little of the neighbourhood as I do? Or someone who knows and loves the forest but who probably has the tact of an elephant?'

Mark grinned. 'Why not postpone the decision in the hope that Robyn returns? You know I won't be offended either way. Now, we didn't cover everyone on that list of the officers involved in the first enquiry — shall I have a go at that? And I might just contact Fi — see how she's coping with her floods.'

What Mark meant merely as an act of kindness had surprising results. Fi had been in touch not with her lover but with a journalist friend who'd covered the case. This woman, Bethan Carter, had been at the same school as Natalie. If Mark thought it would be useful, then Fi would get Bethan to phone him. Mark, of course, wanted to be more proactive: he'd like to call Bethan himself, provided Fi didn't think it would be counterproductive.

Fi didn't; Bethan didn't. In fact, she was happy to tootle over since she was in the district, provided Mark would guarantee she would have nothing to do with the dogs. He hoped she was only joking. He and Fran tossed a coin; she got to do the interview.

Afraid she might be late greeting her visitor, Fran ran down the stairs more quickly than usual. The entrance hall was still empty, but from her vantage point some six or eight stairs up, Fran could see two women outside, one petite, the other probably five foot six; the light was too bad to see any details. The taller one was doing all the talking, as the shorter struggled to yank off wellingtons. Fran went unobtrusively into reverse. Now the smaller woman was arguing, palms spread. She bent again — to put on shoes? The taller woman disappeared. In came short woman, to be greeted apparently spontaneously by Fran.

'Ms Carter? I'm Fran Harman. It's more than kind of you to give us your time.'

'Bethan. Actually I don't know what I can contribute after all this time, to be honest.' She stowed her brolly in a bucket doubling as an umbrella stand and put her wellies beside it before walking straight over to Iris to sign in. She must have been about fifty if Fran's sums were right; she certainly looked very good for her age. 'It doesn't seem to know how to stop, does it? At least it's rain, not snow. Not like it was twenty years back,' she observed. Her faint local accent became more pronounced as she called out, 'Hello,

Iris! How's things? How's that knee of yours? She had it replaced last year,' she added parenthetically. 'The left one, wasn't it?'

Fran was suitably shocked and impressed at Iris's total lack of a limp. She had an idea that the three of them could have nattered happily and meaninglessly all day, and was wondering how to wind up the conversation without appearing brusque.

It was Bethan who announced, 'Well, as my grandad used to say, *There's work to be done, ere the setting sun*. Though I've no idea where he got that from. Where have they put you, Fran? Oh, it must feel so grand to be popping up and down this staircase all day.'

* * *

'I was actually a reporter in Wolverhampton when Nat went missing,' she told Fran. She sipped the tea she'd asked for instead of coffee. 'So I got to know a number of people like Iris.'

'You must have been an invaluable source of information.' Which was a polite way of asking her to share it. Now.

'My editor might have seen it that way, but I don't think the police necessarily did,' Bethan said cautiously. 'Of course, I was trying to pick their brains, not the other way round, hoping to keep the story going. In those days the press office wasn't as obliging as it is now — there was this residual belief that if you gave the public too much information it would somehow undermine police authority. It's all changed now, thank goodness. Anyway, back then . . . the snow — all that snow . . . and she and Hadrian were under it.' She shrugged resignedly.

'You were happy with the theory? About a friend of yours?'

The younger woman raised a finger. 'We weren't bosom pals, Fran. I'd be in the upper sixth, as we called it then, when she was in the third or fourth form. Stourport High School. She probably knew more about me than I did about her, as you do about prefects. But she was in a number of sports teams: netball, tennis, that sort of thing. Represented the school, too, which is how I knew the name. I suppose that's why she got into sports administration. Not my scene at all.'

Fran could have smiled and agreed it wasn't hers either, but she didn't like lying, and her county championship level badminton was coming into its own on the tennis court.

'What about other school-friends? Are you still in touch with any of them? Was she?'

'I'm not. I didn't really enjoy school, and you know how it is . . .' She spread her hands. 'All these people trying to discover people they didn't even like when they were penned in a classroom together. Do you see any point in it?'

Fran wasn't to be drawn. 'Anyway,' she recapped, 'Natalie caught the fitness bug young. You wouldn't know if she kept it up after school? At uni for instance?'

'Other things to do there, surely.'

Nonetheless, Fran made a note to find out. And about gym and sports club membership in Birmingham. 'You said it was hard to extract information from the enquiry team back then. OK, that was the ethos then — but did you have any sense they were making a particular effort to be obstructive? As a team? Or any individual?'

Bethan blinked, as if the enforced return to the original topic disconcerted her. 'Oh, I don't think so. But I was only a cub, back then, of course.'

'And probably more observant than blasé old hands?' Fran pointed upwards. 'At this stage, it'd be strictly sub rosa. We're not investigating the police; we're trying to find out what happened to Natalie. Quite different.' Though there might have to be conversations with Police Standards later.

'No, no one sticks out. And actually I don't think they were obstructive. Just professional,' Bethan declared. Not necessarily truthfully.

'OK. Do you think the ethos of non-disclosure was stronger here than in other areas where you covered cases — presumably all over West Mercia?'

Bethan chuckled. 'I always used to say that the nearer to the Black Country you got the fewer questions you had to ask. Talk to someone in Dudley or wherever for five minutes and you were their new best friend. Lovely people, Fran, Black Country folk. The people you're dealing with are country folk. Like *The Archers*! Are you a fan?'

Fran ignored the question: this wasn't supposed to be just a conversation. 'And country people prefer you to mind your own business. I get it,' she said, thinking about Ted. 'Living in the country, as we do. Do you think they'd take sides if, say, one of their own was threatened by something? Someone? Yes, I'm talking about Phil Foreman. Did you ever meet him, by any chance?'

Bethan looked blank. Carefully blank? 'Why do you ask that?'

Fran spread her hands: 'You're a journalist: you might have got the chance to interview him when he came down here to see how the search was going — I presume he did?' she added, despite what Stu had said.

'If he did I never saw him,' she declared, with something of a snap.

'Are you suggesting he didn't? To see where his wife and child had disappeared? I know today we're all touchy-feely and leave flowers and teddies everywhere, but not to appear at the scene — and not to have an entourage of national media representatives swarming round — seems strange.'

'All I know is that I never saw him.'

Fran nodded her thanks, as if she believed her. 'You must have interviewed Natalie's parents — particularly as you were at least acquainted with their daughter. Tell me about that. Did they react as you'd have expected them to react?' she prompted.

'How would that be?' Bethan countered.

What was going on? Since Bethan had volunteered to come in, Fran had expected her to be cooperative and forthcoming. She said quietly, 'You've probably interviewed a lot of parents who've lost children, before and since. Bereaved men and women. OK, the vast majority would know their child, their grandchild, was dead. They'd have closure. If you knew how many families I've delivered that closure to . . . You must have acted as unofficial counsellor. I know I did, many a time. I was a sort of midwife to all sorts of emotions the bereaved didn't know how to deal with. And to be honest I didn't either.' She waited for Bethan to pick up the conversational ball and run with it. Waited in vain. 'Do I gather that the Garbutts weren't ready to talk?' Even now they wanted to wait forty-eight hours before talking to Fran — their readiness must take a long time to come to the boil.

'They were very distressed. But stoical. They wanted to concentrate their efforts on getting Julius a Christian burial.'

Something new at last. Wouldn't that be the father's responsibility? Or was he too grief-stricken to think of anything like that? 'Didn't Phil want to do that?' Again she felt she had to fill the silence she had hoped would elicit a response from the other woman.

'He'd be working,' she said with an air of finality.

Really? Did he carry on playing all that time? Another job for Stu. Fran smiled, hoping to find another way to skin a cat. 'Do you still work, Bethan?'

'Redundant about a year back. These days I freelance. I thought it might be nice to do a piece on you and — what's his name? — Mark. I bet that would sell.'

'As soon as we get this case sorted, we'll be all yours. Until then, we hardly have time to breathe, as you can imagine.' *Especially when confronted with someone as unhelpful as you*, she added mentally. What was going on? Did Bethan somehow feel she'd got fobbed off with the monkey when she was expecting to see the organ grinder? Perhaps she should try a new tack. 'We haven't got a very big team, you see. Mark — he's the one who phoned you — tends to do most of the admin work, which is a bit of a comedown from being an assistant chief constable. I do more of the hands-on stuff, because I retired more recently than he did. We've only got a couple of West Mercia officers helping us, which makes things more difficult because their systems are slightly different from how ours were in Kent.'

'Kent?'

Why was the question full of sharp interest? 'Like you, we're freelancing. It's not just West Mercia Police we're new to — it's the whole area.'

'So you're nothing to do with the local police.'

And why was that important? 'Only inasmuch as they pay our fee, which we donate to charity. All — all — we want is to find out what happened to Natalie. No recriminations, no nothing. We just want facts.'

'Like Mr Gradgrind,' Mark supplied, popping his head round the door.

Bethan Carter blossomed under the warmth of his everyday smile, getting to her feet and putting her hand in his, tiny, confiding. Feeling elephantine, Fran stood too. 'Mark, sweetheart, Bethan and I have been having a lovely girlie gossip, but I've not written anything down yet, have I, Bethan? Why don't you do the pen-pushing stuff, darling, while I keep my appointment with — heavens, I'm late already. Sorry, Bethan — see you when we do that piece for you, if not before!' She felt ashamed of herself for so obviously laying claim to her man. Or perhaps not.

Mark hesitated. 'Might I just have a word before you shoot off?'

They stepped outside. He closed the door. 'The skeletons,' he murmured. 'Hugh tried to call you but your phone was off.'

She nodded, jerking a thumb in the direction of the door. Then it was the fingers-and-thumb-closing *we were yakking* gesture.

'Anyway, they're not our skeletons. About twelve centuries too old. And no, I've not heard officially. But it might pay you to find out what official notification the Garbutts have had before you and Robyn go marching in.'

CHAPTER ELEVEN

'Hi, gaffer,' a very smart Robyn greeted her as she walked into the incident room. 'You look as if you've lost a pound and found a rusty button.'

'I've just spent half an hour trying to get a possible witness to talk, and Mark comes in and she eats out of his hand.' She demonstrated a winsome smile and flirtatious body language.

'Pity she's not going to find her teeth closing on a wedding ring. Why don't men wear them?' Robyn asked rhetorically. 'We do, both of us. Hers and hers, you might say.'

'Mark had one but he kept taking it off to do dirty jobs, and now it lies unworn in its little chamois bag. Very sad. Now, I take it the court didn't sit.'

'Nope. And there's this *flood* of top brass descending on the city, too — army, Environment Agency, city councillors, MPs. There's a big meeting to decide what to do if the water gets any higher — it's already up to its previous highest, which is a couple of hundred years back. Oh, and the media have descended. Can't move for satellite dishes.' Robyn smiled shyly. 'You said something about going to Buttonoak? With you?'

'If you don't mind. You know the roads; I don't. You've got people skills. Let's use them.'

'Wouldn't Mark—?'

'Between ourselves, I wouldn't mind betting he ends up having to buy that woman lunch as the price for two pieces of information you couldn't rub together to make a clue. Paula and I had a trip out yesterday. It'll probably be Stu's turn tomorrow. So are you up for a trip? You'll have to drive, of course, unless I take our car. But first, and since you'll know exactly who to ask, we need to know how your colleagues reacted to the news of the skeletons yesterday and now today.'

'Today? Oh, Fran—'

'I gather they might be Saxon. Anyway, we must know what the family liaison people told the Garbutts — and how, of course. Both pieces of news.'

* * *

Calm and charming Mark may have appeared to Bethan, but when Fran nipped in to get her coat and boots, he sent up a clear distress flare. She responded with something that popped up in her head from nowhere — and which should have popped up a good deal earlier.

'Sorry to interrupt.' Yes, she genuinely sounded it. Amazing and ironic that working for the police taught you to lie beautifully. She grabbed her things and made to leave. At the door she stopped. 'Mark: don't forget you promised to call Gerry Barnes. He said it was urgent, remember,' she lied.

'Damn. So he did.' Maybe Mark's reaction, hitting his forehead with the flat of his hand, was a little melodramatic. But, checking his watch, he stood swiftly.

'Can you call me and let me know how you got on? Robyn and I are just leaving,' she added, so he'd know he wasn't in on the Garbutt interview. She blew him a kiss and left.

* * *

There was no doubting the anger in Jeanette Garbutt's face, watching them from her kitchen window as they pulled up slowly outside her bungalow. Anger that this was the third visit by police officers in the space of twenty-four hours: the first had been to bring news of the remains; the second to confirm that the remains weren't those of her daughter. And now she had two completely different officers who claimed they were still investigating Natalie's disappearance. Fran would probably have felt the same. Flat anger.

The two women said all that was proper, Robyn referring to her family liaison colleagues by name and echoing their apologies for raising expectations in the first place and then for dashing them. Mrs Garbutt nodded briefly in acknowledgement, and put the kettle on.

Consciously or not, Robyn set about justifying her claims that she was a people person, not by crudely insisting on carrying a laden tea tray through to a sitting room that occupied the whole of one side of the bungalow — Fran did that — but by emanating a gentle but specific interest in her target. Body language? Facial expression? Her voice? Fran would have loved to have time to sit back and analyse the young woman's performance. Except it wasn't a performance: Robyn was clearly relating to this stranger in a way Fran wasn't, however much she tried to pretend she was.

Mrs Garbutt carried her five foot six or seven inches well, with still broad shoulders refusing to stoop. Her short grey hair was well cut, and her outfit — trousers and a shirt topped by a waistcoat — no-nonsense. Her only concession to age was Velcro-fastened shoes. Mr Garbutt lurked in a corner, next to a bookshelf. Fran headed towards him, shaking hands with him and finding a seat near his. He was stick frail, but his eyes suggested that whatever was harming his body hadn't reached his brain yet.

Robyn shook hands with him, introducing both herself and Fran formally.

Mrs Garbutt raised a quizzical eyebrow as Robyn added the prefix *ex* to the rest of Fran's former rank. 'We've never had such exalted police company before,' she said. 'Ex or not. It used to be constables we got; yesterday and this morning, of course, it was a sergeant. First to say they'd found skeletons; now to say they may not be the right skeletons. So what brings you now — *ex*-Detective Chief Superintendent Harman?'

Fran raised a placatory hand. 'Perhaps you'd be kind enough to call me Fran. The only connection I have with the West Mercia Police now is that they've asked me to recheck their investigation.'

'Ah, digging up the past's quite fashionable these days, isn't it?' Mr Garbutt observed. 'Jimmy Savile and all that. So what do you hope to find, ma'am? That's how they speak to people like you on TV,' he added, with a twist of a smile.

'Ex-ma'am, too,' Fran retorted. 'And you know what, I never did get used to it. Really I'm here as an adviser. Robyn's the one doing all the work.'

Robyn responded to Fran's smile with one of her own. 'I'd call her gaffer. But she insists on Fran. Lovely cake, Mrs Garbutt—'

'Co-op.' Mrs Garbutt clearly wasn't a woman for blandishments.

Robyn didn't wince, but carried on, missing hardly a beat. 'As I said on the phone, we just want, without intruding on your time or your privacy, to see if we can complete the original enquiry all those years ago.'

'Is it to do with some crazy government target? You have to solve x number of crimes? Like you suddenly target speeding motorists you've ignored for months?' Mr Garbutt asked.

'Not this one,' Robyn said. 'Forces can always improve current investigations by learning the mistakes of past ones.'

Mrs Garbutt snorted. 'You've come sniffing round here, you and your other friends, churning up memories, so you can do better next time?'

'So we can do better with other grief-stricken families in your position — not just us, but our colleagues all over the country. As I said on the phone, we want to make this as short and painless as we can. If at any time you want us to leave, we will.' Robyn paused.

The Garbutts exchanged a glance. Fran suspected that for all his frailty and her truculence, the husband's will was stronger than the wife's, and that his desire to continue with the conversation would trump hers to end it.

'What would you want to ask us? I thought we'd answered all your questions at the time,' he said.

'Of course. These are what you might call supplementary questions. Again, if there's anything you don't want to answer . . .' Robyn looked from one to the other. 'I understand you've moved here from what was the family house at the time,' she began, neutrally.

'We moved about five years ago: there was no point the two of us rattling round in a place that size. So if you were hoping for another rake through her room you'll be disappointed. We took everything to a charity shop, the whole lot. It might as well do some good, mightn't it?'

Robyn's expression was neutral. But Fran saw her let her eyes drift in the old man's direction. What was his view?

'He'd have kept everything,' Mrs Garbutt declared. 'Wouldn't you? As for the grandchildren — we kept . . . precious things. But I don't want to go poking through them now, thank you very much. If you want to do that, you can take the box away. Father'll show you where it is. Not that he can lift it down himself. But a strapping woman like ex-ma'am here should be able to.'

'Thank you. Would you prefer us to get it down now or when we leave?'

'On your way out.'

'Very well. Just one thing: do you ever remember Phil asking for keepsakes of her, or offering anything from their marital home you might have cherished?'

Mrs Garbutt pursed her lips. Her raised eyebrow told Robyn not to ask such stupid questions.

Fran, however, thought it was a very good one. 'Nothing at all? No? Tell me, how did you decide what you wanted to keep?'

'She'd know,' Mrs Garbutt declared, nodding in Robyn's direction. 'If she's got children.'

Robyn responded quietly, 'Not yet. Now, I hope these questions won't be too intrusive. One concerns Natalie's friends. Did you ever meet any of them? Did she ever bring any of them here?'

'Her school-friends, some of them. But they've all grown up and moved away, haven't they?'

'So you're not in touch with any now? What about friends she made later in her life, at university or in London? Can you recall any names at least?'

'After all this time?'

Nodding as if in sympathy, not frustration, Robyn tried a different tack. 'Now, I know this will be painful. I'm sorry. Little Julius. It must have been very hard for you . . .' She left the question unfinished: was it having the disabled grandchild in the first place that was hard or having him die in such difficult circumstances? When there was no reply, she continued, 'We know Edwards' syndrome can be detected before the baby is born. Yet Natalie continued with her pregnancy. Did that surprise you?'

'You mean why didn't she have another abortion?'

Robyn said nothing, but her whole body conveyed a sort of shocked sympathy. 'Did the first fetus have the same problem?' she asked eventually.

'Oh, she said it wasn't viable, whatever that means. But we always thought it was just because she thought it was inconvenient. Anyway, it broke up her relationship with young whatshisname. Nice young man. He offered to stand by her. But no, off she went and . . . Anyway, young Hadrian came along, bright as a button. Oh, he was a little gem, that one. Apple of his father's eye.' And his grandparents', evidently. 'And then Julius . . .'

'Did they hope that the doctors had made a mistake, perhaps? That Julius would be OK?' Robyn was evidently not going to get an answer. Perhaps there wasn't one that the Garbutts could give; perhaps not one that Natalie could have offered either. So Robyn tried a different approach. 'What did you feel about Philip Foreman?'

'What do you mean? Us feel? Nat made a dead set at him, by all accounts.'

'And why shouldn't she?' Mr Garbutt put in. 'Fine well set-up young man. More money than sense, I'll grant you. But Nat had enough sense for both — she was the first from our family to go to university, and I tell you straight, if she could have come and worked with me, I'd have been pleased as punch. Talk about a head for figures. And she knew her stuff. Even when she left work to have the baby, young Hadrian, she kept up with things — always reading the financial pages of the paper, the parts I always use to start the fire. So Phil made the money — a lot, they said — and she invested it. They made a good team.'

'Did you see much of them? Babysitting and such?'

'Grandparents' privilege.' Mr Garbutt turned to Fran. 'You got any?'

'I share my husband's two. And pour his G and T when they go home. He brought them up to the railway up here.'

'Good job it wasn't yesterday when they found the skeletons,' Mrs Garbutt said.

Fran made sure she didn't react; Robyn too stayed neutral. They were both used to black humour in the police, but neither expected to hear it from her. Was that because she was bereaved, Fran wondered, or because old people weren't expected to make such mordant remarks? Well, they knew Mrs Garbutt was no knitting-by-the-fire grannie, so let her have her quip.

'According to local radio the archaeologists think there may be more,' her husband added. 'That sergeant won't be round each time they unearth one, will she?'

Fran framed a response: *No, it'll cost too damned much.*

Robyn asked, 'Would you rather she simply phoned?'

'I'd rather she did nothing at all till she's got something useful to say. Now, is there anything else?' Mrs Garbutt demanded.

'We were just asking how much you saw of your grandchildren. You said you had a big family house — did Natalie bring them to stay with you?'

'Not after poor little Julius was born. He needed a lot of specialist equipment we didn't have. And then there was their nanny. Nowhere to put her. We used to see them in their posh house in Birmingham more than here — especially when the Albion were playing away from home.'

'You never saw them with him?'

'Did I say that? I said *especially*. Of course we saw him. As Father says, he didn't have a lot between the ears. Kept talking about a cure for Julius, daft lump. Thought he might walk and talk. Not that Hadrian ever did anything else. He was a handful, that lad. And his dad would egg him on, when he should have disciplined him. Said he needed to grow into a man, not some niminy-piminy mother's boy like his brother.'

'Just think, talking about poor Julius like that,' added Mr Garbutt.

'How did Natalie react when he did?' Fran asked.

'She didn't. Ever. Not in front of us, anyway. Or in front of the children. She was a good mother. Even with Julius, she did everything. She only had that nanny because Phil thought she was doing too much. And she was, too.'

Fran nodded. If it had been any other woman she'd have pressed her hand in sympathy. Instead, she was about to kick her, metaphorically at least, in the teeth. 'Natalie wasn't there, of course, to do the final act of kindness to him — organize his funeral. Did Philip . . . ?'

'Him?' Mrs Garbutt was silent for a long time, her face increasingly grim. But at last she said grudgingly, 'Well, to do them justice, the Albion welfare people were really helpful — some young woman kept in touch by phone until the roads were cleared, and I'll swear she was one of the first through to see us. She helped a lot. We wanted him buried here, of course, since Phil never went to church. Some idiot said it should be in Birmingham Cathedral or in some posh church where they lived. But they'd never put down roots, and weren't going to, were they? So this woman — Lizzie, I think she was called — helped set up the service and dealt with a lot of the paperwork. Of course, she knew Natalie by sight, didn't she, Father? So the little mite's in the churchyard here, where we can keep an eye on him.'

No mention of her daughter or the other child. Meanwhile, Robyn personified intelligent sympathy, but she said nothing. Neither did Fran. At last Robyn must have sensed Mrs Garbutt wanted to move the conversation on, and took up the questioning again.

'You mentioned that Philip insisted they have a nanny. You must have met her: what did you think of her?'

'Was it our place to think anything of her?'

Fran couldn't let that one pass. 'Come on, Mrs Garbutt, no one loves kids more than their grandparents: of course you'd have opinions, good or bad.' She wished the words unsaid the moment they left her lips, but Mrs Garbutt actually smiled.

'Father and I didn't agree. You liked her, didn't you, Father? Young Anna? I wasn't sure how far anyone could trust her. And then, of course, she left just like that!' She snapped her fingers. 'Walked out. Only a couple of weeks before — before . . .'

'I still think Phil sacked her. He had a temper, that lad. And if something wasn't just so, he probably yelled at her, and either she walked out, because there's only so much you can take, or he sacked her. And — come on, Mother, admit it — she still keeps in touch. We get a card from her every Christmas.'

Mrs Garbutt flashed him a look of undiluted fury. As offhand as she could be, she demanded, 'Well, what's a card?'

Robyn asked, 'Do you send her one — for old times' sake?'

'Just a cheap one. Nothing fancy.' Mrs Garbutt's mouth shut like a door in a gale.

'In that case, would you be kind enough to give us her address? Just for our records.'

Fran could have sworn that Mrs Garbutt would deny she knew where it was, but Mr Garbutt struggled to his feet and shuffled over to an antique bureau rather too large for a modern house. In his place, though, Fran would also have wanted to keep it, even if its elegant proportions made those of the room seem prosaic.

He picked up a family-size address book and found a page. 'There you are. Fratello. Anna Fratello. Bury St Edmunds.' Then he headed out of the room. 'I'm supposed to move around every few minutes,' he said over his shoulder. 'And there's all that tea . . .'

Robyn jotted before Mrs Garbutt could gather breath to stop her. With a smile, she replaced the book on top of the bureau. But she didn't sit down, catching Fran's eye.

What? Did Robyn want to end the interview? Just as it was getting interesting? Fran stayed put, but made a show of gathering herself together as if she was going to follow Robyn's lead.

'There are just a couple more things,' Robyn said, 'if you don't mind my asking. How did you feel when Phil employed a private detective to help find Natalie?'

Mrs Garbutt shot to her feet, white to the lips with fury. She made a visible effort to appear calm. 'Well, you do surprise me. Well, if you're telling the truth and he did, I suppose he thought he and his money could achieve more than a whole force of policemen out all hours and in all weathers. Well, he couldn't, could he?'

All that anger: it almost looked personal. She felt sorry for Robyn, now raising her hands pacifically.

Fran decided to draw fire to herself by asking a really tendentious question. 'Forgive me asking, but it really is my last question: sometimes when people lose loved ones, they find legal closure by having them declared dead. Did you or even Philip ever contemplate that?'

Her reward was a hard stare. 'I know she's gone. Why should I need a piece of paper? As for Philip, who knows? We've not seen hide nor hair of him in over nineteen years

— not that we expected to, and certainly not that we wanted to.'

Fran nodded. 'Yes, I quite understand. I know these questions have been intrusive, and I'm sure you'll be glad to see the back of us. Are there any questions you want to ask us? We'll do our best to answer.'

'Only the obvious one: why should you start to dredge through this all over again? After all this time?'

Fran shook her head. 'It was a management decision, Mrs Garbutt. We're just doing what we're told.' That was what the Nazis said, of course. A supine response. But at least it was an honest one. 'As for me, as Robyn told you, I'm just a hired hand.'

'We want to sort everything out and leave you in peace as quickly as we can,' Robyn said earnestly. 'Should we get that box now, Mrs Garbutt? We don't want your husband slipping a disc trying to lift anything heavy.'

'When you've got it you'd best be off. The roads like this you'll want to tackle them while there's a scrap of daylight left.'

* * *

Robyn drove tight-lipped as the wind buffeted the car, first one way then another. She might have slowed down to cut through standing water but other drivers weren't so considerate — or indeed sensible — and sent car-wash-size drenches of water over them. The wipers slapped relentlessly, unless the wind lifted them and rendered them momentarily useless.

'On a scale of one to ten,' Fran asked, 'how happy would you think our enquiries are making the Garbutts?'

'I'd put it on the minus scale. It's sort of like picking the scab off a half-healed wound — but you'd think they'd want to know the truth after all this time. Like you said, to get closure.'

'Can you think of any reason why they don't want us sniffing around again?'

'I've never met any response like it before. You don't think — you don't think they had anything to do with their own daughter's death? It was clear they had a very . . . uncomfortable . . . relationship with her.'

'Quite. I'm dead sure they're concealing something. Maybe a lot. Not that I think for a single second that they harmed her in any way. Just that — my God!'

Before their eyes a high-laden lorry tilted slowly and inexorably to one side and finally tipped over. Enough of theorizing about the past: it was time to leap into immediate action. Robyn made the emergency service calls, crisp with authority. Fran, unable to reach the cab, let alone get to the driver, took it on herself to flag down traffic. There was nothing else she could do. And once the place swarmed with police vehicles, ambulances and fire service vehicles, she wasn't required to do even that. All those years when she'd have been a welcome, useful part of a team trying to save a living man and now she was reduced to digging up the past.

* * *

Even in the comparative shelter of the car park, she had to hang on the tailgate while Robyn wrestled the Garbutts' box from the boot. They carried it between them, trudging watery prints through Iris's precious entrance hall and up the stairs. They were still dripping when they dropped it on the incident room table.

'I thought I might skip off now, if it's all the same to you,' Robyn said, pushing her fringe out of her eyes. 'When Traffic have debriefed me, of course.'

'No problem. This can wait till tomorrow,' Fran declared, trying not to sound regretful. 'I won't look at the goodies you worked so hard to get hold of. Not till you're here. Off you go — and have a nice hot bath as soon as you can. Oh, before you go, let me have Anna Fratello's address: I'll see if I can find a phone number for her.'

'Oh, I can do that!'

'You're dithering. Go and talk to Traffic and take yourself home.'

They walked down the corridor together. Fran had always prided herself on being as tough as old boots, but she was out of practice at standing round in soaking clothes, and was going, she told Robyn, to spend a few minutes in the company of the hand dryer. But she couldn't direct it up to her hair or down to her legs, so she gave up, returning to the incident room. She was in time to see Robyn letting herself in again. It was only as she bustled in after her she realized she really should have watched her, to see what she was up to. Spied on one of her team, in other words. But it was too late now.

'You're still dripping!' she sang out.

Robyn wheeled round. 'Traffic aren't quite ready for me. Another ten minutes, they said. So I just thought — Anna's number. I'd have a look. Oh, sod it.' She checked the incoming text. 'Now they're saying tomorrow. So I might as well push off, if you're sure it's OK.'

'Off you go, Robyn. I promise I won't look in the box. Go on. I'll get Fratello's number.' She added in a mock-quavering voice, 'If I can remember how to use the phone book . . .' If Anna was ex-directory, though she might no longer be entitled to ask favours of local police forces, she'd bet her pension she'd get more action more quickly than even the willing and efficient Robyn would.

She could almost see the young man she spoke to, DS Tony Woolmer, stand to attention as he promised to go round personally and have a word with the lady. One day she'd ask him what a man from West Yorkshire was doing down in Suffolk.

CHAPTER TWELVE

Standing in driving rain having a conversation — a more user-friendly, if less accurate term than *confrontation* — was hardly the best way to start an evening out. But Fran had things to say to the ACC, Colin Webster, and the more uncomfortable they all were the shorter the encounter was likely to be. She also manoeuvred him so that the rain was to their backs and thus straight into his face. She told him, though in slightly more polite terms, that communications left a great deal to be desired and that if he wished to scupper any chances of cooperation with the Garbutts, invading their privacy three times in less than twenty-four hours was a really good way to do it.

The weather must have agreed. While the umbrella she and Mark were clutching propelled them forcibly towards Webster, his simply blew inside out, and then took off towards North Wales. He set off in pursuit. Mark, tennis fit, got to it first. He took the chance to tell Webster, too puffed to argue, that he and Fran had had to leave the cottage, but he himself was rendered speechless by the ACC's angry riposte: 'I told you, you shouldn't have been wasting money like that in the first place. You should have been instructed to use the accommodation block.'

By then Fran had joined them. 'We're too old to do Spartan,' she declared cheerfully, with the smile that had closed a thousand conversations. One day she'd have a lot of questions for the little drowned rat to answer, but it wasn't just her who was too old to hang around in dripping wet clothes.

At least they could text Hugh to tell him they'd be late. A return text told them they'd be wiser to abandon the evening. Hugh was up to his axles in a flood near to his home, and would be glad to have an excuse to turn round and put his feet up. He was free for Sunday lunch, weather — and surface water — permitting.

Relief outweighing disappointment, Fran drove carefully to their B and B, deep puddles nearly but not quite meeting in the middle of the road. Did they constitute floods? If not, the lakes engulfing the fields either side of them, glimmering in the fitful moonlight, certainly did. At times the water in the fields actually seemed higher than the road: what invisible meniscus held it back from inundating it and sweeping away even their heavy car? How difficult it was not simply to accelerate as hard as she could to get away from danger — but who knew what might be waiting for them round the next bend? And engraved on her heart was the police-driver training dictum: if you don't know what you're driving into — don't drive into it.

To their surprise Edwina Lally was waiting to greet them when they got back. 'My meeting was cancelled,' she said, scooping up their coats as they parked brolly and boots in her porch. 'And suspecting yours might be too, I slipped into Checketts in the village just before they closed and bought in some supplies. I've kept the receipts so when I charge you what I paid you can see I'm not diddling you.'

'Edwina, if you charged us quintuple, it'd be worth it not to have to go out again tonight. But are you sure you're safe here? There's a lot of water around.'

'Safe as an ark. It's never once flooded all the years I've been here. And just for my peace of mind, they said, though

I suspect it's more to do with theirs, the flood warden and a couple of hefty lads from the rugby club came round a couple of days ago. They checked the floodgate upstream was closed, and just for good measure they've been busy with sandbags too. The back of the house looks like a gun-emplacement.'

* * *

'As I see it,' Fran began, fresh from a hot shower with all the luxury of Edwina's pampering unguents, 'we may need Ted, quirks and all, to push this through quickly. We know how to manage quirks — we've dealt with enough oddballs between us. At the very least we can use him to filter people like Bethan Carter, from whom I got nothing to justify the time I spent with her.' She sat down, taking a sip from a wonderfully strong G and T.

'Nothing?' Mark pulled back from the log fire, which he'd taken it upon himself to cherish.

'I got a distinct sense that she was economical with the truth on a number of occasions. She dropped out that Natalie was once sporty, but then quickly implied she wasn't. We need to check, don't we? She also kept trying to drift me off course — can we turn any of those into something? Or did you fare any better?'

'I might have been trying to pin down a jelly. But I did suspect that she might be shielding one of the investigating officers — someone senior in those days. And, though I'm probably misjudging her, I suspected she had a thing for, if not a fling with, Phil Foreman.'

'She told me he was too busy working to organize a funeral.'

'Bloody hell. Perhaps I was wrong about her and Foreman. You know, I have a terrible fear that she wants to come back to talk to me some more. About nothing. Thanks ever so for dropping me in it, sweetheart.' He leaned across and kissed her.

'That might be a job for Ted, then. He probably knows enough about whoever was on the case to work out who she was protecting. Actually, Iris might have some info too. If Bethan knows about Iris's new knee, you can bet your life Iris knows about Bethan's old liaisons. And her new ones. Sorry, that's not very sisterly of me. Did you know she wants to do a piece on us?'

'I gathered as much. And I made it absolutely plain that if she printed anything at all about us and our activities before we were ready to talk, then she'd get nothing. Are we singing from the same hymn-sheet? Heavens, I hope it's not a strict Baptist one — this drink's gone straight to my head. Didn't get much time for lunch, thanks to Bethan. But I did have time to call Gerry Barnes.' He broke off as Edwina came into the room to tell them their starter was on the table. 'To cut a long story short,' he said, 'we're eating with Gerry tomorrow evening.'

* * *

Edwina was inclined to chat between courses, and didn't need much urging to join them in a glass or two of wine.

It turned out that she was an actor — 'resting, darlings' — who'd never found roles easy to come by, and hadn't minded settling down when she'd married. Bored was a word she didn't permit in her vocabulary, so she'd thrown herself into the life of the local community. She'd sung in all the local amateur operatic companies, made costumes for the WI, organized talent contests and generally kept herself occupied — what else could one do, she demanded, opening another bottle, 'when one's husband's cantering round the world trying to sell sand to Eskimos, or whatever? Oh, but Wally was a lovely man. Every girl's dream: handsome, kind and a very good provider.'

'So you never returned to the professional stage?'

'Too busy. And now I've got time on my hands the dear Dames have cornered the market for older character actors. Bear with me.' She returned to the room a few minutes later with a pile of scrapbooks. 'Darlings, I only do this when I'm a touch tiddled and sentimental. Just tell me when you're bored. Two snores apiece and I shall know I have to stop.'

Striking now, with her chignon of snow-white hair, in her dark-haired younger days Edwina had been a beauty; the portraits might have been by the likes of Angus McBean, but the photographers had good material to work with. And presumably she'd been earning enough once (unless Wally had chipped in) to command the fee the top photographic artists of a generation could demand. They oohed and aahed their way through her professional days, but she seemed just as keen to riffle through her more recent memories.

'Now these are when the local schools discovered Drama and Theatre Arts A level: it wasn't just end of term plays, it was proper acting training.' There were pages of young people miming, dancing, making each other up. 'Now here's an end of term production I was very proud of: look. *The Crucible*. Or this one — *As You Like It*.'

Mark was relaxing into the sort of pleasant torpor he rarely, as a driver, enjoyed: as if on a self-denying ordinance, he usually stayed below the limit even when it was Fran's turn at the wheel. He hardly bothered to look at the endless images, mostly shot with no regard for lighting or focus, let alone composition. And he had absolutely no interest in the young people Fran feigned so much enthusiasm for. But there was something different about the two more recent ensemble snaps.

'Who's your *fair Rosalind*?' he roused himself enough to ask. They'd seen *As You Like It* the previous summer in a low budget open air production in the grounds of St Augustine's Abbey. A performance plagued by wasps, as he recalled.

'Not to mention Abigail Williams?' Fran was far more interested. And he didn't even know she knew the Miller play.

'She was one of my best actors. No hint of stage fright, and a real stage presence. I knew she'd go far — my dears, forgive a gruesome joke from an old woman — but not as far as people imagine she must have gone. *The undiscover'd country from whose bourn No traveller returns*. Poor Natalie.'

There was no need for Fran to kick his ankle; he was fully alert now. 'This is Natalie Garbutt?'

'Yes.' She swigged more wine. 'When they found those remains yesterday, they raised a lot of hope. Sad hopes. *One auspicious and one dropping eye*. And now they say they're not hers. Roman or Saxon or something.' She sounded personally aggrieved.

Fran put a hand on Edwina's. 'I'd really like you to talk about Natalie. But before you say a word, I want you to understand exactly why we're interested.'

'You said something about visiting the police here. Not assisting with their enquiries?'

'Not in that sense. Assisting them in making enquiries, more like. They've reopened the Natalie Foreman case. They asked us to help. Fresh pairs of eyes.' She was speaking with the sort of abrupt clarity needed for someone old and deaf. Or drunk.

'Batman and Robin. No: you're both too tall for that. And I'd be hard put to tell which was boss and which side-kick. Superman and Superwoman.' She clapped her hands and spread them wide as if bidding them join her on some imaginary stage. 'Now, contrary to what you may believe, I really am compos mentis and happy to tell you about the lovely girl. What do you need to know?'

'Paint a picture for us,' Mark said with that seductive smile of his.

'I think she was more admired than loved — like that wretched girl of Wordsworth's. No, I've got it the wrong way round, haven't I? *A maid whom there were none to praise and very few to love*. My apologies. She was, as you can see, born to play Rosalind: tall and lovely, with a decidedly androgynous air. To be honest, I always thought she might be gay. Certainly shoals of younger girls had crushes on her. The lead actress, the house captain, the tennis captain, the hockey captain: she was an icon for those lower down the school. But she dated the most attractive young men in the area and obviously made what my mother would have called a very good match with her footballer. Except match it was not. Oh, perhaps I exaggerate. I couldn't have had higher hopes for Natalie had she been my own child — grandchild, perhaps.' She sipped absently at the empty glass. After a moment's silent discussion with Fran, Mark poured in half an inch, measured almost by the eye-dropperful. Fran shook her head, waving her hand over her still unfinished drink.

'Marriage apart, what did you make of her career choices?' Mark asked.

'A degree in French and Spanish? A good option: after all, one can pursue one's interest in the stage at an amateur level, as I did myself. But then to throw that up and become an accountant? It's not a career one imagines will set one on fire, is it? And to end up running a football club . . .' She shook her head. 'My darlings, I fear I have bored you to tears, and I am about to retreat to the last refuge of an old soak — my bed. Another full English breakfast tomorrow? Or might I interest you in some excellent smoked salmon, courtesy of Checketts, and some of my speciality scrambled eggs? Excellent. A worthy choice. Till eight tomorrow, then.' With a waft of her hand she was gone, though her progress up the stairs was slow.

They looked at each other. No, it was anathema to leave a table uncleared, even if it was someone else's. And the dishwasher was just like the one they had at home.

Despite their fears, the following morning Edwina showed no sign of so much as a headache, let alone a full-blown hangover. The promised smoked salmon and scrambled eggs appeared at exactly the time they'd asked.

'We're meeting a colleague for supper,' Mark said as she poured coffee. 'So maybe we'd best take a key.'

'Maybe you'd best take a boat. At the very least pack your glad rags — a whole overnight bag, if you want my advice. No, I'm not joking. The forecast's worse than yesterday's: you may go into a restaurant and come out to find it's an island. And don't forget, if your engagement falls through, just telephone and I'll be able to provide you with a morsel or so . . .'

* * *

'First of all,' Mark said to the little team, 'congratulations on managing to get in at all through the floods. A lot of people would have given up. I'm glad you didn't.' His smile warmed the room. 'Now, any updates?'

'Bad news from the Professional Footballers' Association. They don't hold the records of retired players. Once they leave a club, all the records go to a GP, just as when you leave your doctor, all your records go to a new one. Sorry, gaffers: dead end there.'

'Win some, lose some,' Mark said. 'On the plus side, before you came in a former senior officer from that list that Webster gave us phoned back to say he'd be happy to talk to me about the way the original investigation was run. But he won't do it over the phone, and if I disclose the information he gives, I'm still not allowed to reveal even to you people who my source is. I'm also meeting a contact of Joe Swallow's tomorrow; Fran and I are going up to The Hawthorns for a little live football and, we hope, a lot more help.'

'Taking your boots, gaffer?' Stu jeered.

'I'm assured the Albion are going to win.'

Cue for derisive laughter. 'Against Chelsea?'

'Well, they've got home advantage. Now, Fran's got an appointment with a private detective in Birmingham at midday: who'd like to go with her? Robyn? Paula? Until I need to leave too, at about the same time, actually, I thought I'd help Stu log the contents of the box of goodies the Garbutts handed over yesterday. Sorry, Fran, I know you wanted to do it, but even you can't be in two places at once. Birmingham for you, Robyn?'

She returned his smile. 'If the court sits today, I'm likely to be called. So this is really a flying visit, though I hope to be back: it just depends on how soon they make a decision.'

Paula grinned. 'Better be me, then. OK, Fran?'

'OK. Shall we go, and leave the men to deal with our Pandora's box?' She stuck her tongue out at Mark.

Robyn raised an admonitory hand. 'Let's hope it's not Pandora's box, then — nothing but bad came of that.'

'But, as I recall, one thing lurked at the bottom,' Mark said. 'Hope.'

CHAPTER THIRTEEN

Crime obviously paid, for a private investigator, at least.

Desmond Markwell lived in Harborne, a chic suburb of Birmingham. His solid thirties detached house lay back from a busy commuter road, with enough space on the drive for two cars, plus the unmarked police vehicle Paula had picked from the pound. The house had been modernized, though it retained some period features such as a black and white tiled hall floor, which positively demanded that they wipe their shoes with extreme care.

A saturnine man of about Fran's age, he showed them straight into his office (once, clearly, the back of his garage), every inch of wall and floor space put to use, with state-of-the-art miniaturized electronics and elegant built-in furniture. Two items caught Fran's eye: a professional quality shredder and what looked like a baby-alarm loudspeaker. Plus two kitchen stools on which she and Paula were to perch, looking down on Markwell himself, who took his office chair. Fran ought to have felt they held the advantage, but she didn't.

'I can't think what brought you to me.'

Fran waited for him to add something — anything — but in the face of his continued silence said, 'As I told you, West Mercia Police have decided to reopen the Natalie

Foreman case. A private investigator, even the most law-abiding and legitimate one in the world, would probably have come across information that the police didn't or couldn't access. You're working for your client, after all, not the Crown. After twenty years, I'm hoping the two roles aren't mutually exclusive.'

There was a brief ring, probably the front door bell, then the cheery call of a woman's voice. Markwell got up and, leaning round the door, shouted something back. He returned to his chair without explanation. 'PIs are paid good money to keep confidential information confidential.'

'At what point do they consider their contracts have expired? Is it a matter of time or — perhaps — a change of opinion about the person who hired them? Or perhaps a desire to do something *pro bono publico*?' Fran prided herself on using the whole Latin phrase, not the usual abbreviated form.

'I don't see how giving you information about a woman who disappeared all those years ago can do the public any good at all.'

Paula spoke for the first time. 'Doesn't that depend on what happened to the woman?'

'Died under a couple of feet of snow, didn't she?'

'Nice to meet someone who believes that,' Fran said, cynically discounting all those who'd spent so many hours searching for her.

A glimmer of a smile softened Markwell's face, taking ten years off it and making him suddenly attractive. Poor Fi Biddlestone. 'You'll understand I can't simply hand over the whole file. But I might answer certain questions. You'll join me in a cup of tea? I usually have one at this time of day.'

'I wonder if I might use the loo first,' Paula murmured.

To their astonishment he looked at his watch. 'Another ten minutes. I take it you'd rather wait for your tea?' he added sardonically.

Flushing scarlet, Paula nodded.

'First question,' Fran said quickly. 'You were paid by Phil Foreman. Why did he employ you?'

'Found me in Yellow Pages? Or because the police search was getting nowhere?'

'A lot of people would have assumed she was indeed under that snow. But not her husband? Did he have any reason to think she wasn't?'

'Is that a question I should answer? Let me ask you one in turn: do you think that he had any reason to suspect she wasn't?'

'I've never met the guy, nor am I likely to. But I have picked up a sense of a mismatch, perhaps.'

There was another yell from the hall. Again he responded. As he returned to his office he said, 'The loo's right by the front door. Helpfully marked *Cloakroom*.'

Scarlet again, Paula scuttled off, Markwell following more slowly. He returned almost immediately with a tea tray — bone china cups and saucers — before leaving again. He waited for Paula to resume her perch before bringing in two tea pots. Fran opted for green, Paula for builder's. Milk. Sugar. Biscuits. All very cosy.

'Was Foreman looking for Hadrian rather than his wife?' Fran narrowed her eyes. 'Or for the money Natalie had invested for him?'

'You know, Fran, you're a woman after my own heart. If ever this retirement of yours gets boring, you know where you can find work . . . Anyway, for what it's worth, I don't think Phil ever suspected she'd spirited away a lot of his cash. But she had. A very great deal. He didn't believe how much when I told him. And then he had to understand I didn't know exactly where it was and doubted if I'd ever be able to get it back. But then, he'd only have spent it on silly cars, wouldn't he? And drugs and booze. And of course, she might have done it for tax reasons, and to make sure there was something in trust for young Hadrian when he grew up. Julius wouldn't need anything long term, of course — wouldn't need anything full stop. Poor little bastard.'

'And were you able to locate the pot of gold?'

'It wasn't at the end of a rainbow, I can assure you. At one point it fetched up in a bank in Panama, but then it moved again. Ecuador. Probably somewhere else equally inaccessible now.'

'Does that presuppose that she's the one who moved it?'

'What do you think? I suppose a kinder deduction might be that she employed someone as her financial adviser, and that even though the goose had died, he still had his mitts on the golden egg. But I wouldn't know. After five months Phil called me off, and it's been a rule of mine never to work for nothing. Especially on behalf of an overpaid lump of testosterone on legs.'

Paula had been looking around in vain for somewhere to put her teaspoon. Now she hopped off the stool, put it on the tray and perched again. As if in response to some private chain of thought, she asked suddenly, 'How did you get on with the police working on the original case? Did they regard what you were doing as interference or did you exchange information?'

Fran managed not to blink. What had happened to tact? Thank goodness Paula knew nothing of Fi's secret.

'Yes and no is the easiest way of putting it. Actually we could have rubbed along — should have done, really. But you know how uptight some of your colleagues could be, years back.'

'And how discreet you're being even now. We've had a nice chat, Desmond, but you've told me nothing I didn't know or couldn't have worked out.' Money apart, of course. She stood, the stool rocking irritatingly behind her, and ushered Paula out before her.

He laid a hand on her arm to detain her. 'There is one thing that would help me remember a bit more, Fran. An exchange of information. There's only one person who'd have thought of me in connection with this. Fi Biddlestone. That's who she was once. I assume she's changed her name. Give me her phone number and I'm sure you'll improve my powers of recall.'

'What a strange request for a private detective to make,' Fran said as she swept out. Before he could close the door, however, she turned back theatrically, disconcerting him as she'd hoped. 'It's a crime, as I'm sure you're aware, to withhold information from the police. As you know, I'm no longer an officer, but my colleague here is and there are a lot more where she comes from. So one more question: what did you conceal from the police at the time? When you're ready to answer that, you may want your tame lawyer with you.'

He laughed. 'You must have been formidable in your day. But I've already told you: the business about the money. I tried to tell them, actually. But the knucklehead in charge, one of them, just didn't want to know. He had it down as Holy Writ that the wench was dead. And I'm quoting Marlowe, not Dexter,' he added cheekily.

'So who was this knucklehead?'

'For that,' he said, 'I'd certainly need Fi Biddlestone's phone number.' And he shut the door on them.

Paula asked, as she let them into the car, 'Fi is that woman you met the other night, right? So is she an old flame?'

'He seems to think so,' Fran said lightly. She fastened her seat belt.

'You're not going to do a deal with him, are you?'

'I'm not in a position to do deals, am I? PIs can do their own dirty work as far as I'm concerned. But if you feel you should overrule me, have a word with Fi herself — her details are on the contacts list. I shan't be offended.'

Paula reversed carefully on to the road, heading back in the direction of the M5. She was silent for several miles, but then burst out, 'That strange business of not letting me go to the loo. Weird or what? Some fetish?'

Fran laughed. 'Come on, there might be a simpler explanation. He called out to someone. Kept you crossing your legs. Called out again.'

'Didn't want us to meet someone? A woman, obviously. From her voice.'

'What sort of woman?'

'How would I know?' In the face of Fran's continued silence, she continued, 'Well, she sounded sort of chummy. Strong Birmingham accent. You'd expect that.'

'Why? He didn't have any trace of one.'

'True. Cleaning lady?'

'She was only there about fifteen minutes — twenty maximum. Did you notice anything interesting about where he met us?'

'It was away from the main rooms of the house? Well, it was his office, wasn't it? All very hi-tech too.'

'Anything out of place?'

'Apart from those stupid stools — fine for a breakfast bar or a high island unit. But way too high for any surface in there. Hell, Fran, this is like those games we used to play when I was a Guide. Sorry: I've got to concentrate now — all this spray.'

So Fran offered her theory: that the oddity was the baby-alarm, unless Markwell was an unusually diligent grandparent. The caller was familiar with the household. She did something he didn't want them to know about. She left. Then Paula was free to use the loo — clearly labelled, remember. 'Do you think that Markwell might have an invalid of some sort in his house who might need to summon him if he's working? Or perhaps he just listens for changes in her breathing, as parents do for sick children? Could the woman caller be one of this person's carers? And that loo — labelled so that new carers know where it is — is out of bounds until certain intimate functions have been performed? Trouble is,' Fran added, laughing ruefully at herself, 'we shall probably never know, unless it has a bearing on the case and comes out when we have our next chat.' She stared at a long line of brightening tail-lights ahead. 'Oh, dear, I don't like the look of this lot.'

Paula braked and came to a halt. So, thank goodness, did the cars behind them. 'We could always do a deal over that Fi woman — of course, I'd warn her first.'

'If this were a live case, I'd do it like that.' Fran snapped her fingers. 'Possibly,' she added more honestly. 'But no, not without her permission. And not for just one name we can surely get from other sources — maybe just a bit more brainwork on our part. Now, would it distract you if I made a couple of calls? I want to see if we've got any news of Anna Fratello.'

They hadn't. Her contact, Tony Woolmer, sounded sincerely apologetic, as if it was his fault. Three days ago Anna Fratello had flown home to Florence. Or perhaps that was news in itself. It had come as a complete surprise to her current employer — apparently she was more than a nanny now, a cross between language tutor and housekeeper. Well, that figured, twenty years on. On Tuesday she'd just announced she was going — that there was urgent family business. It was totally out of character, apparently: she was something of a workaholic, and often had to be persuaded to take her annual leave. But she'd promised to be back within a week, two at most.

'Work apart, is there any reason for an Italian woman of forty or thereabouts to work in the UK? Don't most nannies head for home after a few years?'

'The employment situation's not great in Italy, Fran. And I gather there was a relationship with an English guy that might have influenced her. No one on the scene now, however, and believe me, that's weird. They showed me photos taken last year — she's still an absolute stunner. Anyway, her boss promised to get back to me when she returned. As a matter of fact, they said they'd ask Anna to contact me, but I just thought . . . a bit of a hunch . . .'

'Tony, there is nothing I like more in a cop than a bit of a hunch . . .' They parted the best of friends, Fran absolutely confident he'd call her if and when Anna returned. 'OK, Paula, do we blues and twos our way out of this, or do we inch our way off at the next junction . . . ?'

* * *

'Bethan Carter?' Iris repeated, blushing as she always seemed to do when Mark spoke to her. 'The journalist who came to see Fran?'

'Who greeted you like a long-lost cousin and knew all about your new knee,' Mark agreed with a twinkle. 'Come on, Iris, dish the dirt. Fran'd ask, only she and Paula are still trying to get back from Brum. The M5's blocked near the Worcester (South) junction and there's a solid tailback, so they're coming cross country. And there are a lot of road closures to contend with. So do me a favour and give me the gossip first — she'll be even more pissed off.'

'She'd be more pissed off still — though I don't approve of that language, Mark, let me tell you — if she finds you went out for lunch with Bethan.'

Mark gaped. 'Where did you get that idea from?'

'Little bird told me.'

'You can wring the said bird's neck then, Iris. I don't do lunches with women like Bethan. Because if you do, they come up with even more fantastical rumours.'

Perhaps he'd passed some test. But he was too old a dog to jump through that sort of hoop. 'Come on, Iris, your old man was a cop. You know how important information of any sort is. We're used to sorting wheat from chaff.'

She looked over his shoulder. 'And I'm on duty. Maybe I'll be joining Ted in the Bull tonight. Fran and I can have a nice girlie natter while you work on Ted.'

He shook his head. 'Sorry. No can do. We've already accepted an invitation I absolutely can't get out of. So if there's dirt to dish, let it be now, to please an old man.'

She blushed. 'There's things you can say to a woman that just sound bitchy if you say them to a man . . . OK, she's a man's woman, not a woman's woman. She may be ever so kind about my operation, but you guess she's storing it up, to use when it suits her. And the reason I'm glad you didn't take her out to lunch is that I really like Fran — and you, to be blunt — and I don't want her telling one and all. Which she would do. And she'd hint and wink and look coy. The thing is, Mark, most of the time that's all she does. Makes up stories with herself as the star. But sometimes it's fact, not fiction. And there are men here who'd have done better to be too busy to go out to lunch. Right at the top.' She looked around. Was she about to name names? 'You know this merger business. I reckon there are some who've been more than happy to move to a different site or even take redundancy just to get out of her clutches. Let's just say we know she got some national scoops because of someone she'd . . . had lunch with.' They exchanged a smile: they both enjoyed the euphemism.

'But no scoops twenty years ago, although she was . . . having lunch . . . with Phil Foreman? Were they on lunching terms before or after Natalie disappeared?'

She looked genuinely amazed. 'Who told you about them? She never did, surely!'

'Only indirectly. I'd give a lot to find out at what point they started eating together. And how it influenced the way the story was used in the media, of course. And if she was lunching with anyone else at the same time.'

'Like Mandy Rice-Davies, Profumo and that Soviet military guy? Pillow talk, you mean?' She shook her head. 'I really don't know, Mark, and Ted never mentioned anything about that. I know he wasn't part of the investigation but gossip spreads faster than flu in the police, as I'm sure you know.'

'I do indeed. What a very good job I didn't take her out to lunch.'

She smiled, eyes wide with possible innocence. 'But you might have been able to find out who she's after now — and maybe get the answer to your other questions. See what Fran thinks about the idea!' She turned from him to greet a dripping police officer. 'You poor thing! Now who did you want to see . . . ?'

* * *

'But that's the Ombersley road,' Paula objected, as Fran, stowing her phone in her bag, pointed the direction they were to go. They'd escaped from the solid mass of M5 traffic by pulling off at Junction Three and were picking a more unconventional route back to base. Just to make things worse, from time to time a promising road would be blocked by floods or fallen trees.

'I know. And I know it's a little out of our way. And I know we've not eaten anything since Markwell's custard creams. But I just want to drive past our B and B, Paula. Don't ask me why.'

'Are you afraid it'll be washed away like your cottage?' Paula joked. At last, with what in anyone else might have been an *indulging the old and frail* shrug, she turned the car.

'Yes,' Fran said, her voice tight; she was suddenly uncomfortably aware of Paula's scrutiny. 'More precisely, our landlady's home may be.'

'Call her?'

'That's who I was trying to reach earlier.'

'In that case we'd better use these, hadn't we?' She switched on the blues and twos. 'Do you want to call for back-up?'

'You might believe the twitching of my thumbs, but I don't think a despatcher would.'

Paula used what appeared to be every one of her advanced driving skills: their progress was exhilarating or terrifying and perhaps both at once. Half the time she must have been aquaplaning, but she managed to keep the car steady. Hedges flashed by. Other vehicles flattened themselves into hedges or were waved back into gateways. Fran clutched her phone as if it was an amulet.

'Nearly there. That's her house. Please God she's all right.'

'Weird place for a badger — bloody hell!' Paula dragged the car sideways. For a second she lost the rear end — but then she straightened out of the skid. 'Is that — is that your friend?' She reached for her radio.

Fran was out of the car and on her knees beside the soaking body without realizing it. Pulse. Airway clear. Check for injury. Recovery position. Her training might be out of date but it all came back. She stripped off her jacket to cover Edwina, whose body seemed to have shrunk.

Paula was beside her, stripping off her jacket too. 'Key? Did she give you a front door key?'

'Edwina? Yes. Mark's got it.'

'Sod it. OK, there'll be thermal blankets in the boot.'

Fran obeyed orders.

Paula yelled into her radio. After a moment of inventive blasphemy, she added, 'Make it the air ambulance then. This is one we don't want to lose.'

'Is she stirring? Edwina? Edwina? It's Fran. Wake up, now. Come on, wake up. There's a good girl.' She spoke more in hope than expectation.

Paula sat back on her haunches. 'Is it my imagination or is she pissed? Can you smell the booze? And she seems to have spilt some on her clothes.'

True, on the evidence of the previous evening, Edwina liked her drink. But Fran'd say nothing of that yet. After all, the problem wasn't how the woman ended up on her front drive but that she was lying there, soaked to the skin, and had been for goodness knows how long.

'We'll need her clothes as evidence,' Paula said. 'Can you feel this bump here? Is there a reason for her to have come out on a day like this wearing only indoor clothes — carpet slippers too?' She answered herself with a doubtful rock of her hand. 'Unless you're drunk out of your mind . . .'

* * *

The paramedics doing their bit, Paula stood to one side, easing Fran out of the way of a couple of police vehicles that were just arriving. 'Look, you ought to change if we're heading for the hospital with her. Nip and get some dry clothes from your room. Has she left her back door open? No? Check for a key under a flower pot: this is the country, after all—'

'And risk disturbing a crime scene?'

'You really are serious, aren't you?'

'Never more so. I simply don't see why a woman who was entirely sane last night should fetch up like this.' She was about to remind Paula why they were staying there in the first place but pulled herself up short. This wasn't the time or place to spout possibly idle theories. Maybe, just maybe, someone wanted them out of this cottage, too — even if it meant assaulting their landlady. But she'd save paranoid fancies until there was evidence to support them.

Paula looked her straight in the eye. After a moment, she called her colleagues over. Meanwhile, Fran searched for the key. She'd rather that no one had to break any doors down to get access. But there was no sign of one.

'No problem: she'll have left one with a neighbour for sure. I'd better go in case they need ID. Sorry.'

CHAPTER FOURTEEN

In the living room of his beamed cottage, Trevor Downs, the contact who had demanded a promise of total anonymity, settled himself into what was obviously his chair, leaving the smaller one opposite to Mark. The walls, Tudor at very least, felt thick and solid enough to last for ever; the windows were set so deep in their embrasures it took an exceptional gust of wind even to rattle them. Since Mark had had to battle with conditions he'd rarely experienced before, he welcomed the solidity. On the other hand, he was already irritated at having come out in the first place — the second time in a week when a simple phone call would surely have done. As yet Mark could see no need for a meeting at all, particularly one involving a long journey following diversion after diversion, with a load of road works on a dual carriageway to slop some icing on the soggy cake. Though he'd liked old Swallow, he didn't feel any warmth at all towards Downs, for all he was in much the same situation as the other ex-cop.

The two men helped themselves to home-made scones, far heavier and less appetizing than Mark could cook, and excellent home-made jam. The tea was strong enough for a spoon to stand up in. A coal fire blazed in a deep-set fireplace, the occasional puff of smoke blown back by the gale tearing into the trees of Downs's mature orchard, making the room smell briefly of steam locos. Of Mrs Downs there was no sign, but since the missus was the one who'd made the scones, Mark assumed she'd taken her chance with the weather and left someone else to keep an eye on the old man. Of course he was old. Those who were senior officers twenty years ago were bound to be retirement age or thereabouts now. No doubt their efficient hard-working little team thought they were working with their parents at very least. But at least he and Fran didn't reminisce endlessly. Did they? This man was into rugby matches he'd won when young, single-handedly by the sound of it, and since Mark's knowledge of rugby was somewhat less than his knowledge of football, his concentration was wandering. He and Stu had had an interesting morning, logging the memorabilia in the Garbutts' box. They'd agreed not to speak about what they'd found till the whole team were together—

Idiot! What was it that Downs had said about Webster? Ostentatiously he fiddled with his left hearing aid. 'Sorry, Trevor, the old ears aren't what they used to be — Webster's list? That's how we located you, isn't it, working from the list he gave us.'

Downs might be a bore but he wasn't stupid. 'You worked from a list *he* gave you? That doesn't sound like very good detective work to me, Mark. But I suppose you big wigs get out of practice at looking at little things. Always go back to basics, that's what I used to tell my teams — rugby or police.'

Mark nodded his *mea culpa*. 'So the fact he gave us the list is a problem?'

'Depends whose name is on it, doesn't it? *His*, for instance, man.' Downs jabbed a finger as if Mark was an inadequate cadet.

'His? He was involved with the original investigation but didn't get round to telling us?' Mark thought back quickly. Whose was the last name on the list? Thompson, Christine. Was it simply a question of a page going AWOL? Or . . . ?

'Perhaps his memory's gone the way of your hearing.'

Mark felt himself bracing. He never made any bones about being deaf, but he hated anyone else taking liberties with his disability. He made himself reply evenly, 'Perhaps it has. I'm afraid nothing can help my ears, but perhaps you could remind me why he'd prefer to leave himself off the list.'

'Like you he took short cuts. He made assumptions. And the worst assumption he made was that the woman and her kid had to be under the snow. Rubbish. We'd have found her if she had been.'

He'd come to the same conclusion himself, of course. 'So how would you have driven the investigation, Trevor?'

'Abduction, of course. A kidnap attempt that went wrong. Obvious. Her bloke had a lot of money — why not help him get rid of some of it?'

'Did a kidnapper ever make contact?'

'Not with us. But I'd bet my pension that someone got in touch with Foreman.'

'And he wouldn't tell his family liaison officer? Or did I hear—?'

'Refused to have one. Refused from start to finish. Which would have me for one suspicious, I can tell you. Nasty piece of knitting if you ask me.'

'Ah! You met him!'

'No. Another assumption there, Mark.' He wagged his finger as if Mark was a naughty schoolboy. 'Just what we picked up on the grapevine.'

Mark nodded as if it was news to him. 'Certainly makes sense.'

'And neighbours in that mansion of his in Brum — they claimed to have heard shouting. The fact that no one ever saw any bruises is irrelevant — you know that.'

Now that was new. 'Quite. One of the worst wife abusers I ever came across was a very senior barrister in the CPS. But would Foreman's domestic violence square with him employing a private detective?'

'Oh, the one who was screwing one of my detectives,' Downs observed. 'Fi Something-or-other. They tried to pretend they were having a purely professional relationship but — anyway, the man was in Foreman's pay, so I had to take her off the case. And keep her off. Stupid bitch. Lost her job eventually.'

'Or unfortunate victim,' Mark said gently. 'Yes, we've met her. And she's given us some very useful information.'

'About that little sod Desmond Markwell? He knew a lot more than he let on — and a lot more than we ever did if you ask me.'

If only Downs would stop interrupting himself with meaningful pauses. He must have known that a nice smooth narrative would have been speedier.

'About the possible abduction?' Mark prompted. 'Or,' he added, going out on a limb, 'what if it wasn't an abduction but something prearranged? What if Natalie wanted out of the marriage and faked her own death?'

He might have sworn at the Pope. Downs was outraged. 'But she was only a bit of a thing! With a child! And to leave another child behind to die! No, we never even considered that. And neither should you.'

So much for not making assumptions. But Mark held his tongue.

'The girl was a victim, you mark my words. Now, hang on: there was another woman involved. One that had made a play for Foreman and was seeing your friend Webster, if I remember rightly. Or it might have been one of the guys that left. Worked for a local rag.'

'I might have met her,' Mark said cautiously. He added, in the way he would have summed up meandering meetings a year or so ago, 'OK, Trevor: am I right in thinking that you blame Colin Webster for the failure to pursue other lines of enquiry? He's gone onwards and upwards since then, of course.'

'That's what they do with useless officers: they promote them to where they can't do any harm.'

Mark tried not to take the truism personally. 'What about the ACC who's been made redundant — Gerry Barnes?'

'What about him?'

'Was he over-promoted or was he a decent cop or what?' His phone warbled. Ignore it as would be courteous or take Fran's message? Somehow Downs didn't make him feel very courteous, but he needed an answer.

'Why do you ask?'

'I know the name, that's all. I know he's unexpectedly been made redundant. It's always nice to know any rumours behind such things.' Though it wasn't necessarily moral to try to dredge up stuff about your prospective dinner host, especially when he'd offered you your job in the first place.

Downs got to his feet and padded from the room. Was he fetching some invaluable evidence? While he waited, he checked Fran's text. Just a mild request to contact her. He frowned. He'd better wait to see what the old bugger had yet to reveal.

Getting info from Downs like extracting teeth. Be with you soonest poss. XXX.

* * *

Fran stared at the little screen as if she could make the words change. It was crazy: all her life she'd been almost obsessively independent. Now, after a few short months, she found she wanted her husband beside her. And she wanted him beside her in the hospital waiting area right now. She was cold and wet. Paula had nipped out to pick up dry kit, at Fran's behest, because she wanted Paula to interview Edwina when she came round. She'd much rather have done it herself, it went without saying, but didn't think the SIO would accept that.

Meanwhile, abandoning attempts to read any of the downloads on her mobile phone, she leafed through every magazine within reach. Why couldn't she concentrate? She'd sat waiting for news of patients enough times in the past. What was different about now? Surely she wouldn't buy the obvious cod-psychology theory that in Edwina she somehow saw her mother, still living in Scotland but rarely in her thoughts? She left her sister and the endlessly patient care home staff to worry about the malevolent old woman. The last time they'd met her mother's blood pressure had rocketed to such astronomical levels that the staff had made it clear that her mother was better off without Fran's company. As for Mark . . .

'Still no news?' Paula plumped down beside her, dropping a Sainsbury's bag at her feet. 'The city centre's under a couple of feet of water so I went for some of their own clothing brand, Tu. And then I remembered Mark saying something about your bringing in a change of clothes on Edwina's advice, and there it was, in your office. I know, I know, I should have got some from Edwina's, but you said about it being a crime scene and . . .'

'These are fine. Don't worry.'

'I'll try and find some news of her while you change.' She pointed to a handy ladies'. 'Oh, and I bought some sarnies too.'

Fran hugged her. 'If you're not chief constable before you're forty I shall eat the wrappers as well.'

* * *

'A couple of last questions, Trevor,' Mark said, sick of an interview that felt like wading through treacle. The older man had simply left the room. Wherever he'd been, when he returned he brought back no bulging package of evidence against Gerry. 'First of all about Gerry Barnes — you were going to tell me . . . ?'

'That he moved to the force from Gloucestershire just as I was retiring. Clean as a whistle, as far as I know. Someone said something about his wife — can't recall it right now. But I'll let you know, if it comes to mind.'

'Thanks. And the last question: what's your take on this new police commissioner?'

'I thought you'd never ask,' Downs said, rubbing his hands with glee. 'If ever anyone needed investigation, it's her.

In my day they'd have called her a trollop. Uses her money to get clout. And I have word that she influences enquiries — which cases get resources, which don't.'

'Word? Do you have any evidence?'

'Take my word for it, she'll have dabbled in this cold case of yours. Can't keep her painted fingers to herself. You mark my words.'

'I really need more than allegations, Trevor. More than rumour. I need hard facts.'

* * *

'Observation!' Edwina snorted. 'Tests! I thought the NHS was on its financial knees! What's it doing keeping a tough old bird like me in for twenty-four hours and wasting all that money? In a private ward, I presume.' She gestured at her surroundings.

'Just a single NHS ward as far as I know,' Fran said. There was no need to tell her it was easier to keep an eye on her there — for the nursing staff and for the pimply constable sitting outside trying to pretend he wasn't playing some game on his phone. 'I think the hospital trust's saving up for a boat to take you home,' Fran said, kissing her cheek affectionately. 'There's an awful lot of water out there. Seriously, at any age a bump on the head is serious: think of that lovely actress who died in a skiing accident.'

'I believe we're all *actors* now, Fran, whatever our gender. Tell me, how and why are you here?'

'I found you. Me and Paula, the forceful young officer who's talking to your nurse there.'

'Found me? Darling, as I told . . . Paula . . . there are a few minutes absent from my memory. You may have to refresh it.'

'Of course I will,' Fran said, taking a seat. 'Just what did you tell the officer who was talking to you earlier?' She was too old a hand to put words — or false memories — into Edwina's mind.

'That I'd followed my usual routine. I'd loaded the dishwasher, but not set it off. I'd run the duster and vacuum round the dining room. I'd been out — I like to go into the village to collect my paper every morning; they save it for me. Some idiot drove too close to me and soaked me. Someone stopped and asked me the way. I went home.' Using both hands, but clearly irritated by the drip attached to her left, she gestured that from that point her mind was blank.

'You've no recollection of answering the front door to someone? Or the back door?'

'Ah, you found the key.'

'Key?'

'There's one under a flower pot.'

'Paula had to ask a neighbour for one.'

'I know there's one there. I always check.' Her hand fretted the sheet.

'Something or someone encouraged you to step outside, where you were socked on the head and left in the rain. Personally I believe your memory will recover as you get better. And don't forget, Edwina, that the greatest healer is sleep, so I shall leave you to your zizz.' She got up and prepared to tiptoe off.

Edwina's eyes snapped open. 'You'll be staying at the cottage tonight? No charge, darling, I do insist.' She managed a smile. 'In fact, I should pay you in your new role of caretakers.'

'Or not,' Fran said, repeating the conversation to Paula. 'And there was a key. And it's gone. You must know a decent locksmith who'll get out there immediately? I'll pay, of course, and have one key. Oh, and someone must make sure Edwina can get back into her own home when she's released.'

'I'll make sure a key's left with that neighbour of hers.'

'Thanks, Paula — I don't know what I'd do without you.'

But Paula was already tapping into that damned phone.

CHAPTER FIFTEEN

Fran had never enjoyed meetings late on a Friday afternoon; though she'd been long inured to ignoring weekends and all the pleasures associated with days off, she always felt others were paying more attention to their watches than to the matter in hand. Not real active officers, to be fair, but administrators — and Webster was an administrator if ever there was one, unlike Mark, who'd much rather have been actively solving crimes. On the other hand, if Webster was desperate to get away, perhaps they'd be able to railroad through a few days' extension to their contract, particularly as they would both swear that they were getting somewhere.

If Mark ever turned up, that is. He'd texted to say he was leaving Downs, and had phoned a couple of times to report that he was caught in traffic, rather than floods.

She stared at the box of carefully bagged and labelled evidence on the incident room table, but didn't open it. She'd have somehow felt she was betraying a tacit trust, like eating the best chocolates from an extravagant present. What would it tell her of Natalie's life as filtered by her mother? After all, it was only what her parents had chosen, not all that she'd left behind in her old home, a choice she as a non-parent couldn't be expected to understand. If pushed, she'd have said she'd expect to see an old teddy bear, first shoes, baby-teeth. She was just about to break her promise to herself and test her theory when Paula came in, just putting away her phone.

'Come on, Paula — it's POETS day.'

Paula jumped violently. 'Sorry? I was miles away. Oh, of course. Yes, I know it's Saturday tomorrow and I know people piss off early. But I've had a word with the scene of crime officer who looked at Edwina's house.'

Fran stiffened. 'I thought you said there was no damage.'

'There wasn't. To the bulk of the house. But there was to one room.' Paula hesitated, as if reluctant to say something. 'That cottage you rented: you said it had been flooded. Well, I did a spot of double-checking, on the basis of the SOCO's report. It seems that the cottage letting agent officially reported that some gully or other had been deliberately blocked.'

'I've got some snaps on my camera if you want to look for yourself. Frankly, Mark and I just didn't have time to check if someone had it in for the owner. But I'm glad young Alex, the letting agent, took it seriously enough to report it. And it sounds as if the SOCO found something interesting? The room that was trashed wouldn't happen to be the guest room — ours?'

'I'm afraid so. Of course,' Paula added quickly, 'the intruder might not have had time to do any more. In fact, we could have disturbed him ourselves, couldn't we?'

'Could we?' Fran wasn't sure of the logic behind such deductions. 'It means whoever did it must have pushed Edwina out into the rain and left her there while he started rifling through the house — pretty callous behaviour. Though not, of course, impossible. And when I say he, I really should have said "he or she", shouldn't I?'

'A woman?'

'Who knows? Anyway, is there evidence that the intruder took anything? Or would you need Mark and me to check? The trouble is, we're due with the ACC any moment now — me solo if Mark can't fight his way through the traffic. And then we're out to supper. Not just a jolly evening but a meal with someone involved in the original enquiry.'

'I've an idea that this ought to take priority over one of them. I'd like to say cut the ACC—'

'But such words would never pass your lips. On the other hand, active crime investigation ought to trump a review meeting any day of the week. Let's see what Mark has to say when he gets here.' Fran covered her mouth with both hands, wincing. 'I never thought I'd say that. I spent all my life taking decisions, sometimes big ones, deliberately avoiding referring them upwards. And now listen to me: that's what nine months' retirement does to your brain. So if you don't want to end up like me, take yourself off home now.'

'But—'

'I can't give orders, Paula, but if I could . . .'

* * *

In the event, the ACC's secretary cut the Gordian knot. It seemed that Webster was going to front a press conference in time for the Channel Four News. The metrocentric media had finally realized that there might be news in these country bumpkins' rain, and the troubles of the Severn Valley were finally being brought to the public's attention. Who better than Mole to represent West Mercia? Fran snapped her fingers in irritation: Rat, of course, or even Otter, though she had no one to share the idea with.

So she phoned to divert Mark straight back to Ombersley; she herself gratefully accepted a lift with the officer in charge of the break-in case. She tried to pretend she was simply Josephine Public, humbly accepting police help. Weird or what?

Sergeant Cole, known, he said, as Andy, a tubby man not many years from retirement, drove with sensible caution; in fact Mark had already parked when they arrived. Parked in a small torrent, sickeningly similar to the one that had pulsed past Snowdrop Cottage.

'Looks as if the floodgates have given way. Best stay here, ma'am,' Cole said, reaching past her for the wellies stowed behind the passenger seat.

'Uh, uh. I can smell a rat.'

Cole grinned. 'Probably a water vole, ma'am — though they say all these swollen rivers will have a terrible effect on the poor little creatures. Flood their little burrows, and maybe if the torrents are fast enough drown them.'

Fran was prepared to be sentimental about nature about ninety per cent of the time. This was one of the other ten. 'We certainly need to know what evil little rodent caused this. Personally I'd suspect it has two legs. What a total bastard. Let's go — hang on, I can't move till you've passed me my wellies from our boot.' She passed him her car keys. 'Thanks. Now there are all poor Edwina Lally's treasures to rescue.'

In a sad reprise of the work he'd done in Snowdrop Cottage, Mark had already ferried as much as he could upstairs. But all of the old house had been spared. It was only the new extension, where Edwina had housed them, that had suffered, largely because someone had managed to open the patio door — unlock it from within, they suspected, because there was no obvious sign of damage — that opened on to the once pretty rear garden. Now it was a muddy mill-race. The bedroom was ruined, with water surging into the bathroom. The passageway between the house and their room was still unaffected, but would make a good escape route for the water.

Now there were three of them, knee deep in water in the garden, they could force the door shut, and then reinstate the sandbag dam — except they needed to do far more than reinstate it. Something or someone had cast the bags to all corners of the garden. But at last they had a decent wall, and had the pleasure of seeing the water heading away.

'You and Edwina mentioned floodgates as well as sandbags,' Fran said. 'Shall we take a look?'

'Don't you want to check your belongings first?' Cole asked.

'Not if we can stop the water doing more harm.'

But nothing they could do would close the floodgates. Apart from the sheer weight and force of the water, something seemed to be stopping the great toothed wheel from moving even one notch.

'God knows what repercussions this will have downstream,' Cole yelled above the roar of the water. 'I'll get straight on to the Environment Agency and warn them. Meanwhile, it's not safe for civilians here — back to the house, please.'

Civilians. But that was what they were. Two no longer young civilians, to be herded from danger. Exchanging a sadly ironic smile, they did as they were told, holding hands tightly.

Mark, who'd collected Edwina's key from the neighbour, gave them all a few seconds' panic when it wasn't in the first pocket he tried. This time they didn't bother to kick off their boots in the porch: there was enough mess already, and they needed to get to the annexe corridor to open the door leading to the front garden, letting the built-up water flow away.

'Funny,' said Fran, as they checked that the sandbag wall still held, 'that at the last place we were driven out by floods someone caused by blocking a culvert; here someone seems to have done the opposite.'

Cole, more out of breath than either of them, ended his call and looked at her sharply. 'Last place?'

'We were supposed to be staying at Snowdrop Cottage, about a mile away.'

'That's the holiday let? Safe as houses, that.'

'Until the culvert was blocked. Then it was decidedly unsafe.' Fran stopped: could the lack of gas and other welcoming necessities have been part of the scheme — or was she being paranoid? She showed him the photos on her phone.

Cole narrowed his eyes: 'Are you saying this flood business is directed at you?'

'Not in so many words. I suppose it's just possible that Mrs Lally might have an enemy? And the previous incident could be focused on our landlady, whose name slips my mind.

But the letting agent, Alex, has notified your colleagues — he seemed a bright, switched on young man.'

'I don't like coincidences,' Cole muttered, reaching for his phone again.

Meanwhile, they stared at the sodden mess on the floor. At least it was simply river water, with no evidence of any sewage. 'It looks as if someone emptied the contents of our cases and anything in the drawers or wardrobe that might be ours before they let the waters rip,' Fran said. 'Andy, this does feel personal, you know.'

He shook his head sadly. 'I'm beginning to think you might be right, ma'am. But it'll be hard work proving it, won't it? Not that we won't try,' he added, without managing to sound positive. 'Now, is anything of yours missing? Are you sure? No portable electronics?'

'Neither ours nor Edwina's — that nice TV of hers is still in place. And we had our mobiles and iPad with us.'

'Jewellery?'

'Apart from what I'm wearing, I didn't bring any on account of Mark's having hocked my tiara.'

'If this has happened twice . . . goodness knows why they're picking on you.'

'There might just be a reason,' Mark said slowly, reluctant to complicate matters for a purely local officer. 'Someone doesn't like us digging up the past,' he explained.

As he suspected, their investigations were news to Cole, but he cottoned on quickly. 'I gathered you were ex-police. And all we knew was that you were poking round in something or other — no one was quite sure what. So someone might be trying to deter you . . . want you to give up . . . Do they think it'll be sufficient to — I don't know — send you back to Kent to get fresh socks?' he added with a pleasant gleam in his eye.

'Put that way, it doesn't sound very convincing as an explanation,' Mark agreed.

Cole got back into his stride. 'Or maybe there's a simpler explanation. That there's some local vandals. And this was a burglary gone wrong: Mrs Lally interrupted the intruder; hence he assaulted her.'

'And dragged her outside hoping she'd either drown or die of hypothermia. A bit extreme for your average housebreaker, Andy?'

He nodded, sucking his teeth. 'According to the medics, by the way, she's well enough to give us a statement now: I shall be heading for the hospital as soon as I've finished here.' He shifted his feet. 'I don't suppose you could look out some clothes for her, ma'am: those she was wearing will have been bagged up . . . but you'd know that, wouldn't you? That'd be very kind . . . Sir, would you mind giving me a hand ripping up this carpet?'

'Sure. So long as you drop this *sir* and *ma'am* business. As you say, we're just civilians now. Mr and Mrs Joe Public.'

'And as such entitled to a bit of respect.'

'Thanks. Let's tackle this carpet — hell's bells, it weighs a ton.'

Fran gathered up the piles of sodden clothes and stowed them in the washing machine. That was as far as she got. Mark was the domesticated one: maybe he'd work out how to use it.

It was only as the laundry whirled round obediently that Mark said, his voice low even though Cole was busy at the far end of the house, 'Downs has made extraordinary allegations against that commissioner woman. I told him I wanted evidence.'

'You'll have to talk as we drive. We're due at Gerry Barnes's place in an hour. And we can't exactly turn up like this.'

'Of course we can't. OK. Let's go and buy something dry and decent.'

CHAPTER SIXTEEN

They might never know what preconceptions Gerry Barnes might have had of his dinner guests and their clothes. But Fran would have offered good odds that he wouldn't have expected them to turn up in brand new Sainsbury's gear designed for the younger and decidedly shorter. It might work well on Paula, but Fran felt all legs and arms, her situation not helped by the fact that Gerry's wife Caroline was both petite and exquisitely dressed.

'Why didn't you bring everything here? We could have washed and dried it for you,' Gerry said, pressing G and Ts into their embarrassed hands as Mark gave a potted history of their peripatetic problems. 'Did you bring your overnight things? Of course not. But we can surely—'

'You're very kind. But we promised Edwina we'd look after the place while she was in hospital: we're just decamping into another bedroom,' Mark told him, noticing that Caroline didn't add her voice to her husband's.

The number of guests had been sharply depleted by the floods. In fact, it was now just Mark and Fran who'd grace their table, using china and lead crystal finer than any Fran had used in any home but their own; you couldn't live, they'd agreed from the outset, in a listed Georgian building and still use IKEA. So, much as she'd have liked to be involved in the police gossip already occupying the men, still infuriatingly dividing the conversation on sexist lines, at least she and Caroline had topics they could share — Royal Worcester porcelain and Stourbridge crystal.

But the hands passing her specimens from a display cabinet to handle and admire were not the manicured and polished ones Fran expected. The nails were as short as Fran's own, and the skin decidedly under-moisturized. Caroline clearly had other interests, other occupations. Of which cooking wasn't one. The plates might be a delight to the eye; what landed on them didn't tempt the taste buds at all. In her situation Fran might have cheated — equipped herself with loads of M and S or Waitrose easy-cook meals.

The initial four-way conversation over an under-seasoned soup was banal enough, and the main course was equally bland until Caroline dropped out that she'd been a SOCO with West Midlands Police, and was now, post-redundancy, retraining as an archaeologist. Suddenly it was sleeves-rolled-up, elbows-on-table time. Gerry was transformed from a genial host to a tough-looking cop with attitude.

'It was you who invited us to look at the case, Gerry,' Fran said bluntly. 'You must have felt this particular case warranted looking at again.'

'And it was me who got made redundant,' he said. 'I'm not complaining, not with the size handshake I got.' Clearly he was.

'Are you implying there's a causal relationship?' she pursued. 'But I'm jumping the gun. You may already have told Mark why you wanted to look at cold cases, and this one in particular, but I've been enjoying moments with Dr Wall and some of my other porcelain heroes.' She grinned at Caroline, who murmured, 'I'll show you the rest of my collection while we have coffee. Cheese, anyone? I've got this lovely Shropshire Blue.'

Gerry spread his hands expansively as she brought it in. 'I don't like loose ends, any more than I suspect you do. It was you who was in charge of cold cases, wasn't it, Fran?'

'Yes. Mark merely ran the whole shebang,' she said affectionately, 'while his chief went to meetings.'

'Meetings! Don't get me started! Anyway, I was one of those most in favour of setting up a small team to investigate cases we'd never closed. Got my own way, too, backed by the commissioner, I gather; I had a good team, led by a DCI and with all the resources of teams working on active investigations. But then the economic climate changed . . . I didn't want the valuable work they were doing to be lost in the chase for efficiency and targets and all the other crap. So I suggested we parachute in people on short-term contracts. A couple of times we used an agency. Then I remembered Mark and found that you were free too — which is how you come to be sitting here wearing clothes some of which still have the store labels on them.'

Caroline got up from the table and returned with a pair of scissors, dealing with first Fran and then Mark, ostentatiously laying their price tags on their place mats.

Smiling her thanks, Fran resumed her questions: 'So you weren't drawn to this case for any pressing reason? No one outside the force asked you to look into it?'

'No. Absolutely not. We've nailed a rapist; tracked a fraudster to Spain and extradited him; linked a murder to a killer doing a natural life term. But this is the only one that seems to have caused any problems. And the only one with any connection to me having the carpet pulled from under my feet. I called you; we agreed terms; I told the boss; he seemed delighted; I got the chop.'

'Was it something we said? Or the way we said it?' Mark asked whimsically. 'Or the very fact that someone — anyone — was going to ask questions?'

'I simply don't know. Of course, some of my colleagues left in post might fight less vigorously to support the investigation. Resources; staffing: those sorts of things.'

'People like ACC Colin Webster?' A man who left his name off the list of investigating officers.

'People like him.'

'And who might they be fighting for these resources? The chief constable? Andrew Barwell? Or this new police and crime commissioner of yours, Sandra Dundy?'

'Commissioners! Don't ask . . .'

For the next few minutes, they engaged in a pleasurable and wordy discussion about the whole concept of elected commissioners, capping each other's horror stories of politicos who were milking a profitable cash cow. From time to time they'd admit that X was honest, that Y was really shaking up a force that needed it, but the verbal hunt for possibly corrupt commissioners was much more fun.

'But what about yours in particular? Who backed you, you said?' asked Mark, still chuckling at the report of one outrageous piece of behaviour. Now perhaps he might get information that would substantiate Downs's allegations. 'How have you got on with her?'

Gerry's face went entirely blank. Studiously blank.

Mark tried to keep any excitement from his face. Downs had said he had nothing on Gerry, but there was no point in giving information away.

Gerry declared, 'Police and crime commissioners do not meddle in individual enquiries.'

'Of course they don't,' Fran said cordially. 'But—?'

'They're duly elected public servants, responsible for conveying the will of the electorate to the force. They can appoint and dismiss chief constables,' he parroted.

'Can and do,' Caroline pointed out. 'I can think of a number of decent chief constables whose faces didn't please the new commissioner. Some went quietly.'

Gerry nodded. 'At least one endured the most horrible humiliation before a very public sacking.'

Damn: the conversation was drifting away again.

'Is your chief expecting that sort of fate? Or any other of the senior team, for that matter?' Fran thought of the anxiety on Webster's face.

Gerry frowned. 'I wouldn't know. They play their cards very close to their chests, some of them, and don't even like being asked what time it is, to be honest. Greg, our previous chief, was very much more accessible. I could have asked him if there was anything wrong. Come to that, he'd have told me. Do you remember him, Mark? Greg Orford?'

Mark nodded enthusiastically. 'I remember. A decent man. Very keen on alternative medicine, of all things. Planned to set himself up in practice as an osteopath or something. But Barwell? I've seen him around, looking harassed, but never exchanged a word with him. I've had no reason to, of course.'

'You'd have to book a week ahead, and then expect to have your meeting cancelled at the last moment while he battles with the latest crisis. They call him the Invisible Man. Not original, but accurate. To be fair, I wouldn't want his job. He spends most of his time haring round the area we police. Correction: we're supposed to police. Geographically speaking it's huge. Look at it on a map. The logic behind the merger was that we were both forces with expertise in rural crime, so a lot of things were duplicated. Anyway, it's not my problem. Not any longer.'

'Nor is the commissioner,' Fran pointed out. 'I've seen her just a couple of times: very smart. Once she seemed inclined to be friendly until it dawned on her what job I was doing, if not who I was. But there's not much of a biography of her on the West Mercia website, though they pretty well give the chief constable's shoe size there's so much detail, and Google doesn't come up with anything special. Which is odd, given her position. All over the country other candidates seemed to have their pasts examined with bizarre thoroughness; didn't one withdraw because he'd allegedly smoked pot forty years ago? But she seems to have escaped any sort of trial by media.'

'Possibly because she came in on a second election: her predecessor managed to crash a police vehicle he had no right to be driving and resigned PDQ. So she came in as the proverbial breath of fresh air.' Gerry looked across at his wife, who was clearly trying to catch his eye: 'OK, coffee in the living room?'

Mark had a sneaking suspicion that the change of location was supposed to indicate a change of topic. However, he was determined to finish this one, bad manners or not. He bided his time, waiting till they were all seated and served. The coffee was as feeble as the food had been. 'I can see Fran's itching to get her hands on your porcelain, Caroline, but I'm desperate to get some line on Dundy. The only opinion I've so far managed to elicit was one-sided in the extreme: she's a fiend in human form, lying, cheating, driven by a desire to make money, power-mad. I'd really welcome something more considered.'

Her hand on the display cabinet door, Caroline paused. 'I've met her socially once or twice. She actually seemed a very nice woman. OK, her politics may not be mine but she struck me as decent and well-meaning. She's also very bright. I know you're no keener on entrepreneurs than on politicians, Gerry, but she set up her own sportswear business from nothing, always buys British products when she can and recruits local workers for her shops.'

'Sounds like an ad for UKIP,' Gerry grumbled.

'Or a stand against sweated labour and economic migration,' she retorted. 'A fair day's pay for a fair day's work; does that sound familiar? Now she sponsors sports like cricket and football, with the emphasis on involving girls both during and after school. She stood on a Can Do platform, Fran. Yes, she had the Tory ticket, but that doesn't necessarily help anyone these days.'

Fran nodded. 'She's achieved a lot for a woman still in her forties.'

Caroline continued, 'She's married. No children. She's a good advert for her own sporting philosophy — very fit, not a gym bunny but plays a lot of tennis and swims. A really good role model for women.'

'And she turns her back on her career and stands as police and crime commissioner on what seems to me a good salary but must be peanuts to her. I wonder why.'

Caroline's laugh was dry, ironic. 'Not a very sisterly question, Fran.'

'Actually, I was thinking about her altruism. All that commitment and drive; yet changing something as huge and amorphous as a regional police force must be like pushing a pea uphill with your nose. Why take it on? And at such a difficult time? Next time I run into her in the Hindlip Hall ladies' loos I must ask her. And, come to think of it, ask her how she manages to walk in those high heels of hers. I'm sorry: we've talked nothing but shop and all that china and porcelain is waiting for me.'

Mark raised a finger. 'I'm sorry. Just one more question, then I promise not to utter another word of shop. Is there still a Mr Dundy and what does he do?'

'Dundy's her maiden name. No idea what her husband's called. I think he's a lawyer of some sort.' End of discussion. Definitely, this time. 'This is my favourite, Fran.' She produced a tiny handle-less cup on its saucer. 'When tea was so expensive that you locked your caddies, you needed cups this small.'

It sat like a flower on Fran's outstretched palm. She ran her finger delicately round the rim. 'I wonder how many lips sipped genteelly from here. I know a woman back in Kent who collects spectacle cases. Sometimes they come with the spectacles still inside. There's a pair I can actually read with. And you think, what was this woman's life like compared to mine?'

'Other people's lives! That's why I took up archaeology!'

'And why I,' said Mark truthfully, 'became a police officer.'

CHAPTER SEVENTEEN

Back at Edwina's, the torrent decidedly abated, they had risked parking in the lee of the house. There was nowhere else for the car after all. To their relief they found that Sergeant Cole or the Environment Agency had managed to stem the cascade — presumably they had some giant spanner to close the floodgates. They'd also organized reinforcements to the sandbag dam and brought in a pump to clear the water in what had previously been their bedroom. The corridor to the outside world was no longer a minor river, though not all the water had gone. Fran did her best to sweep it out, but neither had the energy to attack the residual mess in what had been their room.

Meanwhile, the washing machine having completed its cycle, Mark reloaded it with soaking bed linen. Edwina wasn't as ruthlessly green as Mark, owning a state-of-the-art tumble-dryer, something he eschewed. Looking almost shifty, he put in the items they'd really need for the next day and set it off, standing back as if it were a petard that might explode in his face.

Trying not to laugh, Fran installed them in their new room, one on the first floor. It wasn't as spacious as the alternative, and the smell of paint lingered. But since Mark had dumped in the other one what he'd retrieved from the flood, it was the obvious option. It was a matter of minutes to make up the bed. Would hanging their new clothes in the wardrobe somehow provoke further meteorological retribution? She hoped not.

* * *

The trouble with sleeping the sleep of the just was that you didn't want to surface knowing that your new day would be spent pursuing the unjust. But the central heating hummed away, and it was Fran's turn to get their tea. She also applied herself to transferring the newly washed sheets to the dryer she'd just emptied; there was nowhere else, after all. The little patio garden was still awash; anywhere requiring you to don wellies to hang out washing was a non-starter in her book. There was the other part of the garden, more a small orchard, but the wind was hammering that so hard that the sheets would soon have been in the next county — Shropshire, she presumed.

Meanwhile, there was something else on her mind: the afternoon's activities. What did you wear to a football match? Something warm and weatherproof was the obvious answer. No doubt Birmingham shops would provide the solution. No lie in for them this morning, then, especially as they might be involved in arrangements for getting Edwina home. But their phone call to the hospital elicited the information that she was more than capable of organizing this for herself and had already drafted in a friend to collect her at twelve. As for the annexe room they weren't even to consider trying to tackle it. All they had to do was leave the central heating on. Silently Fran added another task: that fine bed linen would have to be ironed, wouldn't it? A job for Sunday.

* * *

All Joe Swallow's organization came together beautifully. Yes, they could park in a reserved space; yes, the welcoming girl in Reception was expecting them: would they sit in the corner for a moment with some of the kids who'd be mascots for the afternoon?

Mascots? It meant nothing to Fran, but it clearly meant a lot to the boys and girls, aged from something like six up to a tall eleven dressed from head to toe in blue and white.

A dapper man sporting a stylish hat appeared, looking around with a quizzical smile.

Mark got to his feet. 'You wouldn't be Joe's mate, would you?'

'Alan Cleverly at your service. You must be Mark and Fran. I'll rescue you from all this enthusiasm, shall I? Come on, we'll find a coffee. Let's take the lift.'

He ushered them into a restaurant overlooking the ground and sat them down at a table where their conversation wouldn't be overheard.

'I know a lot of the old Baggies players,' he said, pouring coffee. 'That's what the fans call the Albion — the Baggies. And of course these guys know others I don't. But I'm afraid Phil Foreman was never in my circle of close acquaintances. For various reasons,' he said meaningfully. 'Look, Joe told me you were football virgins,' he added with a disbelieving smile.

'We've got no Premier League club in Kent,' Mark confirmed. 'And it's a long time since either of us was on Saturday afternoon duty at the Gillingham ground.'

'So at least you know it's a round ball, not an oval one. Well, that's a start. So you've no idea what a modern football ground is like? Well, let's take a look round the ground while we talk.' Alan's eyes twinkled with obvious pride in the place. 'I usually give a history of the club and the players, but that might not mean much to you.' He gestured: the restaurant was already filling. 'Early birds, come for a bit of atmosphere.'

'You start them young,' Mark said.

'Ah, those mascots. And why not? We're a club that values kids. Later on I'll point out the academy, and tell you what we do in the community. Ready? And then I'll introduce you to the guy who'll be your host this afternoon, someone who knew young Phil better than most. No, you're not sitting on the terraces: you're in a hospitality suite.' Waving away their surprised thanks, he set them in motion. 'One thing you need to know is that the Baggies have a reputation for being decent people. Some clubs are proud of being hard, with hard fans. Not the Baggies. We pride ourselves on being family-friendly. Decent folk like to have decent players in their team. They don't think it's clever for them to collect yellow cards, let alone red ones. So though they'd be the first to say that Phil Foreman was a terrific striker, they didn't like his tactics. Broke an opponent's leg once, just because he could. That sort of man.'

Mark nodded.

'Presumably we're actually under one of the stands here?' Fran gestured at the thickly carpeted corridor, which reminded her of one in a well-managed hotel.

'Quite. Let's find a window so you can get a better sense of where you are. There! Over there we've got an indoor pitch, a gym, of course, an all-weather pitch — and it's not just our academy and the players that use the facilities, it's the community too. We've got really good links with players with disabilities.'

Fran nodded with genuine admiration. 'It's like brand new shiny jewels set in an old, tired setting!'

'Yes, poor old West Bromwich like all our industrial heartland has suffered in the recession. Not pretty, is it?'

'But all those trees.' She hoped she managed to sound pleased rather than disbelieving. Success. She was rewarded with a charming smile.

'We've got a whole urban forest of them these days. But they say that when a Black Country native's been away, he knows he's back when he sees poplars and blue engineering brick.' His pride and pleasure mirrored Ted's their very first night. 'Let's have a look at the media centre — not as huge or space age as the one at Lord's, but state of the art, believe me.'

They even saw the home dressing room — but were fiercely denied access to the away one. Finally they had a look round at pitch level. 'Up there's the sort of place you'll maybe be familiar with: the police command centre.'

'All I can say is that it wasn't like that in my day,' Mark said, bracing himself against a rain-bearing gust of wind.

'This is the highest Premier League ground in the country,' Alan explained as they huddled against it, 'just as Edgbaston is the highest test cricket ground. We're on the Midlands Plateau — that's why we're not so bothered by floods as the folk in the Severn Valley. And the next high point as you look east is the Urals.' He gestured as if to conjure distant mountains.

Mark was peering at something altogether closer: the pitch. 'It's so lush,' he marvelled. 'I wish I could have a lawn transplant.'

'You'd have to mow it every week by hand,' Alan retorted, 'and be prepared to wave it goodbye at the end of every season. This'll be a ploughed field by the end of May — and within weeks it'll be playable again. Now, Fran, you look frozen. Would you like me to take your photo under the Albion badge? Inside, then . . .'

Their photos duly on camera, he took them briskly along, pointing out en route the academy he'd mentioned. They climbed to a much higher level, that of the executive suites, which Fran would have called hospitality boxes. But this one was certainly no box. It was a room ready to feed sixteen in some elegance, and Dean Redhead, whom Alan introduced as their host, was on hand to greet them, exchanging a few minutes' chat with Alan about the prospects for the game before the older man bade them farewell.

'This has been such a treat,' Fran declared, beaming with pleasure as she shook his hand. 'I'd simply never expected anything like this.'

'Not if you've not been to a ground since Gillingham's twenty or thirty years ago,' Alan agreed. He shook hands with Mark. 'Enjoy the match — probably more than we West Brom fans will, to be honest.' He tipped his hat and was away.

* * *

It was a good job they'd gone for the layered look, with smart underneath the layers. Their host sported smart casual clothes, with the emphasis on smart, which might, had Mark worried about such things, have made him feel underdressed.

Tall as Mark, but broader and more self-consciously muscled, Dean had apparently been on the Albion staff as a physio when Phil was a player. Now he ran several sports injury clinics; not just physio, he assured them as he held their hands in greetings he prolonged, as if assessing by touch possible treatment programmes for them. He listed massage, hydrotherapy, acupuncture, Pilates and also a whole range of other therapies they didn't recognize by name. Such quasi-medical treatments always made Mark nervous, as if the very mention of a torn muscle or snapped hamstring would prompt the tennis gods to fix him in their gaze. Fran, who had spent much of last spring on crutches, drew Dean's fire, mentioning her leg injuries and eliciting a further barrage of remedies. She took more interest in his suggestions for preventing further damage, though she had no intention of attempting heroics again. Come to think of it, however, she'd not intended to be heroic at the time, so she could make no promises, even to herself.

He checked a Rolex she didn't expect to be fake. 'Let's get those questions of yours out of the way fast — or you can stay behind after the game for an extra tipple. It's best to wait till the traffic clears,' he said. 'There'll be a lot of away supporters. Probably victorious away supporters, Chelsea being the club they are,' he concluded sadly.

'Thanks. That'd be lovely, result apart,' Fran declared. 'So you're happy to talk to us?'

'I wouldn't have invited you if I wasn't, would I?'

Mark smiled. 'Apart from Natalie's parents, who might have been biased, you're the one person of all those we've spoken to who actually knew Phil Foreman well — or the only one who admits to it, at least.'

'Yes. I should imagine I saw more of him than most while he was here. In both senses,' he said drily. 'He was a bit injury-prone, was Phil. But he was a client; I can't tell you anything that would violate practitioner–patient confidentiality. So why me?'

'You answered that question yourself: you saw more of him than most,' Fran said. 'And people are unguarded while other people are stretching and bending them — talking distracts you from the pain of someone's fingers delving into parts of muscles best left in decent torpor.'

He gave a bark of laughter. 'You may think you're walking well, but that calf of yours is still pretty tight, you know.'

'Wading round floods in wellies should stretch it a bit! Actually, after a broken leg and a torn muscle I owe my mobility to your NHS colleagues. Until then I was physio-phobic. Was Foreman?'

'Professional footballers can't be. Most carry an injury most of the time. They're young, they're fit, they're highly paid. Most of all, they've got a limited shelf life: they have to do whatever's necessary. No argument. Things have got much more sophisticated than when he was a player: ice baths, cryotherapy, that sort of thing. And no,' he added, 'cryotherapy's nothing to do with having a good weep on someone's shoulder.'

'I thought it meant freezing dead bodies to wait until a cure had been found for their illness,' Mark quipped. 'But did he weep on your shoulder?'

'Yorkshire lads aren't in the habit of weeping.' Redhead grinned. 'Some folk think because he played a lot of his life for Arsenal he was a southerner. But they come from all over, these kids — because that's all they are, most of them, remember. And in most Premier League clubs, despite academies like ours designed to bring out the best of talented players in the area, you'd be hard put to find many local born lads. Many UK-born lads, to be honest. Anyway, young Phil was tough as they come — came from mining stock, I shouldn't wonder. No, he'd be a bit tall. He could have played rugby, only the game wasn't professional in those days, or cricket, but again, there wasn't so much money. He just had ball skills to die for — could always pop the ball into the net just when you needed him to. But he was already on a downward trajectory when he came to us, to be frank. He still had the miracle feet, but, my God, he was a rough player. And, between ourselves, he let fly at one or two of his team-mates during training sessions. He was on the receiving end of endless verbals from the manager. From us he went to Millwall, then a couple of overseas clubs. Don't think we didn't try to help him, though; someone who does that's troubled, isn't he, as well as trouble?'

'So what sort of support could the club offer him, Dean? Theoretically. I appreciate we may have to wait to see his file to get specifics.'

'There's the club doctor for starters. It's hard to pull the wool over his eyes. All our medics care about the game and they care about the players. So if he'd seen the doc back then — and I've every reason to believe he did — he'd have been assessed for specialist treatment. A shrink, maybe, or an anger management course. All that testosterone, all that adrenalin: he's not the first player to need to learn to calm things down.'

'When he was hurting other people, did he ever get hurt himself? Did you see injuries that might not have occurred on the field of play?'

It was clear that Redhead was reluctant to reply.

'Put it another way, could you imagine him being violent with people off the pitch?'

Redhead got to his feet, staring down at them. 'Let's get this straight: you're asking if he could have killed his wife. Right?'

'Wrong. At least for the time being. Technically he was never in the frame. His alibi was absolutely watertight: he was in Newcastle with the team. There's no evidence that we've seen that made us think he hired a hit-man or anything like that.'

'That wouldn't be his style at all. Strictly between ourselves, I can imagine him taking a swipe at her — back of the hand stuff when he was in a temper. But he wasn't a forward planner, young Phil. He was an impulse man.' He sat down again.

'When the police found no trace of her he hired a private detective,' Mark said. 'Why would he do that?'

Redhead smiled grimly. 'Plainly you don't think he simply wanted to find her. But I do think he'd want to find his son. He worshipped that lad. Can I tell you a little story? My kids and his Hadrian used to go to toddler tennis. Half a dozen kids with oversized tennis balls and racquets with very large heads. I know, I know: it's like Baby Mozart and whatever. Four he was, Hadrian, just. And he was good. Even a doting dad like me could tell he was going to be better than my Thomas. He could see the ball, move around the court, put the ball where he wanted.'

'At that age? Why do I bother?' Mark groaned.

'You play? Well, maybe it's a good job you don't play like he did. A couple of times Thomas was crying after coaching. I spoke to the coach: what the hell was going on? Coach said that another kid was the problem. It wasn't bullying or anything like that. It was just if this kid missed a ball, or walloped it out — and he was only four, remember — that kid lost it. He literally hit his head on the wire netting. Made himself bleed.'

'A kid of four?'

'Right. Then the coach asked me to step back a bit because he was going to have to have a word with this kid's dad. At this point Phil turned up. I made myself invisible. Best I could, anyway. Must have worked because I heard the weirdest conversation. The coach explained the problem — the headbanging and everything — and asked Phil to explain to Hadrian that he must do as he was told and cool it or he couldn't come back. And do you know what Phil said? He said he liked Hadrian that way. Hard. He wanted him hard and hungry. "Not," Phil said, pointing at Thomas, "like that little poofter over there." Funnily enough, next time Phil needed a treatment session, I wasn't available. Within two months Natalie had gone and soon after Phil signed for Millwall. That's the kind of bloke Natalie was married to.'

'Be straight, now: did he hit her?' There were people outside the door. There was only time for a blunt question.

A swift nod. 'Skin off his knuckles a couple of times.'

Fran asked another, less threatening one, because she wanted to know and it didn't matter if people heard. 'And does Thomas still play tennis?'

'He switched to badminton.'

'Lovely game; I used to play myself.'

'I've lost count of the hours I spent ferrying him around for tournaments, and then sorting out his niggling injuries afterwards.'

'My dad just did the ferrying,' Fran laughed. 'I had to deal with the niggles myself.'

Dean looked at her with renewed approval. But his guests were swarming round. He put a hand on her arm. 'Do hang back afterwards, remember; maybe we'll have a chance to talk again. Especially about that private detective: that worries me.'

The seats might have been outside, up near the roof, but they were comfortable and, to their amazement, heated. The noise from the PA system pop music and the crowd was overwhelming. From somewhere came the visceral pulse of drums — or maybe fans rhythmically hitting barriers. Talk about *The Rite of Spring*! Even Fran would have danced herself to death impelled by this tribal force. No matter she couldn't hear what people were saying; they weren't out there for conversation. She was on her feet too, yelling, baying with the crowd. Yes! She'd never dreamed it would be like this. She turned to Mark to share the force. But Mark wasn't there. Before she could get to her feet, Dean was moving, gesturing her to stay put.

* * *

'I'm fine, Dean. Honestly. I just needed to take these out.' He held out his hearing aids. They were both equipped with a mini-switch with which to raise or lower volume, indicating their position on the scale with a number of beeps only audible to the wearer. However, their tiny sounds had been completely drowned, and he truly didn't know whether he'd been making things worse or better.

'They're so unobtrusive I didn't realize you wore them.'

'They're life savers, normally. And usually I can just turn them down. But it was like being smothered in sound. I'll be fine now.' He returned them to his ears. 'Please: I don't want to spoil your afternoon.'

'The Chelsea goal's spoilt it already! Sit down a second — no one's allowed to see us drinking, you see.' He tweaked the blinds. 'I've been thinking about this PI thing, Mark: it's so out of character for an action man. Phil was more the sort to be out there scouring the area himself.'

'But according to a number of people he never even visited the place where they were last seen. There was some tussle about little Julius's funeral, too. His in-laws can't say a decent word about him. Nothing new there, I suppose.' Not that he'd been bothered much by his own decidedly eccentric mother-in-law — though he knew Fran's relationship with her was desperately difficult.

Dean topped up their glasses and nodded.

'Are you still in touch with any of his team-mates?'

'They're scattered to the four winds. But what about her friends?'

He'd keep the missing nanny under his hat for a bit. 'The weird thing is no one's ever remembered a single name.' Which must of course be significant in itself. 'Unless . . . ?'

'Sorry. I hardly knew her. I wonder . . . look, I'll give this some thought and maybe call you.'

Mark did the unforgivable: he fixed him with the stare he'd used on a thousand witnesses. 'You did know her, didn't you? You treated her.'

Dean raised his hands. 'OK, I did. Which means, Mark, I'm bound, since she may still be alive, by patient confidentiality. I'm sorry. You're a decent guy doing your job. I'll try and work out what I can tell you and what I can't.'

Mark put an apologetic hand on his shoulder and passed him his card. 'I'm sorry to press you. I'd be grateful for anything. Anything at all. But I'm keeping us from the match. The view's stupendous from up here, isn't it?' But he made sure he turned his aids to minimum before following his host.

* * *

The post-match celebrations in the hospitality box would hardly have been excessive if the Albion had actually defeated the opposition. They hadn't — they'd just managed a 1–1 draw. But they'd certainly dented the collective ego of Chelsea, a team that, according to the people almost dancing for joy in Dean's suite, seemed to regard their position at the top of the league as a right. It probably was, given the huge sums of money and world class players the money bought. But they'd been brought low by one of the least experienced attacks in the Premier League. A draw! A wonderful opportunistic goal just minutes from time! Dean Redhead called for champagne all round.

Mark and Fran were everyone's best friends, southern mascots that had somehow kept the club out of the relegation zone. Mark found himself with an invitation to play tennis at the Priory: it seemed his putative opponent was a Warwickshire cricketer. As for Fran, it was fortunate she was no longer afraid of physios: Dean insisted that he'd give her a morning's free treatment on her leg. Both, without reference to the other, accepted — for a day when they'd finished their short-term contract.

Fran could have partied all night. But as she looked across to Mark, she caught a brief glimpse of horror before he rediscovered his social smile. His ears, of course: his aids might work wonders, but they couldn't replace the miracles that were human ears.

In any case, what were they doing here when they should have been keeping an eye on Edwina? She was straight out of hospital, for goodness' sake. She collected a relieved-looking Mark, and thanked Dean for all his kindness. Would he join them for a thank-you supper on Monday evening? He couldn't do Monday, but Wednesday was good; he'd await a text with the details.

CHAPTER EIGHTEEN

They'd have liked to go to church on Sunday, but there wasn't a service at St Andrew's, only one at a neighbouring village. But this was inaccessible because of the floods, or Edwina, who insisted she was completely recovered, would have asked them for a lift.

The other thing that was inaccessible was the restaurant Hugh had chosen. Since his house was separated from the main road by thirty yards of two-foot deep and rising flood water, the news was academic anyway. 'And I'm busy moving furniture upstairs at the moment: I know you need to cross-question me, but this really isn't a good time. Maybe this evening?'

The decision to go into Hindlip to work was easy enough. Edwina wanted to cook them lunch, but admitted that she'd been planning to spend the afternoon playing Scrabble with a group of like-minded old friends. But she did insist that she'd prepare an evening meal for them all — they'd made themselves part of her family, she said, with all they'd done for her over the last two days. And surely one of her packed lunches would be tastier than anything they'd find in a police canteen?

Who could argue with that?

'And have you got a change of clothes?' she called to them as they were about to set off. 'Excellent. You never know in this weather.'

* * *

'Do you remember that TV quiz back in the mists of time,' Fran said, 'when the audience used to yell at the contestants to *open the box*?' She slowed as a four by four came too quickly towards them, like an ugly Viking longboat bearing people inclined to do a spot of raping and pillaging. The bow-wave swiped at old red-brick walls as if deliberately undermining them. She waited for the troubled waters to subside, located the middle of the road and set off more circumspectly, but making sure to maintain the engine speed.

'That was *Take Your Pick!*, wasn't it? Michael Miles? My parents loved it. I suppose I did — but I chiefly remember sneering about it. Horrible teenage superiority.' Mark sighed at the thought of his younger self. 'What about you?'

Now clear of the flood, she kept pressing the brakes to dry them. 'I was too busy playing badminton all over the place, wasn't I? But what I want to do now, more than anything else, is open the Garbutts' box. OK, I know that technically it's been opened and examined and that Stu's logged the contents. But I really want to see the items and handle them myself. I don't want to wait till tomorrow and I know you've been dying to tell me what you've seen.'

'We've both been paragons,' he agreed. 'I just thought it would make more sense if you saw things through unprejudiced eyes. Look at this devastation,' he said, gazing out at the countryside spread before them. 'You almost feel that it's not just the locals who don't want us to investigate properly — it's the whole environment. Not being able to get here or there, people trapped in their own homes. Who knows if any of the team'll be able to get in tomorrow? Who knows if we will?'

'I'd hate to take up Webster's offer of single accommodation,' she said glumly. 'Look, would it speed things up if we did ask Ted to join us, even if it's just for a couple of hours a day? It seems silly to look a gift-horse in the mouth.'

'Assuming, of course, that he's a gift-horse, not a Trojan horse. And remember, you should fear Greeks when they come bearing gifts. *Timeo Danaos et dona ferentes*.'

'Don't I remember you having a long discussion with someone about the meaning of that? Isn't there some debate about whether it means *even when they come bearing gifts* or *especially when they come bearing gifts*? Sometimes I wish I'd had the benefit of a Latin education,' she added, shaking her head. 'Then I'd know if Ted was a Greek or not. Assuming a Danaan is the same as a Greek anyway.' Then she became altogether more serious. 'I really do not like the look of that tree!' No time to tell him which. She slammed the protesting car into reverse, accelerating as hard as she dared. 'When I have to stop, get out and run! Now!'

* * *

'Shock, that's what that'll be,' a traffic officer declared, as they stood dithering on the grass verge, staring at their car. He found them another foil blanket.

'Or it might be something to do with the fact that we're ankle deep in icy water,' Mark said with a grim smile. 'Heavens, it isn't much more than a twig that's done all that damage. If my wife hadn't reacted as she did . . .' He drew his hand across his throat. 'Now, sergeant, if you think it's safe, we'd like to retrieve a few items from the boot and thumb a lift with someone to Hindlip Hall. And if it violates Elf and Safety, just look the other way. We've got important police documents in there I really wouldn't want to let into the hands of a scrap merchant.'

'We're answering direct to the ACC (Crime),' Fran added, wondering how two sets of clothes and shoes could mysteriously have become confidential information, but not arguing. Not laughing, either, though she was near to it. Shock, that's what the officer would have called that too.

And perhaps he wasn't far out. She'd probably have preferred to retreat to the sybaritic comfort of Edwina's B and B; but Mark was right. Working would be a more therapeutic option. Possibly.

* * *

Not that many people were working today, not if the Hindlip car park, where their temporary chauffeur decanted them, was anything to go by. Cars were clustered away from trees or anything else likely to blow over, apart from a Bentley daring the elements to do their worst.

Mark widened his eyes. 'That's bravado for you. And who in the force drives a car like that?'

Fran pointed at the registration plate. The letters and numerals managed to form the name Dundy. 'Three guesses. And who's that pulling up beside her? Another nice set of wheels.'

The driver, a woman, pulled up her hood as she scurried in. Rain or guilt? Rain, they decided.

Showered and changed into the clothes Edwina had once again insisted they bring, they turned on the coffee machine. Perhaps soon their hands would stop shaking. They helped themselves to extra biscuits.

'Tell you what,' Mark said, 'why don't you look at the stuff in the box while I go back to our office and deal with the car insurance? That way you can be sure I won't interrupt your thought processes.'

'Such as they are.' She managed a grin. 'OK. Gloves.' She snapped them on. 'Notepad. Ball-point. Action.'

Something in her voice stopped him even as he opened the door to leave. The building, buzzing during the week, was echoingly quiet, though there must still be a hundred people working there somewhere. 'Will you be all right on your own?'

She turned slowly. 'You know what? I'd feel much better if I had another hug.'

'You know what? So would I. And I'd also feel better if I phoned Caffy to find out if our rectory's still in one piece. Hug first, though.'

Much restored, she pulled herself up straight as if that would shake her thought processes back into shape. And then she did indeed open the box.

Perhaps she would have felt a more immediate, more vivid response if everything hadn't been properly bagged and numbered, and if she'd had a sense of how the contents had been packed. Had there been a formal order, or was everything jumbled together? Stu had certainly imposed a scheme. First there were family snaps of children. They were almost generic children at first — hard to pick out anyone as a cherished daughter. But then came a girl with higgledy-piggledy teeth crying out for the work of an orthodontist. A few photos of the same girl, mouth snapped tight shut: perhaps the vital braces had been fitted. And then — as if to testify to the dentist's skill, a couple of a teenager not so much smiling as ironically saying *Cheeeeeeeese*. There was a jump of a couple of years; there was a recognizable Natalie demure in Puritan cap and pinafore, and then one of her in a tracksuit brandishing a medal. Fran burrowed. Yes, here was the medal, in its own tiny bag. Fran tipped it on to the palm of her hand. And cursed. Though her eyes were good enough for most things, they'd started to let her down when she needed to inspect something closely. Time for a trip to the opticians. She returned it to its bag, making a note to ask Mark — already equipped, of course, with reading glasses — to check it.

Next came a bag with what were clearly professional portraits taken much later. Despite the care with which the photographer had lit his subjects, he'd been unable to disguise poor Julius's disabilities. Hadrian gave the impression of loving every moment of the attention. Phil Foreman might never have existed except as a sperm donor.

Fran rooted round for other photos. None. So what had happened to all the years in between? Natalie's graduation ceremony for a start? Not to mention her wedding album. No, there was no sign of them. Whether the Garbutts liked it or not, she'd have to ask them about that. Or maybe Robyn should go on her own? Or with Mark, famous for charming even the most cynical old ducks off the water?

She returned to the box. Next came a couple of school play programmes — Edwina would have been pleased to see those there. Natalie had got the cast to sign them. No exam certificates; no degree scroll.

Here was a teddy bear. Who had that belonged to? If it had been Natalie's wouldn't the fur show more signs of wear? Her own, Old Ted, now carefully dressed to conceal the baldest patches, certainly did. More to the point, he would have done even when they were both thirty years younger. And this was a very small bear — the sort you associate with babies. Perhaps it had belonged to poor Julius. Another question for the Garbutts. But there was nothing else that might have belonged to Julius or to Hadrian. Perhaps Phil had refused to be parted with anything. And yet the loving grandparents she knew who regularly hosted grandchildren either for visits or for longer stays all kept a supply of toys; like Mark's train set, ostensibly meant for his son and grandson.

All gone to a charity shop, as Mrs Garbutt had said? Somehow she couldn't believe it. Mark might see nothing at all of his daughter or her children, but there was certainly a box of mementoes of them tucked safely away. If ever they were reconciled, it would prove how much he'd loved them — how he still continued to love them.

She pushed away from the table to lean her head on the cold of the window. Why was there so little love in this box?

* * *

'Why is there so little anything?' was Mark's rejoinder to her question as he reappeared for a top-up of coffee. Looking as weary as she felt, he sank on to one of the chairs. She bit her lip; she'd let him deal with all the phone problems associated with the insurance, hadn't she? Why hadn't she thought through his offer? The audiologist had said it might be a year, maybe two, before he got the full benefits of his aids; meanwhile the phone was one thing he still found irritatingly stressful. Should she draw attention to it even more by asking how he'd got on? She'd phrase it as a tactful question about their cover and a replacement vehicle.

'Oh, that's all sorted. Our poor car amongst many poor cars. They've had Range Rovers taking to the water like giant ducks, they've had cars submerged in flash floods, they've had high-sided vans blown over — the young woman was very chatty. She seemed to think our tree was more dramatic than most when I emailed her the photos. Actually, she sounded quite shocked.'

'I think I'd feel shocked if I saw them now. I felt quite calm, quite dispassionate, while we were at the scene.'

'They'll get a temporary replacement to us as soon as their computer clears it — but as you can imagine, it's a very busy little computer at the moment.' He managed a pale smile, and then upgraded it to a proper one. 'The good news is that everything's OK at home. One or two branches down, Caffy says, but only from those trees we'd had scheduled for a visit from the tree surgeon. One tree's gone: that ash — it chose the Dignitas option rather than hanging around to wait for ash die-back, she says. The trees the surgeon's already dealt with are all fine. The ditch at the far end of the garden is now a stream, but still well within its banks — and Caffy's organized some sandbags just in case. All the slates and chimneys are safe and sound.' His voice told her far more than his words. He wished he was back there, longed as much as she did for its comfort and security, for people they knew and trusted, for dear friends who loved them and were loved in return.

But now he was back in investigative mode. 'I could have sworn there was more than that,' he said, picking up and replacing the items she'd left spread on the table beside the box. 'An evidence bag with some papers in it.'

'Maybe I put something down on top of it,' she said. 'It wouldn't be the first time I've messed up since I've been here.' She grabbed, lifted, patted, shook.

He took her frantic hands. 'You're over that now — time and again you've proved that. We wouldn't be here now if it hadn't been for your quick reactions this morning. Here as in alive, in case you'd forgotten.'

Still checking the table, she nodded. And then sat down, hard. 'Let me see the photos of that tree. Yes, I need to. Bloody hell, another twenty metres forward and . . .' She clapped her hands, left them palm to palm. 'OK, switch it off. Please. I was stupid to look. Perhaps it's why I feel edgy. Funny, when I was at work I used to be able to hold a post-mortem report in one hand and eat a sandwich with the other.'

'It wasn't a report on you, though, was it? What's that, under the lid?'

'Just my notebook.'

'Weird. I really could have sworn . . .'

'Stuart logged everything, didn't he? So there's a computerized record. No?'

His irritation showed with every tap of the keyboard. 'No access. The system's down. Essential maintenance, according to the screen. However,' he said, 'I remember copying it to the iPad. Just in case. And the iPad's back in our office. On the desk with that wonderful lunch Edwina put together for us.'

'So long as that hasn't gone walkabout too,' she said, gathering up her bag.

CHAPTER NINETEEN

'Can't see it anywhere in here,' she said, as if they'd spoken of nothing except the evidence bag on their walk along the corridor. She touched and moved items as before — even looking under the picnic basket.

Mark joined in, increasingly anxious. 'Funny thing is, I can't see the iPad either. Shit!'

'I know you said you'd left it here, but maybe you took it to the incident room after all? I don't recall seeing it there, but that doesn't mean a thing these days.' Her fingers to her temples, she shook her head as if to clear it. 'I'm just off to the loo — do you want me to check en route?'

'I'll go and look myself. But I really do not remember taking it there.'

Fran got back first. She'd been horrified to look in the wash basin mirrors and see how pale she looked. Would a bit of what Edwina no doubt called lippie help? She dug in the drawer she'd commandeered for her odds and ends — and found not just some make-up but also the elusive iPad. In *her* drawer? What was Mark thinking of? Or perhaps, like her, he hadn't quite reassembled his marbles after the tree incident? She popped it on to his desk, in full view.

'Where the hell—?' he demanded the moment he returned.

'It had gone to look for the evidence bag — in my tat drawer,' she added carefully.

'What on earth was it doing there? I know technically it's yours but—'

She spread her hands. 'You tell me.'

'I never put it in there. Why should I? Did you?'

'Not that I remember. Anyway, there it is. Is it OK? Do you want to fire it up while I unpack the picnic? Bless her, Edwina's even given us a tablecloth. There's enough here for six, you know.' She smacked her head. 'Hell! I forgot to iron those sheets . . .'

At last Mark managed a smile. 'It's all here. Here — Stu's list of evidence.' He passed her the iPad and, arm round her shoulders, tracked down the screen. 'Sod it! Bag 7A/TH: containing documents, various.'

'Bloody hell! Why couldn't he be more precise? I've a good mind to phone him now and tell him to get himself in here, Sunday afternoon or no Sunday afternoon. No? OK, think back. You were with him some of the time: did you see anything?'

'Not to register it here.' He tapped his forehead. 'There's been stuff going on to make me forget it, to be honest; forgive the pun but a lot of water's gone under the bridge since then.' He switched off. 'Call me paranoid, but I'd rather keep this with us.'

'Plenty of room in my bag,' she declared optimistically, easing it between keys and hairbrush. 'But you've had enough to make you paranoid. Two sets of flooding which probably had some human intervention. On the other hand, a missing file — these things happen in busy offices.'

'Our office? Busy?'

'OK. But the other missing thing's safe and sound. And the tree — that was more an act of God. Who looked after us, rather than the reverse. Anyway, enough talking shop — time to enjoy this wonderful poached salmon . . .'

* * *

Fran would have given a lot to be able to leap into the car and go home. Even if neither was an option, she didn't want to be at work. From the look of him neither did Mark. But eventually they caught each other's eye and got up as one. 'We've still got the problem of getting back to Edwina's,' she murmured, checking the iPad was still in her bag.

'Be nice if they lent us a car from the pool,' Mark observed, looking round the room — no, they'd left nothing where it shouldn't be. He even checked that the drawers were in their usual state — Fran's chaotic, his anally neat — and locked them. Groaning, Fran gave him a hard stare, but not about his security fad: it was that awful reference to the pool, wasn't it? Hand in hand, they returned to the incident room.

'One last hunt for the missing bag?' she asked.

'Let's just ask Stu tomorrow. Maybe he took it with him by mistake.'

'Some mistake! Heavens, a sackable offence in a live case. What are you doing?'

'It was here all the time!' Fran exclaimed, moving the box a couple of inches and flourishing the missing evidence bag.

'No, it wasn't. I checked under the box. Unless it somehow stuck to it,' he added with less conviction. 'OK, let's go through it — unless you'd rather do that alone too?'

She held out her hand. 'I'd rather do it with you. So long as you only laugh at me when my theories are crazy.'

'What about if they're just odd?' he asked, taking it.

'Odd can be useful. And weird. At least that's what I've always said.'

Mark raised a finger. 'What's that?'

She squeezed his hand. 'It's just footsteps.'

'But our team's the only one using this corridor at the moment.'

She grinned. 'I don't think anyone with sinister intent would bring along a posse of kids, do you? Can you hear them yet? Good.'

'Hi, both.' Rain still dripping from her raincoat, Paula stepped in, pushing rats' tails of hair from her face. 'I heard about your car on the grapevine and thought you might need some wheels to get home. Only you'll have to share the car with my lads. Their dad's out with the other men from the village filling and laying sandbags and they'd rather have helped him.' She rolled her eyes at the prospect.

'I never imagined . . . this is so very kind . . .' Fran found she was close to tears.

'Look, if you're in the middle of something, so long as you don't mind them sitting over there with their games, I can go and get them out of the car and maybe even help?'

She was out of the room before they could demur. Within minutes, she reappeared, more or less dragging two little boys.

Fran gripped Mark's hand: how on earth had Natalie managed to make Hadrian go where she wanted?

Peeling their soaking jackets, which she hung on the backs of a couple of chairs, Paula shooed the kids to the furthest corner. 'No you can't play with my phone! Look, you've got your own games and stuff, for God's sake.' Then she disposed of her own and literally rolled her sleeves up. She gave a mock salute. 'At your service.' Returning to her usual voice, she continued, 'And I know there's no overtime. Oh, is that the Garbutts' famous box of goodies?'

'I'm afraid so: I just couldn't wait,' Fran admitted.

'Can I see?'

'You're more than welcome,' Mark said. 'Fran and I have just had a joint senior moment: we thought we'd lost an evidence bag, but it's just turned up again.'

'You're kidding me. You're not like that. My nan, yes — but not you two. Either of you. After that first morning, when for a few minutes you seemed on a different planet, Fran, I've never seen such a switched-on pair. Despite all your adventures. And another one this morning — you're lucky to be alive, according to Zeb in Traffic.' Her eyes widened as Mark showed her the photos on his camera.

'More than lucky: Fran saw what was happening and managed to reverse. Then we scarpered.'

'I should think you did . . .' She seemed to make a conscious effort to change the subject. 'How's Edwina, by the way?'

'Back home,' Mark said. 'Back on form. Bossier than Fran. Criticized my porridge-making this morning.'

'I thought *she* was catering for *you*!'

'I don't think she's quite as steady on her pins as she makes out. Besides, I pride myself on my porridge.'

'Horrible stuff. Invention of the devil. Anyway, what was the evidence you lost?' Paula peered inside the box. 'Not a lot to show for thirty years on this planet, is there? Of course, her husband would have kept most — and you know what in-laws are like. Armed truces at best. And Robyn didn't think the Garbutts had much in the way of the milk of human kindness. Mrs G especially. So if Phil was as grief-stricken as even the toughest guy would be, I can't see him handing over much, can you? I wonder what he did with it all when he moved in with that model. Photos. Little things meaningless to anyone else. Binned it? Or kept some items just in case . . . You know, you couldn't imagine Madeleine McCann's parents ferrying bin liners full of her toys to the tip, could you?'

A brief tussle broke out between her sons. She shouted. It subsided as quickly as it had arisen. Nearly. Fran clocked a swift kick their mother missed — or tactically ignored.

Mark used the diversion to flick a quick glance at Fran: should they look at the peripatetic evidence? She shrugged: there was little point in making Paula feel they didn't trust her. Mark nodded, and put it quietly on a table out of the boys' line of vision.

'We've not yet looked at it ourselves,' Fran said. 'Why don't you have first pop?'

Paula broke a fingernail removing the paper clip. She nibbled it flat. 'I don't think that's a good omen, do you? Oh, look — baby handprints and footprints. These must be Hadrian's. The poor little dabs must be poor Julius's: some babies with Edwards' syndrome haven't got proper thumbs, have they? Ordinary poster paints by the look of it, and ordinary A4 paper. The Garbutts must have done them when they had the kids at theirs.' She dug in her bag for an emery board and tackled her nail again, blowing away the dust. It took her some time to get it to her satisfaction and return her attention to the papers.

'You can't get much more personal than that,' Mark said sadly. 'Or this: I think it says *Nanna*. A portrait of her. Look! And this says *Grandad*. Possibly.'

'The rest are just more of the same — it was a bit grandiose of Stu to log them as documents,' Fran observed. 'Do you reckon there could be anything here from Natalie's childhood, Paula, as opposed to the boys'? No?'

'I'm not exactly your art expert,' Paula said, assuming a pompous voice, 'but I'd say the paint and paper were all from the same source.'

'So would I,' Mark agreed. 'And there's very little point in getting them checked forensically — it's not as if we're investigating art fraud, is it?'

'It's weird, isn't it? Keeping just your grandchildren's paintings, not your own daughter's. As for her driving licence and passport and all the serious stuff, perhaps Foreman kept them. When are you going to nip across and talk to him, Fran?'

'When a fairy godmother touches our zero budget and transforms it into a crock of gold? The thing is, we know he couldn't have abducted her — he wasn't in the Midlands. We know he employed a private detective to find her; if he had had her abducted, he wouldn't need to do that. Not unless it was a double bluff, which means he's a lot brighter than people give him credit for. So I can't see any justification for a trip to Cyprus. Not really.'

'I got a sense the marriage wasn't a happy one,' Mark mused. 'And she's alleged to have been squirrelling away his money, whether with or without his permission we don't yet know.' He snapped his fingers in irritation. 'Did Stu ever report back on whether she'd got any driving convictions?

There was talk of her having taken points on her licence to keep his clean.'

'I'll double check now, shall I?' Paula suggested.

'Thanks for offering, but the computer system was down earlier — essential maintenance, whatever that means for a computer. It's not urgent. Tomorrow will do. In fact,' Mark said, as a squall made a fresh assault on their windows, 'I think we should remind ourselves that this is all unpaid overtime, and that we should go home while there's light to see where the roads are. Assuming the route is clear. If you take the kids down, Fran and I can lock up and pick up our things. See you in a minute?'

Fran snapped her fingers. 'There's one thing I need to ask Paula — meant to ask you, but I'll bet her eyes are even better than yours. Can you make out what it says on these medals?' She jiggled the bag at her.

Paula manoeuvred the bag under the light. '*English Schools Cross Country runner up* — she'd be sixteen then. *University Women's Cross Country. Home Counties Cross Country, third in class* — and that'd be the year before she disappeared. All awarded to Natalie Garbutt.'

'It gives the cliché *doing a runner* a whole new meaning, doesn't it?' Mark said. 'In other words, tricky though toddlers are—'

'Sorry,' Fran broke in, 'but I think we should have revised that definition of Hadrian too. He's too old to be a toddler. Toddlers are uncoordinated and wilful.'

'You're telling me,' Paula put in sourly. 'And worse when they lose the uncoordinated bit.'

'Hadrian may have been wilful, but not uncoordinated. In fact, he played startlingly good tennis, according to the father of another kid having lessons at the same time. So he was a mini-sportsman. Capable of running fast and maybe walking a decent distance. Paula, is it humanly possible to get through to the Wyre Forest again? Are some roads clear?'

Paula pulled a face.

'Back to our OS map,' Mark said briskly, spreading it on a table. 'Let's see. She parks here — right?'

'If park is the word you choose,' Paula chipped in.

'And according to Marion Roberts the footprints on the verge led towards the road. Maybe they crossed the road.' His index finger traced the route. 'Back towards Buttonoak there were a couple of paths heading south — right? There's a car park for one — Earlswood or something.'

Paula nodded. 'Earnwood. Earnwood Copse. There's quite a good trail towards the disused railway line. Once you get there you can follow the line west or east, or you can cross it and reach the visitor centre. Lots of car parking there. Or you can simply fetch up on the A456. It's a long schlep for a child though, even a fit one.'

'But what if his mother was an expert cross-country runner? What if she carried him on her back?' Fran persisted.

CHAPTER TWENTY

But there was no time for the others to respond as they no doubt wanted. Paula's kids, sensing the adults were messing up their chance to escape, started a loud and physical spat. The usually cool, competent Paula yelled threats of all sorts of retribution she probably had no means of imposing. Mark caught Fran's eye: they must get on the move before she smacked them and had to spend the rest of the afternoon apologizing for breaking the law. It was time for him to become a good grandpa.

So he spent the journey in the back seat of Paula's car, trying to work out what electronic games the lads were playing; the double-slap of the wipers, the road noise and their excited and heavily accented explanations left him completely at sea. Paula, talking them through the route she'd chosen to avoid tree problems, complicated things even more, firing occasional comments at him. Fran covered for him, as she usually did. She didn't understand the deafness, but she at least no longer thought him simply stupid if he missed things altogether — or more confusingly misheard them. In a barrage like this it was all too easy for him to switch off, retreating to his own thoughts. The kids didn't seem to mind anyway; it was easier for them to pursue arcane targets without having to bother with someone else's useless grandfather.

He turned to look out of the window at the entirely alien landscape. Dimly he recalled a poem he'd had to learn when he was a kid. Not all of it. Everyone in the class had had to learn just a few verses. His bit included the words, *Water, water, everywhere, Nor any drop to drink.* Coleridge had been writing of a mythical ocean; here there were all too real sheets of water covering what were no doubt lush pastures or rich arable land. Snowdrop Cottage might have been flooded opportunistically, but had the perpetrator waited, his or her work would probably have been done by nature; all around, he could see cottages whose only meagre defences against this wash of water were vulnerable sandbags — though he could see some with what looked like commercial barriers by front doors, and hoses, gushing with water, emerging from cellars. Dare he, dare he thank God that their rectory had been spared? And ask that it would continue to be?

* * *

Scrabble had left Edwina with a headache she only feebly attempted to deny, so she adjourned with Fran to the living room with a couple of paracetamols while Mark yet again loaded the washing machine with flood-soaked clothes and applied himself to the vegetables. He was interrupted by a loud and urgent yell from Fran. Something about the car? On television?

He dashed to join them, wiping his hands on the pinafore he'd borrowed. And there it was, indeed, the offending tree now swarming with men with chainsaws. He couldn't for the life of him understand why they'd not guessed that such an arboreal disaster would attract coverage. Wouldn't it have been a splendid opportunity to appeal for witnesses, for fresh information? In fact that was the first thing he'd do the next day: he'd talk to the press office and see if they could at very least get on to the regional news and, aiming higher, on to *Crimewatch*. Fran had enjoyed such excellent relations with the people working on the programme she'd surely be on there in the click of her fingers.

Why had this idea come so slowly? There was all that business of the missing file and iPad too; was he really losing the odd marble? He'd had a terrible fear about Fran only a week ago, but now, thank goodness, she seemed very much back on song. Or perhaps they were simply out of practice and indeed seriously short of staff. There was still the problem of Ted, of course. He found himself smiling: the very fact that he'd used the word *problem* told him that his subconscious really did not want Ted as part of their little team. If only his conscious mind would tell him why.

By now the news was over. Weather forecast time. More tight isobars. And lots more rain to join the gales.

And, of course, no car.

Edwina declared that her head had cleared enough for her to start cooking dinner. 'You have your uses as a scullion, Mark,' she said grandly, holding out her hand for the apron, 'but I am the chef. And since the medics would prefer me not to imbibe for another few days — such penance, darlings — I will leave the choice of wine to you. There are some very decent Riojas to tempt you . . .'

* * *

'Access CCTV footage?' Fran repeated, as they laid the table — nothing sloppily casual for Edwina, despite the change in circumstances. 'Why on earth?'

'Because I don't believe the temporary disappearance of the evidence and the iPad were signs of our incipient dementia. Do you remember that writer friend of Caffy's said she mowed the lawn when she needed her brain to produce fresh ideas for her next book? That's what peeling the spuds did for me. I think that the temporary disappearances today are more connected to our being flooded out than to any carelessness, absent-mindedness or whatever on our part. And — you know what? — it also dawned on me I'm absolutely sick of the whole business and for two pins would tell Colin Webster to stuff the whole exercise somewhere painful.'

'But?'

'But I'm like you: the more someone tries to deter me, the more I want to dig my heels in.'

Fran abandoned her attempts to make the linen napkins look like anything other than linen napkins. Lilies and other variants were simply beyond her, at least while she was thinking. She pulled a chair from the table and sat down. 'Let's talk this through. The guy who employed us is sacked — OK, made redundant, which is better for him but comes to the same thing for us; our resources are negligible; our mini-team is depleted before we even say hello; one of the team keeps disappearing — though admittedly that's through no fault of her own—'

'Assuming she is indeed in court,' Mark observed dourly. 'OK, I like Robyn, but I'm prepared to believe the worst of anyone at the moment. And there was something distinctly weird in management letting her join a team she simply couldn't be part of.' Spotting a minuscule smear on a glass — whatever Edwina had said, he'd put one out for her, if only for symmetry's sake — he polished it with a napkin, which he carefully refolded. Into a neat fan.

Fran eyed his creation and passed him the other two linen squares. 'Technical support arrives eventually. A plus. The evidence is negligible and today it comes and goes. And if something has disappeared, we don't know because Stu's summary is sketchy at best. It'll be interesting to see if he comes in tomorrow, and, if he does, how good his memory is: will he know what — if anything, of course — has been removed? Thanks.' She took the first napkin and put it on a side-plate. 'Have you checked the iPad since it turned up? It'd be interesting to see if anyone had a go at your password.' They'd installed software to warn them of tampering.

'I'll go and check now. It's in your bag, isn't it? But who'd bother trying to access it when they could simply have nicked it? After all, they didn't have long, did they, to get the techies involved?'

'Stealing it would have been too obvious. There'd have had to be a proper investigation. But you're absolutely right: the CCTV will be the key. Assuming we can get hold of it.'

'And assuming we can get in to work.'

'There's no problem there,' Edwina declared, emerging from nowhere to make Mark drop his third napkin. 'The medics don't want me to drive for a couple of days. You can use my car. It would do it good to get its wheels wet.'

Mark gently removed the glass — gin and tonic — from her hand and placed it on the table, easing her on to a chair. 'There'd be all sorts of insurance problems, Edwina — but we're truly grateful for the offer. And before you offer to drive us in, no, you're not going to treat the doctors' advice about driving as cavalierly as you're obviously treating their instructions about drink.'

'Well, then, you'll have to do what Eliza Doolittle did — take a bloody cab, darlings.'

* * *

But, thanks to their insurance company and the nearest Audi dealership, both of which came up trumps, they learned, via an email on the tamper-proof iPad, that they'd have a temporary vehicle by nine the next morning, floods permitting.

'That's the good news,' Mark said, as they sipped their own, considerably weaker G and Ts. Edwina was back in the kitchen, leaving them to enjoy the warmth and comfort of the living room on their own. 'The bad is that someone did try to break our password. Several times. And failed. What's the betting they'll have another go?'

'No takers. There's only one conclusion, isn't there? That at least one person doesn't want this case solved, and that this person has not just influence over the police, but access to Hindlip — directly or via the person they're instructing. It'll be very interesting to see how our request to see the CCTV footage is taken. And who acts.'

'Assuming, of course, that the camera system didn't have the same down time as the computer system. A big assumption, I'd say. Do we explain why we need it? In full?'

Fran pulled the sort of face that suggested she was sucking the lemon in her glass. 'Remind me — does the iPad record the time someone tried to get in? We'd need to be able to say it wasn't happening some time when we weren't in the building.'

'It does. It puts it fairly and squarely at a time when the CCTV cameras will show we were in the incident room without it. Will possibly show,' he added. 'This is the worst thing, Fran. Police corruption. I'm almost wondering if this isn't too big for us — if we shouldn't inform their police standards unit, assuming they have one, so they can give them a fully official high-powered going over.'

'If we find there is corruption there's no question we have to hand everything over. Tell me,' she asked suddenly, 'that wretched journalist woman. Bethan Carter. She really didn't want to talk to me. She wanted to talk to you. She didn't . . . there wasn't . . . ?'

'Iris told me flat out that it was a very good job I hadn't taken her out to lunch, though for some reason there was already a mini-rumour beginning to sprout that I had. So though you have a nasty suspicious mind, I have one too. And yes, I do suspect her motives. Why else make eyes at a deaf old wrinkly like me?'

'I can think of several reasons,' she said, kissing him emphatically enough to elicit a round of applause from their hostess, entering the room to tell them that their starters were on the table.

* * *

'We have a WI meeting tomorrow evening,' Edwina told them over decaf coffees. 'Would it help you if I asked people for their memories of young Natalie? It isn't just old stagers like me — we have younger members too. In fact,' she continued, warming to her theme, 'provided I make a few telephone calls, there's no reason why you shouldn't speak to the group yourself for a couple of minutes. And — we're very broad-minded, Mark — we welcome male guests to our meetings now. Excellent. I'll go and speak to Sandra Mould — that's our chairwoman, though she insists on being known as Madam Chairman — immediately. Always best to strike while the iron is hot.'

'And to prevent us raising any objections,' Mark said under his breath as she swept from the room.

'Corn in Egypt!' Edwina declared, returning within moments. 'Our guest speaker is marooned in Somerset and we hate to cancel. You may even claim a fee — not generous, but a fee.'

'What was he or she going to speak about?' Mark asked, unable to keep the doubt from his voice.

Edwina gave a crack of laughter. 'Preserving the legacy of our countryside. But any talking head is better than none.'

Fran raised a finger. 'Just for the record, Edwina, we won't be talking directly about this investigation: it's simply not allowed. But we can talk about how we came to do the job, and maybe elicit information — discreetly, shall we say?'

'Goes without saying, my angels. I think that calls for a little celebration, don't you? You'll find an interesting range of liqueurs in that cupboard, Mark darling, and a supply of regrettably minuscule glasses . . .'

CHAPTER TWENTY-ONE

Mark had never been much of a fan of Monday mornings. In his early career there'd always been an influx of weekend crime to deal with; in the latter half there'd been the first meeting of the meeting-crammed week. He rather thought that on balance he'd preferred crime to endless management speak. This morning all — all! — he and Fran had had to do was get in to work. Instead of nine, it was nearly ten when an exhausted-looking Audi driver had at last found Edwina's cottage; he'd then needed a lift back to base.

While Mark did a quick stint in their office, dealing with emails, Fran obtained a new parking permit from Iris.

'You don't really need this anyway,' Iris told her, updating the computer. 'There: the car's on the system already.'

'Even so,' Fran shrugged, and paddled out to stick it on the windscreen. She even remembered to email HR to tell them.

* * *

They entered the incident room to find themselves on the receiving end of a round of applause, not even ironic. Their poor car's TV appearance had obviously been watched by all three of the younger people.

As if they'd ever doubted it, at this stage trusting their mini-team seemed the only option. Partly trusting them, at least. And not bollocking them for inadequacy in the matter of logging evidence — they needed an unresentful Stuart on side. As it happened, he was the first one to report anything — whether he'd been prompted by Paula they'd never know.

'I've been checking Natalie's licence, as you asked,' he said, passing Fran a cup of coffee.

She smiled her thanks. 'And?'

'She took several points, spaced out over the period of her marriage. She never argued, always pleaded guilty, never appeared in court. No other convictions. But there's no indication either way whether they were hers or his. Sorry. Another dead end.'

'Thanks for getting what you have, anyway,' Fran said. 'Could I ask you to check something I meant to look for last week — was Natalie a member of any sports clubs in Birmingham or nearby? Running clubs for preference.'

'Right.' He jotted. 'Paula says one of the evidence bags went missing,' he continued, voluble for once. 'I can't think how. I logged everything and put it all back in the box. Everything.'

'I don't suppose you remember exactly what was in the bag?'

'Kids' drawings; baby hand prints and footprints. A pile of cuttings from old newspapers.'

'Cuttings?'

'Yeah. Hang on, I'll show you.' He rifled through the touching pictures they'd looked at yesterday. Twice. He looked up. 'Why should anyone want to nick a load of old press cuttings?'

'Depends what they were about,' Robyn said. 'Or who. And how old.' She was leaning forward, making encouraging gestures with both hands as if she were helping him reverse a small car out of a tight space.

Fran suspected that Stu was enjoying their impatience, playing up to a village idiot image. 'Now what might they have been? There was a pic of a man in a kayak. Then there was half a page of hatches, matches and despatches — but nothing to show which paper it was from. The names were just normal names, so not much to go on there.'

'Any town names?' Fran asked, urgent despite herself.

'I'm sorry. I didn't take much notice. It was my first bag, and there was other stuff to get through and I wasn't to know it would go missing, was I?'

'Of course not,' Mark said briskly. 'You've remembered some really useful stuff, actually. Did you get a chance to find out about the kayak man?'

Stu's blank expression told them he'd not even wondered if he should. But he added, 'If there's nothing else you need in a hurry, I'll have a look now.' He hunted and pecked his way around the keyboard.

Fran pressed her fingers to her temples. Kayak man? Or did he mean canoe man? Of course he did. What was the man up to?

But Paula was already speaking. 'Hang on, gaffer. Things like that don't just go missing because they want to. Someone wants them to go missing. And that someone must have come in here and known exactly what to get. My God,' she added, looking from face to face. 'One of us?'

'Of course not,' Mark said, briskly, because he'd been thinking exactly the same thing himself. 'We're a team. We wouldn't let each other down like that. But as you say, someone must have come in. So I'd like to ask one of you — you're serving officers, and Fran and I have no authority, remember — to go and retrieve the footage for the relevant period CCTV. Could you do that, Paula?'

She flushed. 'I'm the only one of us who was in the building yesterday — you're not thinking—'

'Hey, I'm not thinking anything, I promise! Why should I? You only came yesterday out of the kindness of your heart to rescue us — and the only time you saw that evidence bag was when we were with you. You're a goodie, in my book. And as I said, one of you three has to go and be nice to your colleagues; I don't believe we've been vetted to go into the CCTV area, let alone ask for anything.'

Paula flushed more deeply. 'OK. Sorry.' She headed out.

Fran followed her. 'Paula?' she called softly. 'Is everything OK?' she asked as the younger woman turned back. 'Come on, if we'd got you down as prime suspect, would we have asked you to go? We'd have done everything in our power to keep you away from any evidence.' She smiled, hoping to encourage a response. After a moment, she added, 'Or is it something else? Anything I can help with?' She set them in motion towards the office she and Mark shared, closing the door firmly. 'Come on.' She gestured to a chair.

Paula stayed on her feet. 'What have you been saying to my DCI, ma'am?'

Fran let her jaw literally drop. 'Eh? What should I have said, since I've never met him or her?'

'Her, actually. Ann Sumner. You can guess what she's called.'

'I feel sorry for her already. Except that if she's done or said something to upset one of my team, I can feel damned angry, too.'

'You really haven't spoken to her? Or phoned her?'

'No. Nor texted her nor emailed her nor sent a carrier pigeon. But someone's said something; could you give me the gist?'

'Just that you told someone I was a waste of space and you're looking to recruit someone else to the team. And how disappointed she was considering she recommended me in the first place.'

Of course, Fran had got the impression that Paula had been volunteered rather than simply recommended. 'We've completely ruled out adding to the team, that's how much of a waste you three are. Heavens, after yesterday afternoon? Can you imagine my saying anything snide like that to a third party? You know me by now, Paula: if I thought you'd done anything wrong, I'd take you on one side and tell you to your face. And you'd not forget. My bollockings have been honed through many years of practice. However, you'd find I'd never refer to it again unless you made the same mistake, and I'd never bring it up in front of other people. Now, would you like me to go and speak to this woman with the unfortunate nickname about the perils of spreading rumours that have no basis in truth? I may have no rank to pull these days, but don't think that'd stop me.'

Paula smiled, then laughed. 'I don't think it would. Tell you what, do you want to come down and have a word with the security team yourself? I'll chaperone you.'

'I'll keep my powder dry, if it's all the same to you. There's no point in trying to flout a rule book if you don't need to. And if you can deal with two kids, you can wrap security round your finger.'

Paula stopped by the door. 'That's the trouble, Fran — I can't deal with them. I came this close to hitting them this morning. Their cheek and arguing and—'

Fran enfolded her. 'I've never been a mother. And I don't know how women manage, either full-time stay-at-home mums or working mums. I'm never going to criticize anyone for losing their temper. But I do know that when you come to work, unless there's an emergency or one's ill, it's best to leave the family pressures at the door. I just had parent pressures. They nearly brought me down.' She eased her away. 'You're a kind woman and a bright cop, Paula. Go and sort out security and come back and have a cup of coffee while we all watch the footage.'

* * *

At first no one took any notice as Fran strolled into the main CID office, once two or three smaller rooms, if the damaged ceiling plasterwork was anything to go by. After all, she had her visitor badge clearly visible, and, more to the point, she walked in as if she owned the place. And it might have been her old base in Kent: there was a familiar buzz of activity, with bright looking men and women obviously trying to make the world a better place. There was no goldfish bowl of a glassed-in office for the DCI or superintendent: no doubt they had solid-walled accommodation close by. So when someone looked up from her computer, she caught her eye. 'Where can I find DCI Sumner, please?'

'Through that door. But she's in a meeting. Not to be disturbed. Really, absolutely not,' the woman added as Fran shrugged and drifted to the door she'd indicated. 'I said she was not to be disturbed,' she said more loudly.

Holding up her hands in mock surrender, Fran stopped. Her presence had been noticed by a dozen or so other officers, many of whom got uneasily to their feet. Perhaps it was time to make a tactical withdrawal. Looking coolly at her watch, she declared, 'In that case I'll email her. Thanks for your help,' she added with a smile as she left. A quick smile. One that left her face the moment she was in the corridor. What had she done to put all those people on red alert? Perhaps talking to the professional standards team, a branch of CID, of course, might not be the best option.

She'd only got back to their incident room, and certainly hadn't had time to open her mouth, when Paula shot into the room, pale and panting. As if in ironic greeting, the internal phone rang. Stu, who'd been punching the air in triumph, picked up; his eyes rounded. The call ended.

'It was the ACC, gaffers. Wants you both in his room. Now. I'm sorry.'

'Sorry, Stu? Why sorry?'

'His voice, Mark. Didn't even get his secretary to call, did he? Sounds like shit's coming your way.'

It must be bad, Fran reflected, if someone who (poetry apart) might not be the brightest star in the sky picked it up. But then, Stu had been edgy all morning. Kayak man. Canoe man. Come on. Out loud she said, 'It's not your problem, any of you. So long as none of the shit flies your way, of course. Ah, perhaps I'll make him wait.' She reached for her mobile and took the call.

'Fran? Hugh Evans here. We need to talk — quick lunch? Nowhere too close to Hindlip.'

'King's Arms, Ombersley — if we can all get to it.'

'Make sure you can. One fifteen?' End of call.

'Curiouser and curiouser,' mused Mark, holding the door for Fran. Then his phone chose to warble. 'The ACC will just have to wait even longer, won't he? I've got a text from Dean. He's like us, thank goodness — doesn't go in for indecipherable abbreviations. *NF: injuries consistent with overtraining — running. No news of PI but working on it.* Which rather ties in with those medals, don't you think?' He grinned cheerily. 'See you all later.'

Halfway down the corridor, Fran drew them to a halt. 'What did Stu find about kayak or canoe man? It was that guy who faked his death, wasn't it, and popped up in Panama? And that case was years after ours. So why on earth should the Garbutts put it in their box of precious things? If they put it there at all.'

'He found exactly that case, of course. And none of us could come up with an explanation either. Do you know what? If Stu was a more subtle man, I'd have said he knew more about the case than he's ever admitted and was trying to give us an anonymous clue.'

'He likes poetry,' Fran said, as if that might be conclusive. 'We need to talk to him in private, don't we?'

'But maybe not yet. It seems we have an escort. An inspector, no less.'

* * *

'Clear your desks and leave the premises,' Webster greeted them.

Mark smiled amiably; he was still, despite over a year's happy absence from committees, meetings-man par excellence. 'I thought you'd invited us down to hear that on the balance of the evidence—'

'I repeat: clear your desks and leave the premises. Make no attempt to contact any of my officers. Any of them. Inspector Fielding here will accompany you at all times.'

Had Webster even registered what he had been about to say? Probably not. So Mark smiled again. 'I don't think our contract is susceptible to that sort of treatment, sir. And at very least, as one senior officer to two former senior officers, you probably owe us the courtesy of some explanation. It may be,' he added, equally smoothly, 'that Inspector Fielding would be happier waiting outside. Or even that you'd prefer him to. We're perfectly happy, on the other hand, for him to be present, though I'd have thought someone from your professional standards unit was more appropriate.'

Fran nodded as if she'd known all along he was going to say this.

'Maybe even someone from another force,' Mark continued, warming to his theme, 'since the SIO in charge of any case should be one grade higher than the officer being investigated. Things haven't changed since my day, I presume? Excellent.'

Before Webster could respond, Fran joined the polite attack. 'While you decide what to do, perhaps you'd like to know that someone has stolen evidence and tried to hack into my iPad. On these premises. I've asked one of the serving officers on our minuscule team to obtain CCTV footage of the relevant passageway at the appropriate time.' She smiled at Fielding. 'That'd be more CID's bag than uniform's, wouldn't it? So perhaps ex-ACC Turner's idea that you might prefer not to be involved is a good one. Can you think of a superintendent or even chief superintendent who might take your place? Ideally another ACC, of course. But someone who would like to hear the rest of what Mr Turner was going to say about the original case.'

Webster was still chewing an antacid, or no doubt he'd have reached for another.

'I told you to leave the premises,' he said, but with all confidence and authority drained from his voice.

'And we're happy to, once the terms of our contract have been met. They include, if I recall, a formal debriefing by the chief constable. Obviously we wouldn't want to forgo what promises to be a most interesting and enlightening encounter.' Mark epitomized reasonable cooperation. 'We would have thought you'd prefer to mount an internal enquiry about the theft of evidence, but clearly you'd like us to contact the Independent Police Complaints Commission direct.' He enjoyed rolling all the syllables round, although there was no doubt that Webster and Fielding would instantly have recognized the initials. 'No doubt there'd be quite a lot of attendant publicity.'

Webster goggled. After a palpable hesitation, he turned to Fielding and gave a minuscule jerk of the head — more of a twitch or tic, in fact. Fielding took the hint. Fran smiled over her shoulder at him as he inched out.

'Missing evidence?' Webster prompted, sitting down as if to assert his authority. In fact, having two tall people towering over him wasn't a good move.

Kindly they sat down, without waiting for him to suggest it. But Mark's smile wasn't kind. 'We have witnesses willing to testify that important documents have been removed from the incident room you allocated to us. As far as we knew, we and the team were the only ones in possession of the key code, and, of course, the key code to the office you allocated to us. It seems we were mistaken. As Ms Harman has told you, one of our team, a police officer authorized to make the request, asked for CCTV footage of the corridor connecting the two rooms. And within minutes we were invited down here. It's hard to believe the two were unconnected.'

Fran enjoyed the word *invited* as a euphemism for a brusque demand.

'I've no idea what you're talking about,' Webster declared.

Almost convinced, Fran continued, 'In that case, you could always contact security and look at the images yourself. You're more likely to recognize—'

'Have you any idea how many people work in this building?'

'About a thousand. Rather fewer yesterday. Look,' Mark continued, reasonably, 'we expected problems with this enquiry. What we didn't expect was to find almost zero evidence had been retained, and to find what little we were given permission by the rightful owner to inspect — not keep, I stress — going missing. Someone has to explain that to the grieving family.'

Webster dropped his eyes.

'Neither did we expect criminal activity to cause a flood at the cottage we'd rented, or to flood the B and B we adjourned to, our belongings being deliberately put in harm's way. I believe some of your colleagues will even now be looking at connections — provided they've not been ordered to close the cases. They shouldn't be: in the second an entirely innocent old lady was assaulted and left to drown or die of hypothermia. At the very least she deserves justice. A civilian, Webster. Right?' Mark looked at his watch, as if it was he who was rationing precious minutes from his day to deal with a miscreant. 'We'll be back here at three this afternoon, Webster, and we'd like some explanations. Good day to you.' As one, he and Fran rose to their feet.

* * *

Fielding might have left the room, but as they left he fell into step behind them. There was no point in arguing with someone at his level, so in silence they strode to the room they'd used as their office. Two boxes of his and hers belongings sat patiently outside.

'There are more of our things in the incident room,' Fran said, 'including our coffee machine.'

In silence, Fielding turned in that direction. But someone had already changed the key code on the door; there was no sign of any of their team inside, nor, incidentally, of the coffee machine and mugs. A series of texts on their phones told them that all three had been ordered to return to normal duties. Despite Webster's orders, three texts went back: *Working on getting you back.* Perhaps a smiley face apiece would be too informal? Fran added them anyway.

Fielding coughed. 'Your orders were not to communicate with anyone here.'

'We may have been communicating with any of our acquaintances, inspector. As for Mr Webster's orders, the trouble is that since we're not officers we don't have to accept orders. But we don't want to get you into trouble.' Fran pocketed her phone and accepted the younger man's escort to the entrance hall.

A tight knot of officers huddled round Iris. Taking one look, Mark and Fran made no attempt to compromise her position by trying to attract her attention.

The replacement Audi had fewer refinements than theirs, but now sported one extra they hadn't expected: wheel clamps. A legend in a plastic envelope told them the car was in a reserved parking area, and was subject to a ninety-pound penalty to obtain release. In smaller letters they were told that an official permit was obtainable from Reception. So much for being on the system, so much for Fran's getting soaking wet to attach the permit perfectly clearly to the screen; in fact it was only the plastic envelope that obscured it.

'Taxi, then,' Mark said, already applying himself to his mobile. 'We'll meet it outside the grounds. Out of range of the CCTV cameras, with luck. And we'll sodding well put it and this — this stupid outrage — on expenses.'

CHAPTER TWENTY-TWO

At the King's Arms, Hugh had grabbed a table next to the loos, not promising aesthetically but giving clear views of anyone who might be approaching. There were no other tables within earshot, a fact for which it was worth sacrificing a table nearer either of the welcoming fires.

'This is all extremely cloak and dagger,' Fran observed, kissing Hugh on the cheek and getting a rather warmer kiss in return. The two men shook hands with less enthusiasm, the old flame meeting the new husband.

'It has to be,' he said. 'Because I've already been warned off you both. Indirectly. Which made me wonder what on earth you've been up to since our mini-reunion on the Severn Valley Railway. Sorry about having to cancel the other night, by the way; it was nothing to do with this warning, just that the council hadn't thought to unblock some road drains since Noah sailed his boat up the cut. They didn't get round to it till he built another ark. Have you seen that joke doing the rounds on the Internet about how Health and Safety issues would impede his attempts to build a new one? White wine, as I recall, Fran? Mark, what about you? Come on, this is the first time we've met since your wedding, so it should be fizz. Prosecco? Lower ABV, after all. Ready to order? I've got a cadaver to deal with at four. Meanwhile,' he said as the waiter distributed menus, 'I've got something for you, since felicitations are in order. A Georgian rectory, I think you said? These might be a decade out of period according to the hallmark but at least they belonged to a Regency rector.' He passed them a small packet each, identically wrapped. A man of style, Hugh.

With a sideways glance, they unwrapped them simultaneously, to find an unpretentious shagreen spectacle case in Mark's, and a pair of silver spectacles in Fran's. A label written in neat letters declared the case to belong to the Reverend Wm Devenish of Stelling Minnis, Kent.

Their thanks were profuse and genuine. The spectacles went in the case, which Mark slipped into an inside jacket pocket. 'Handbags can be snatched,' he said flatly.

'As bad as that, is it? Look, to cut a long story short, pressure was put on me to declare that I'd made a mistake, and to confirm the remains revealed by the landslip to be those of Natalie Garbutt — it was funny to call her by her maiden, not her married name — and her son. But I didn't know of any modern women wearing Saxon jewellery when they're buried, and told them so.'

'Saxon jewellery?' Fran's eyes rounded.

'It's really nice stuff. About the same period as the Staffordshire Hoard. Birmingham Museum's got its eye on it already.'

'Sorry: I sidetracked you,' Fran said.

'You always did. The instruction came via a phone call. The speaker muffled their voice. I demurred. Anyway, this person insisted. I said tests would prove my theory; they said they'd prove theirs since they'd paid for the privilege. The tests rarely lie, but when they didn't fit their theory they asked me to lie instead. I declined.' He stopped short.

A waiter appeared with the Prosecco and glasses, which he filled. They gave their orders. He left.

Fran counted to ten. 'And *they* would be?'

'A woman. Don't think,' he added with a grin, 'that I didn't check the number she was calling from. Oh, yes, I can play the detective too. I did. It was withheld. On the other hand, she called my mobile, a number which isn't common knowledge.

'A woman? That only rules out seventy per cent of the force, unfortunately,' Mark sighed.

'Who says she's in the force anyway?' Fran asked slowly. 'Just because she says so? Who knows how many women know Hugh's number?' she added with a grin. 'Don't answer that, Hugh. I'm sure you're a man of discretion. Seriously, do you know any women who might conceivably want to influence this enquiry?'

'Such as?' Hugh spread his hands. 'I can tell you which women officers have the number.' He produced the phone and scrolled down. He reeled off half a dozen, none of whom either of them recognized.

When he got to the name Sumner, however, Fran raised a finger. 'She's the DCI who reduced Paula Llewellyn to tears, alleging I'd bad-mouthed the poor girl. Paula's a DC we borrowed for our team. I don't suppose *she*'s on your phone?'

'She is, actually — she's made calls on Sumner's behalf once or twice. But a DC? She wouldn't be in a position to tell me what or what not to say.'

'Neither would the chief constable himself. Or even,' Mark said, drawing a bow at a venture, 'the commissioner. Herself.'

The waiter approached with their bundles of cutlery. All went very quiet. He left.

'How would she know my mobile number?' Hugh objected.

'She could ask someone who did.'

Mark took another sip of fizz. 'We've had one or two problems ourselves.' He recounted them baldly. 'The question is,' he said, 'would you be prepared to talk to the Independent Police Complaints Commission about this?'

'I don't suppose, now I've told you two, that I've any option, have I? It'd be like taking a bone from a pair of bulldogs.'

* * *

For some reason Iris wasn't on duty when they returned to Hindlip Hall in the hope, rather than the expectation, of seeing Webster; her place was taken by the young woman who'd greeted them on their first morning, whose name Fran had inevitably forgotten but whom Mark greeted immediately as Charlie. She responded with a very cautious nod, backing away as if he were suffering from smallpox. He decided it was better to let the photos on his phone tell the story. The clamps; the polythene envelope; the parking permit centimetres away from the envelope. Charlie deduced pretty sharply that ninety pounds was not about to change hands. In the most charming, affable way, Mark stood over her while she made a phone call to get the car liberated.

But that was as far as they got. They were not to be admitted to the building. Full stop. Neither wanted the indignity of being escorted from the premises by security guards, even (or especially) by kids as tiny as Charlie, or — worse — by officers, people they still thought of as colleagues.

Once back in the newly free car, they waited until they were out of camera range before they started talking — as if suspecting that some evil genius would be lip-reading their conversation from a hidden room. Then Fran asked, 'Why are we going this way?'

He touched his finger to his lips, briefly meeting her startled glance and raising an expressive eyebrow.

So he suspected a bug, did he? And maybe a tracking device? And where better to get a new car checked over than the impartial provider of the vehicle, the Audi dealership? They explained to an immaculate receptionist what they wanted, were asked to sit in a comfortable waiting area and even given cups of excellent coffee. But Mark soon abandoned his drink, prowling amongst the impossibly sleek showroom cars as if already planning an upgrade when the insurance money came through. Fran, staring at a glass-fronted cabinet full of car goodies, for some reason including a teddy bear in racing strip, fretted when she couldn't reach Edwina, cursing that she'd never bothered to ask for her mobile number.

At last a sleek young man invited them over to a desk in the sales area, producing as they approached two polythene bags, which he laid on his blotter. As they pulled back chairs ready to sit, he waved them back to the far side of a gleaming Quattro. 'Are those what we were looking for, sir? Because if they are, I should warn you that they're both still working. On the other hand,' he added with a grin, 'you see that lorry there? It's come to take away our waste . . .'

'But it's evidence,' Mark said, nonplussed for the first time. Then he smiled. 'You must have a safe? For all your car keys? So could you hold them until the police come?'

'Uh, uh,' Fran said. 'Until some police come. Because others might want to get their sticky paws on them too.'

'Maybe you should bring the police you want to have them to collect them?' suggested the young man. It was impossible to detect any sarcasm. He just seemed helpful, obliging, alert.

'Maybe we should. If we knew who were the good cops and who were the bad. Can I make a call using your phone? Just in case.'

The young man — Si — opened his eyes wide. 'You think yours might be—?

'Who knows?'

'I think my boss's office might be more private.' He ushered them backstage, as it were, and closed the door, delicately as a butler making himself scarce.

* * *

'Carry on as normal!' Mark repeated the advice of the IPCC representative he'd spoken to in a voice so calm and controlled Fran knew he was trying not to explode. 'OK, they said they'd organize someone to watch over us. But we're to continue talking to the witnesses with whom we've made contact! Dear God, it's not much of an ask, is it?'

'It's the advice we'd probably have given if we'd been in their position. After all, we've sent them everything on the iPad. Meanwhile, we can get new SIM cards and put their number on speed-dial. This isn't some crazy Middle Eastern state. It's the heart of England. Isn't it?'

At a discreet distance from the office door, Si was waiting for them as they emerged. 'All well? Maybe you'd like another car? One's just come in. We can change all the documentation for you? We'll just say the original one had an irritating squeak . . .'

'You're more than kind. Actually, your suggestion about the lorry was an excellent one. Not for the devices: the IPCC will arrange for their collection, using a password they'll email to us. We'll phone you personally just so that you know it's kosher. But meanwhile we've got our SIM cards to dispose of . . .'

'So they can't track you? All this is so amazing! It's like TV.'

'So it is. But it's a programme we'd rather you didn't discuss with anyone. Not yet, at least. Not, in fact, till the good cops say you can.' If he could wait that long; however mature and serious his face, his eyes were like those of an excited puppy. He bounced alongside them as he took them to their replacement car, apologizing that there hadn't been time to valet it.

'Si, you could have rolled it in mud: we'd still have been grateful.' Mark shook his hand, man-to-sensible-man.

Fran hugged him.

* * *

Safely anonymous in a Kidderminster car park, armed with new SIM cards, they sat staring at the rain which was sheeting down again.

Fran put her head in her hands.

Mark put his arm round her. 'Bother the IPCC — let's get out of town. Fast. Birmingham's a nice big anonymous city: we'll lose ourselves there.'

'Even turn ourselves in? West Midlands Police must have safe houses. We're meeting Dean Redhead there tomorrow anyway.' She took a deep breath and straightened her shoulders. 'Edwina's WI meeting? Can we really chicken out of that?'

'Edwina'll understand.'

'She might. Her friends might not.'

'OK.' Mark couldn't have sounded less enthusiastic. 'For Birmingham read Ombersley, I suppose.'

* * *

There weren't many faces in the rows in front of them. Nor was there much enthusiasm on any of them, apart from when they all sang 'Jerusalem': *And did those feet in ancient time Walk upon England's mountains green?* Was Fran alone in finding the lines they sang throat-closingly ironic in connection with Natalie's disappearance? Had her feet indeed not just walked but walked away? As for *England's green and pleasant land*, she always cried.

Many of the women, mostly of Edwina's generation, folded their arms implacably. They clearly regarded a talk on lives spent maintaining law and order as of considerably less interest than preserving the countryside. Or was there more to it than that? Fran was sure she saw active hostility in some of their eyes.

They introduced themselves as the Fred and Ginger of crime fighting, including the joke about doing the job backwards in high heels. Cue for laughter? Not so much as a mild giggle? OK, press on. They'd knocked up a sort of organized conversation, and had primed Edwina to ask a light-hearted question at the end, just to get the others started, as they said.

She obliged. But when the next hand went up — that of Madam Chairman, a woman so beautifully made-up and elegantly turned out she might have been heading for a night at a West End theatre — it wasn't to ask about the problems of courtship under constant surveillance from your police colleagues.

'Can you tell me,' she asked, 'what right you have to come to our village and poke your nose into things that don't concern you? Things that are best left undisturbed anyway?'

Fran turned to look her straight in the eye. 'When someone deliberately ruins someone's livelihood by flooding their cottage? Oh, yes, someone blocked a culvert and was well aware of the consequences to an entirely innocent woman. When someone lures another householder from her home — a friend of yours, sitting here — and beats her unconscious? When, just for good measure, whoever it is deliberately opens floodgates? Edwina could literally have drowned. Are those crimes best left uninvestigated?' She shifted slightly so that she was addressing the audience. 'Oh, I assume no one wanted Edwina to die. They just wanted to be rid of us. But, ladies and gentleman, whoever is making serious efforts to be rid of us is just attacking the messengers.'

She thought she might have won over the majority of the group. But Madam Chairman smiled implacably. 'In that case, the messengers should convey to their masters what I have just said.'

* * *

'Which told us,' Mark reflected, his hand wrapped around a glass of the finest single malt in Edwina's extensive collection, 'more than anything else we've learned in this investigation. Or at least,' he conceded, 'confirmed what we already suspected. That Natalie did not die in the snow, but escaped. How? Clearly some people know more than they're letting on. And they absolutely do not want her found. Not just people round here, of course — that nanny skipping off to Italy as soon as she hears we want to talk to her . . .' He leaned back in his chair. Somewhere upstairs a still embarrassed Edwina was retiring for bed, so furious with her fellow WI members that she said she'd sink a whole bottle if she touched so much as a drop of alcohol. She'd claimed that she found their continued presence reassuring; perhaps she might not if a lynch mob turned up on her doorstep the next morning — or perhaps they left hanging people out to dry to the local police round here.

Fran nodded, swirling the contents of her own cut-glass tumbler. 'Her parents' lack of cooperation; the attempts to make us leave the area; the obvious corruption in the force, from the moment that they got rid of Gerry Barnes; sacking us and moreover tracking us — there's only one conclusion: Natalie's certainly alive and kicking somewhere, isn't she? Why didn't someone just say as much on our first morning? *We've cocked this up. We've discovered her after all. Thank you and goodbye.* Should we just put in a short report — half a page even — and walk away?'

'We could do. On the other hand, it'd be nice to discover why—'

'Easy-peasy. Her husband hit her; she robbed him; she's in Panama or Ecuador, anywhere where they don't have extradition, and she's living on the proceeds.' She helped herself to another thimbleful of whisky — it'd probably stop her sleeping, but rest seemed a distant prospect anyway.

'We need a bit more on the record evidence. Dean Redhead might help. After all, he's broken confidentiality once today — who knows what he'll do over dinner tomorrow?'

'Dean Redhead — it sounds as if he's a Victorian divine known for his excellent sermons. I don't want to waste another day hanging round to have dinner with him.' Her anger terminated on a sob.

He leaned across and took her hand. 'Maybe we can see him earlier. Officially. Remember, the IPCC asked us to carry on as if nothing has happened. Let's think about doing just that. Another talk with Mr and Mrs Garbutt, to explain that some evidence has gone missing and ask what it was: that'd be useful. Redhead — even if we do have to wait for dinner. That excellent witness, Marion Roberts. Every damned person we've spoken to, if necessary. Find out who flooded two cottages and could have killed Edwina in the process. And we should pursue some of the police problems Gerry and his wife spoke about. There's a lot to do before we draw a line under the enquiry. Come on, we'll feel better in the morning — especially if we don't have another top-up.'

CHAPTER TWENTY-THREE

The home of Sandra Mould was appropriate for someone who preferred to be known as Madam Chair: the handsome four-square Edwardian house, spoilt in purist terms (though not in terms of heating) by the sixties porch, stood on a rise, a huge bay window overlooking flooded fields and drenched gardens. She did not seem pleased to see them on her doorstep the following morning, but neither did she seem surprised. 'How did you find me? Oh, I might have known that Edwina Lally couldn't keep her mouth shut,' she said, stepping back and admitting them to her porch, at least. Not for their protection, probably, but so the driving rain wouldn't spatter her tiles. She touched her immaculate hair; Fran registered the understated make-up. At ten in the morning? On your own in your own house? 'Well, what do you want to know?'

'Very little now, in connection with Natalie Garbutt, at least,' Fran said, continuing to drip despite the temptation to shake herself like a dog. 'It's clear that she's alive and well somewhere or other — that when she went missing that day it was planned pretty well down to the last detail. Probably the only thing that went wrong was that poor Julius died when he did, forcing her into the dreadful decision to abandon him where he was and leave with Hadrian.'

'You'd best leave your things here,' Sandra said, pointing to the wrought iron coat and umbrella stand.

They slipped off their shoes too and padded in behind her. Mark couldn't hold back a smile at the elegance of the room she led them into. Sandra caught the appreciative glance, and addressed herself to him. 'So what did bring you here?'

'Edwina's attempted murder, for a start,' he said. 'Because I live in a hamlet, I can understand that you're all closing ranks to protect a woman who had to protect her child and escape an unhappy marriage, even if she took with her a rather greater share of their joint finances than she was legally entitled to. That's fine. But as we said last night, endangering other people's lives is not fine. But we can't tell our masters to pull us out of the enquiry because they're not our masters any longer.'

'You've given up the case? Excellent. I think that calls for a glass of sherry, don't you?'

'It might be a bit early in the day for us, thank you,' Mark said. 'We still have a lot of work to do.'

'But you said—'

'We're working for a different team now. As from this morning. We're investigating police corruption. A civilized country stands or falls on the incorruptibility of its police. If you know anything, we beg you to help us.'

Silently Fran was humming 'Nimrod' but her face assumed the earnest expression Mark's appeal deserved.

'You're so right. I just wish I could. At least let me offer you coffee or tea. I have some excellent gunpowder.'

Mark was ready to accept when his phone rang. 'It's Edwina,' he told his hostess. 'Can you excuse me while I take it?' He stepped into the hall. Within two minutes he returned. 'I'm afraid we shall have to decline your kind invitation. Your friend needs us urgently.'

Under her make-up Sandra paled. 'Is she ill? Shall I call the ambulance? Or the police?'

Mark laid a reassuring hand on her arm, and channelled Dixon of Dock Green: 'Just leave it to us, Mrs Mould. But bear in mind what we said earlier. This is my mobile number, in case you want to contact me.'

* * *

'It was my day for cleaning under beds,' Edwina declared, looking like Boudicca on the warpath. 'And having found one, I found another under the sofa and a third under the dining table. They're in the compost heap now. I didn't think you'd want them to overhear our current conversation.' She sat down suddenly. 'In my house, darlings. Bugs! Whenever could they have got here?' She sounded as disgusted as if she'd been invaded by cockroaches, not listening devices.

'When our water-loving friend hit you and used your key to get in.'

'Oh, and I never paid you for the new locks! Oh, Fran.'

'And I never paid compensation for your whack on the head. So let's call it quits.'

Edwina looked at her with narrowed eyes. 'Are these people paying your expenses? Well then, put it on their bill.'

* * *

'Email from Tony Woolmer?' Mark queried, passing Fran the iPad. They were in the kitchen, which appeared to be bug-free, making Edwina a cup of tea, on the grounds that though she, like Sandra, favoured a glass of sherry (in her case restorative), tea would do them all so much more good.

'Suffolk Police. It'll be about Anna Fratello.'

It was. Anna had returned and promptly departed again, this time by car overnight. Suffolk Police had her registration number and were circulating it to all forces. Fran chewed her lip. That made her sound like a criminal; should she ask Tony to cancel the alert?

Someone else it might be fruitful to speak to further was Desmond Markwell, that weird private detective. Dean Redhead had said his presence was the most troublesome part of the case; should she pay him another visit? Just call him, maybe? But first, retiring to the Audi, just in case they'd missed any bugs, she called Fi Biddlestone. Not to ask permission to respond to Markwell's blackmail. Just to talk, one ex-cop to another. She should have done it earlier, out of courtesy, shouldn't she? Like a lot of other things. But as Macmillan might or might not have said, *Events, dear boy, events*. And they'd experienced a lot of events.

* * *

Fortunately for Fi Biddlestone, one of her neighbours drove a tractor, and he kept her in supplies. Boredom or loneliness, however, prompted outpourings of nothingness far longer than Fran felt she had time for. On the other hand, she owed Fi at least one favour, and she didn't bring the one-sided conversation round to the topic she really needed to raise. At last, however, Fi came round to it herself. 'Did you ever get to see Desmond . . . Desmond Markwell?'

'I did indeed. He asked after you.'

The tiny gasp was audible. 'Did he? How was he?'

According to Mark, Downs had described her as a silly bitch; Fran thought she sounded more like a lovelorn girl — not good at sixty. But then, hadn't she felt the same at the start of her relationship with Mark? 'Enigmatic, I'd say, Fi. Not very helpful. Sorry.'

'Would it help if I spoke to him?'

Fran was sure that Fi would hear her deep breath. 'It might help our enquiry. But if it wouldn't help you . . .' She waited a long time before adding, 'He did ask for your phone number.'

'He's a detective, for goodness' sake! Couldn't he just have looked me up? Oh, there's his wife, of course. But he still wanted it?'

'Mischievously, I'd say. As a bargaining tool. But I didn't want to betray your confidence without asking you first.'

'Bargaining tool as in he wouldn't give you information till you'd given him my number.' Fi seemed to be mulling it over. Did she see the blackmail as the sign of a desperate man or the mark of a total bastard? To be honest, even Fran would have been hard put to make the call. 'OK,' Fi said, surprising her, 'give me the number. I'll call. What did you want to know? Go on, shoot.'

'Only if you're sure, Fi.'

'Of course I'm not sure. I got the sack because of him. Did he take up with me simply because I was on the case and nosing things out? Or did he . . . But I'm a big girl now: if I messed up then I need to put things right now.' Her voice cracked. All these years later.

'Let me deal with him,' Fran urged. 'I'll give him your number, but I'll ask the questions.'

'But that way I might never hear his voice again.'

* * *

'So it's a matter of sitting here and waiting for things to happen,' Fran said, huddling up against the Aga.

'Not for long. While you were out there, I took a call too. In that little corridor, before you ask. Just in case. The IPCC guy, Dan Wilson. I shall know if he isn't who he says he is: I was on a course with him at Hendon.'

'All the same . . . dear God, I hope he's kosher. What if he's bent too?'

'His front tooth should be — unless he's had it straightened. That looks like him now.' An unmarked car sidled up to the Audi, as if unsure of its welcome.

'We can't talk here! But what if he . . . abducts us?'

He grabbed her shoulders. 'A week ago, would you even have had such a fear, let alone voiced it? How many bent cops have you ever known? Yes, it's Dan. See that tooth? What's up? Your face is a study.'

'The guy that's with him. The Asian guy. He seems to be waving at me.'

'Wave back, then. OK, let's talk to them outside.'

* * *

'They call me Elephant Man, ma'am — I mean Fran. Nothing to do with my ugly mug either.' Unconsciously he smiled with the knowledge that some might even call him handsome. 'Because I never forget. I can't help it. Once I've seen a face I know it. The Met even call me in sometimes to look at a crowd scene and see if I can pick out the face of a criminal they want. There's quite a team of us.'

'Super recognition. Like having perfect pitch,' Dan explained.

Mark scratched his head. 'Let me get this straight: you two had the briefest of conversations in Birmingham — what — six or eight years ago, and you still recognized her?'

'Of course,' Naz said. 'Fran's easy to recall — her height, of course, her demeanour, and a very memorable face, too, sir.'

Fran grimaced. 'You wouldn't expect me to remember a name, would you? But I dimly remember the occasion. Naz was in uniform then,' she said, with increasing certainty. 'It was the time I made the old chief eat a speciality Birmingham curry. And you, of course. But you've moved on, Naz? A DCI.' Progress indeed.

'Only acting, to be honest.'

'Even so.'

By now the four of them were dithering with cold.

'DCS Wilson recruited me when he heard about my visual memory. And here we are, ready to listen to anything you have to tell us. But maybe,' he added, 'we do it somewhere warmer and drier. Dan's car, maybe. We can talk as we go to pick up those bugs.'

'We shall need our own wheels,' Fran pointed out. 'Mark, why don't you and Dan catch up while I tail you? If he doesn't mind, Naz can fill me in with news of some of my old friends in Birmingham. Provided I can remember their names,' she added, not entirely joking.

* * *

'Young Si, arrested!' Fran squeaked, staring in disbelief at the chic receptionist who'd dispensed coffee and sympathy the previous day. 'You're joking. Call the manager, please.' She had no legal authority; she shouldn't be the person doing this. She stepped back smartly to let Naz and Dan flash their IDs and talk the talk. Naz, anyway. Dan was snarling into his phone. Mark morphed back into senior officer mode with a single footstep forward.

The manager, sleek as his cars, addressed himself exclusively to the men, even the preoccupied Dan. A year ago, Fran wouldn't have let him get away with such sexist behaviour. But now she confined herself to staring at the fully dressed teddy bear in his glass cage, which bizarrely became the personification of the helpful young man. She'd thought there was a pattern: the injury to Edwina apart — and even that was amateurish — the attempts to deter them had been irritations, harming property rather than people. Even the Hindlip Hall thefts were on the scale of things trivial, things meriting only a local CID investigation, not really the full might of the rubber heel brigade. But arresting a man they knew to be entirely innocent could ruin his career. That was going altogether too far.

Mark came over, putting his arm round her. 'It seems that young Si changed the safe code without telling anyone, because he was so concerned when he saw the police car turn up without any warning from us. So the manager is frothing at the mouth — no one can access any of the keys and his business is at a standstill. As you can see. Or not.' He spread an arm to indicate the hordes who, if they'd been present, might have been tearing impotently at car doors. 'My mate Dan is arranging for Si to be brought back. Fortunately he wasn't arrested, just invited to help with enquiries. So he won't have a stain on his escutcheon, whatever one of those might be. He'll open the safe; Dan and Naz will get their evidence. We could go home.'

Arms akimbo, Fran stared. 'Why *could*, not *can*?'

'Because I want us to go in person to apologize to the Garbutt parents for losing their treasures.'

'You might say that but you mean something else, don't you? Even if I'm not quite sure what.' Fran looked him in the eye. 'Mark, they didn't take to me any more than I took to them. This is a gig you'd be better doing without me. Truly.' Her phone rang. 'Fi Biddlestone: I'd better take this.' She retreated behind a scarlet Quattro.

'He'll talk to you. Somewhere neutral, he suggests. There's a service area on the M5, near Junction Three. The east side, in the ordinary coffee area. Eleven. You know his number if the time doesn't work.'

'Fi, are you all right?'

Her swallow was audible. 'You don't know what I'd give to come with you. But barring a helicopter, I shall have to sit this one out. And perhaps it's for the best.' She ended the call before Fran could say any more — assuming, of course, that she could have thought of anything.

She wandered back to Mark. 'Do you have any particular time in mind to talk to the Garbutts? Because we have a slight logistics problem. One car; two different directions.' She explained.

He ran his fingers over his hair, as if checking it was still there. Most of it was, at least. 'How would you feel about getting Dan to request the return of our team? Just until all the loose ends have been tied up? They'd be useful for ferrying us around if nothing else.'

She took his hand. 'My heart says yes. But my head's trying to shake all by itself. Just in case. In case . . .'

He raised hers to his lips. 'That's what I hoped you'd say. This is the first time I've ever had even the tiniest doubt about people I want to trust implicitly. I know you've not been quite so lucky.'

'No. But I wasn't totally impotent then. And I could conjure a driver from thin air when I needed one,' she added with mock bitterness.

'You could conjure me,' Dan said, materializing by her shoulder. 'I could commandeer the car bringing this man Si back here, couldn't I?'

'Much as I love the idea of the poor driver being made to walk back, no, you couldn't and no, Fran couldn't,' Mark said quickly. 'Because I've got to grovel to these good people and the more senior the officer beside me the better. In any case, I suspect the guy Fran's going to meet will run a mile at the sight of a proper officer.'

'In that case,' Naz said with a saturnine grin, 'I'll do the commandeering: the sooner one of us starts talking to people at Hindlip the better. And if you're busy, gaffer, it had better be me. But I might just let the poor guy drive me, not walk.'

CHAPTER TWENTY-FOUR

'Dear God,' Desmond Markwell declared, looking around him in disgusted despair at Frankley Services, 'this has to be one of the worst places in the country.'

Fran couldn't argue. 'Your choice,' she retorted. 'As was the coffee. We could have spoken over the phone, you know.'

'I may have every anti-bugging device going, but I still prefer not to take risks. And I take it you're not wired?'

'If I was, it'd be hard for anyone to hear any conversation above that lot.' She jerked her head. A loud and numerous family had arrived at the next table. 'Over there? Your turn. You choose the table.'

The one he picked was still covered with detritus. She watched him move it all to another table, dusting his fingers in surprisingly finicky movements to clear probably non-existent crumbs.

'The sooner you get everything off your chest, the sooner we'll be out of here,' she pointed out, as he sat down at last, but now played with his disposable stirrer.

'Very well. Here goes. Phil Foreman paid me a great deal of money to discover why the police were making no progress in their search for his son. Bother his wife, or words to that effect. No, just where his son was. And he gave me enough money to bribe the chief constable if necessary. You're supposed to ask me if I tried,' he said, conscious charm in every millimetre of his smile and his crows' feet. Poor Fi.

On the other hand Fran was inclined to resent being used as an opportunity to hone his flirtation skills. 'Whom did you attempt to suborn — not necessarily with cash?'

'If you're thinking I was simply using Fi, forget it. She was the love of my life, that woman.' He turned eyes lustrous with tears towards her. 'My wife—'

'Is an invalid, I gather.'

His eyebrows made an appreciative leap. 'Has been since before I met Fi. And even I am not sufficiently beyond the pale to think of leaving her. Not — not yet. But Fi — you've no idea how much I've wanted to hear Fi's voice. Wanted to hear it for twenty years.'

Fran was beginning to feel queasy. 'As if you couldn't have run her to earth like that by looking in the phone directory.' She snapped her fingers. 'Any other attempts, with or without money?'

'The locals closed ranks. Many of the police were locals. QED.'

'You said that Phil was only interested in finding his son. His marriage was as flaky as everyone believes? How did he feel about her helping herself to his money?'

'He was more than ready to do a deal: *you keep all the cash, so long as I get Hadrian.* But there really was no sign of her. Or Hadrian. In the end, he paid me in full, again in cash, because without Natalie that was how he did things, and had a huge bonfire. I was there. I saw.'

'Why on earth should you be?'

'He didn't have a lot of friends, Fran. And he saw me as having some spurious legal status as a witness. Anyway, everything that had been hers went on it.'

Fran's mental thumbs began to twitch. 'Including?'

'Clothes. A lot of good clothes. I babbled about charity shops, and such, but on the pyre they had to go. Shoes, ditto. Books, ditto.'

‘So she was expunged from his life. What about Hadrian’s stuff? He surely never burned that?’ Irritatingly her voice changed.

He noticed. ‘You see, you are capable of sentimentality. He isn’t a perceptive man, Phil, but even he registered the shock in my face. In the end, I washed all Hadrian’s things, soft toys and clothes, and sealed them in one of those storage bags you pump the air out of. Some of Julius’s too. He put it in a storage unit when he moved south. I’ve got a key and authorization to remove it, should Hadrian ever show up. Only if he ever shows up.’

Fran nodded; she wouldn’t try to force the issue on that point. ‘You’re assuming he hasn’t taken it to Northern Cyprus?’

‘I could check. But I really doubt it. He’s had other relationships since, and that sort of thing might not go down well with new partners, might it? Interestingly he’s never had any other children — I am a PI, you know!’ he added with that wretched winning smile. ‘Do you think it might be connected with Julius’s condition? That he’s the carrier?’

‘You’re the PI,’ she retorted, grinning despite herself. ‘But it’s hardly germane to our enquiry, is it? But that bonfire might be, you know. Was there anything that didn’t go on it? You’ve told me a lot that did. Was there anything that struck you at the time — or since — as a notable omission?’ She smiled. ‘Confession is supposed to be good for the soul.’

‘No passport. Everything a woman might need was there — even make-up and tampons, for goodness’ sake. But I never saw her passport. And before you ask, no, I didn’t point this out to him at the time. Or, in fact, to the police. I might be a city lad, Fran, but after that afternoon, I agreed with her parents and everyone else that she was better off without him. As a matter of information, I had my own bonfire: the bill I’d prepared, and the entire file.’

‘But not the cash for the bribe?’

He might have blushed. ‘Come on, I’m only human. But I can see from your face the information about the passport was what you were after. Unless Natalie's parents kept it?' He sounded very dubious.

She decided to trust him, for the time being at least: 'What do you think? Quite. Did he ever say anything about his parents?'

'Dad died down the pit. Didn't get on with his mother, though I know he paid her a good allowance. He may still do. If he filled in a standing order, then he's probably forgotten all about it. Not my problem. His accountant's. I made sure he had one of those when Natalie left him, by the way.'

'What about her parents? Did he see much of them?'

'Liked her dad, loathed her mother. Surprise, surprise. I never interviewed them: even I would have thought it was intrusive.'

'According to Mrs G, they didn't even know you'd been employed.'

'Fi said that she'd go berserk if she knew. The police certainly did, which is why Fi got the boot. Well, impugning their honour and all that. How do they feel about your talking to me now?'

'I'm not answering direct to Colin Webster anymore.'

His eyebrows shot up. 'Now that is interesting. I wonder why. Frankly, I'd never have recommended working for him in the first place — a supine little man, as I recall, even in those days obsessing about budgets, with a weather-eye, of course, on promotion. *Plus ça change, plus c'est la même chose*, eh? Who's he toadying up to these days? The new CC's as milky-mild as they come.'

'We've never had the pleasure,' she said. 'I did meet the commissioner once — in the loo,' she added, ready to employ a bit of charm herself. 'As one does. Opinion about her is sharply divided, isn't it?'

'Alpha female, locally born, good-looking — she's bound to have enemies,' Desmond responded mildly, looking at her under his lashes. 'Though I gather she's thrown her weight around as commissioner more than you'd expect and got up some male noses. That's all.'

'Just dish the dirt, Desmond. I can't believe you don't have any. We've both got jobs to do.' She looked him straight in the eye. 'Connection with Foreman? No? Don't tell me there's a connection with Natalie! They must be pretty well exact contemporaries. Her parents claim they don't recall any of her friends; she's not one of them, is she? Dear Lord, fancy missing that one.'

'I don't know. Seriously. But there'd be a sporting connection, wouldn't there?'

Fran clapped a hand to her forehead. 'Between Natalie and Dundy! Of course. And at this point we're supposed to bow out gracefully,' she added furiously.

What's your budget, Fran? I could sniff round for you. Maybe get a result within twenty-four hours?'

'Zero in answer to your first question. Sorry. Oh, shit.'

'If I do it anyway?'

'I'm sure you'll get your reward in heaven, if not elsewhere.' She dug in her bag. 'If you get anything, these are the guys to call. IPCC. You see, Desmond, it's them I'm working for now.'

'As a matter of fact,' he said, getting to his feet and shaking her hand warmly, 'I wish you were working for me.' She smiled a dry negative, but he kept her hand. 'In fact, you and your husband. The BOGOF principle.'

'As in supermarket offers on lettuces? If you want to get Mark for free,' she declared, throwing her head back and laughing, 'you'll find the initial unit price is pretty high.'

* * *

She was about to nose out of the service area car park when an idea crawled belatedly into her mind. They shouldn't ever have been looking for just a missing woman; they should have been looking for her grown-up son, too. Phil Foreman's son, the one with amazing ball skills. She killed the engine and texted Naz. With IPCC resources they could enhance the photos of young Hadrian to add twenty years to his life, and, with Naz's extraordinary ability, he might just pick out from a load of sporting mugshots a young man with ball skills good enough to put him in the public arena. Probably not football — she couldn't imagine that having gone to all the trouble of leaving Phil so deviously, Natalie would risk someone in the game recognizing him.

A reply warbled back almost immediately. *Can do!*

But what could she do? Nothing. And where should she go?

She texted again, asking for a renewal of her visitor's pass to Hindlip. Access All Areas, this time.

* * *

'Independent Police Complaints Commission?' Mrs Garbutt repeated, staring from Dan to his card and back again. 'But we haven't made any complaints.' Standing impregnably on her doorstep, she folded her arms and watched the rain drip from her visitors.

'You may be about to, Mrs Garbutt.'

Mark noticed that his colleague made no attempt to ask to use her first name. As Fran had realized, she was not a likely candidate for first-name informality.

'Well, complaint or no, you'll have to come back another time. It's not convenient. You should have phoned to warn me. I'm doing my housework. And before you say you don't mind, let me tell you, young man, I do.' She looked at her watch, a handsome modern one, and smoothed her skirt, which was surely far too smart to wear while wielding a duster. 'Four at the earliest. Understand?'

They understood, retreating to the car and driving away. But not very far. Just out of sight. Obbo time. Just like when they'd been young officers. Mark could almost taste the cardboard-flavoured tea and coffee.

'Just who might she be expecting?' Dan asked, releasing his seat belt and leaning back. 'Someone she doesn't want us to meet, evidently. Any ideas?'

'Too many for any of them to be worth sharing — from the police commissioner down to our landlady, via the chair of the WI and the nanny Natalie once employed. The last two would almost certainly fill in the pieces about Natalie's disappearance, which I'm sure, apart from wasting police time, of course, involves a reasonably harmless conspiracy. They weren't to know about Natalie's financial activities, and would probably have considered siphoning funds away from an unlikeable husband a good idea. The first, of course, would be — no, could be — much more serious.'

'Who else would have the clout to get an ACC sacked and the investigation suspended?' asked Dan.

'Apart from the commissioner, the chief constable himself?'

'Quite. I must say, Mark, between ourselves, you seem to have had a bit of a blind spot where he's concerned, if your emails to me are anything to judge by.'

Stung, Mark stared straight ahead. 'You're right. Possibly because we've never met him. He's given us not so much as a nosy look in the corridor, let alone a polite welcome. To do him justice they say he's forced to spread himself very thinly, and we've heard nothing bad against him. Mind you, if we'd not been chucked out of the building yesterday we'd certainly have wanted to talk to him.'

'OK, and have you actually interviewed the commissioner?'

'We focused our informal enquiries on her. Yesterday was the strangest in my police life: I felt like a victim, not an investigator. Vulnerable. Impotent. We didn't even know if one of our own little team was involved in stealing the documents and trying to hack into the iPad. Still don't, actually. And then the villagers turned on us. Not quite a lynch mob,' he added with a chuckle, 'but when I said that one of the people Mrs G might be expecting was the chair of the WI, I wasn't joking.'

'As a matter of fact,' Dan said quietly, 'we may just be about to find out. There's a car pulling over on to their drive now.' He clocked the reg and spoke into his radio. The

ID crackled back immediately. 'Now who might Ms Anna Fratello be?'

'The Foremans' nanny. Sacked a couple of weeks before Natalie went missing. Fled to Italy as soon as she knew we wanted to talk to her, but now — as you can see — back here. Do we barge in now or let them start talking?' He added, though he hated the words, 'Your call — you're the boss.'

CHAPTER TWENTY-FIVE

As she pulled over her head the Access All Areas lanyard handed to her by a bemused-looking Charlie, Fran did a double-take. Sandra Dundy had walked straight past her in the direction of the women's loos. Talk about déjà vu. This time their conversation wouldn't be about haircuts.

She ran a mental check. Posture — non-threatening; face — open, relaxed. Her breath might match her pulse rate for speed, but she mustn't let it show. Right. Apparently reading all the safety notices, she hovered long enough to let Dundy retire to a cubicle. Now it was time to stroll in as if all she was worried about was finding her comb. Except she leaned heavily on the door: she didn't want anyone else to come in and certainly didn't want Dundy to be able to escape. So far so good. Except that two of the five cubicles were in use. She might just have to wait outside to pounce; if it came to running, there'd be no contest between her shoes and Dundy's.

But when one woman started to speak to the other she abandoned all thought of lurking outside. Sensing the conversation wasn't going to be about hair or hormones, she switched her phone to record. One voice was Dundy's, of course. Thank goodness it was neither Paula nor Robyn she was speaking to. She really didn't want them implicated in any of their misfortunes. So whose was the other?

* * *

'Time to go in?' Dan asked, as if he needed Mark's permission.

'Sure,' Mark agreed, already shifting in his seat when his phone warbled. 'No. Hang on one second. This is from Fran. Sandra Dundy's at Hindlip.'

Dan nodded. 'Excellent. Right — no, hang on.' A text on his phone this time. 'Naz. Look at this, Mark. This might stir things up in there.' He rubbed his hands in glee at the understatement. 'Let's go. Oh, bloody hell. Who's that?' he added, as another car joined Anna's on the Garbutts' drive.

Mark smiled grimly. 'I told you I wouldn't be surprised if the WI were involved. That's their chairwoman. Correction: Madam Chairman. Sandra Mould.'

Dan rolled his eyes. 'All these women! Or are they ladies?'

'That remains to be seen. When I was a beat bobby, I always thought girls were far harder to deal with than blokes.'

'Absolutely. You knew they'd be violent — but the women were transformed into biting, scratching harpies, with language to match.'

'These women may turn into harpies, but I think we can rely on them to be genteel, well-spoken harpies. I'd suggest we go for our very first plan, which was a formal apology. And take it from there. Ready? No, hang on. Someone else is arriving.'

A man this time. He emerged from a car that was weirdly familiar — though heaven knew there were enough silver Fiestas on the road. He could have done with Naz's powers of recall. Except that as soon as the driver stepped out, Mark knew him straight away. 'An ex-cop,' he told Dan. 'Part of the original search party, but not part of the investigation itself because he had a family connection with the missing woman.'

'Do you want to intercept?'

What was Dan doing deferring to him? Perhaps in the younger man's eyes an ACC trumped a chief superintendent despite his year's retirement. 'Let's let him join the others, shall we? Day's his name, by the way. Ted Day.'

* * *

If Fran's reaction to the sight of Dundy emerging from the cubicle was surprised pleasure, Dundy's was one of fury mingled with terror.

'What the hell are you doing here? This is harassment. You're stalking me! Leave me alone!' Her voice was loud and shrill. In response, the other woman emerged too, eyes blazing.

Fran's smile broadened. 'DCI Sumner, I presume.' She texted Naz to come and ride shotgun.

At first Naz ushered all three women not to an interview room, which would, Fran admitted, have been crude, but by a stroke of typical police irony to the room that she and Mark had briefly occupied. Some of their notes were still on the wallboard. She stood near the window, so that had there been any sun her face would have been shaded. The interview, after all, was between Naz, Sumner and Dundy; her role was primarily to observe, though Naz might well call on her to participate if necessary. She toyed, but very briefly, with making tea or coffee in the mugs she and Mark had disdained, but rejected the notion. Meanwhile, a nervy plain clothes officer, presumably someone who knew her well, came to escort Sumner to another room.

How would the young man play this? It would have been nice to plan the interview beforehand. Would it have been disrespectful to the commissioner to leave her to stew a while on her own? Or even more so to question her ineptly? But there was nothing inept about Naz, who was swift to remind Dundy that this was simply an informal talk, prior to a formal investigation of possible police corruption.

'I'd like you to look at this, Ms Dundy, and tell me who it is.' He slipped a large photograph from a card folder. Fran was as nonplussed as Dundy. Then it dawned on her that Naz might be showing the result of the party trick she'd hoped he would perform. From somewhere he'd conjured a colour photo of a bronzed young god clutching helmet and gloves and schmoozing up to a glossy horse.

Dundy shook her head dismissively, but then stared, as if despite herself. Her eyes slid from it to Naz, back to the photo and then to Fran. Fran had no trouble looking impassive, since the photo was just the wrong distance for her eyes. But she'd have placed bets on it being the lad who once shared tennis coaching with Thomas, Dean Redhead's son.

'Why are you showing me this?' Dundy gathered her assurance round her like a cloak.

'You tell me. You do recognize him, don't you? Once he was called Hadrian Foreman. Now he's Adrian del Castro. I've looked for one of his mother, maybe Mrs del Castro now, but she seems to have slipped from the photographic radar. If I have time to scan the crowds at one of this young man's polo matches in Argentina, I've no doubt I'll find her.'

Fran nodded. Argentina would be a good choice for someone with a degree that included Spanish. And, as she recalled, extradition between the two countries wasn't almost automatic in some cases, unsurprising given the Falklands issue.

Naz picked up the questioning again. 'Would you like to tell us what part you played in all this? No? You see going missing isn't an offence. Neither is investing your husband's money, provided you have permission. Nor is leaving him if he's abusive, though it's nice to get a proper legal settlement. I wouldn't cross the street to question Natalie, let alone the Atlantic. What is infinitely more problematic is when someone in your position breaks the law.'

'It was minor. It was trivial.'

'In that case there's nothing to worry about.' Naz looked at her as if he was about to paint her portrait. He held up another photo. 'Is this of you?' With a quick sideways smile, he turned it for Fran to see. 'Of course it isn't. It's Natalie, isn't it? But you're as like as two peas.'

Fran nodded. 'You could almost have been sisters. Swapped clothes.' And then she knew. 'You could have swapped passports.'

'What proof do you have?'

'Your reaction for a start. But we can easily check to see if you reported yours lost when you were in your late twenties. Did she pay you? Or did you do it out of friendship?' Fran added more kindly.

Dundy looked exclusively at Naz, as if to blank Fran. But she got no help there.

'Answer the question, please, Ms Dundy. As I'm sure you know, the more cooperative you are, the more lenient any sentence is likely to be. Though I have to confess I don't see you being able to continue in your present role.'

Fran tried hard to feel sorry for her, but remembered her lucrative business would probably welcome her back and become even more profitable, assuming the community accepted what she'd done as a mere peccadillo.

Perhaps the word *confess* had a subliminal effect. 'We ran a lot together. Sort of rivals, I suppose. But we became close. Funny, I'd always thought of myself as being as hetero as they come. And I do now. But — I loved her. I'd have done anything for her. Lending her my passport didn't seem a big thing. OK, giving.'

Naz frowned. 'But yours wouldn't have Hadrian on it.'

'Of course not. He must have had his own, because sometimes he travelled with her, sometimes with his dad. He worshipped him, Phil did. That was the only part I didn't like, leaving the man absolutely distraught. They say he couldn't even face seeing the spot Hadrian had disappeared. Anyway, I got my new passport, and got on with my life. Until all this unsolved-cases business came along. I was all in favour of the force improving their clean-up rates but never imagined they'd look at this one.'

'And you leaned on them to stop it?'

'I told them I wasn't at all happy. For heaven's sake, why pick on a missing person case when there were a load of others involving real criminals? I think they thought it would be — shall we say, a soft target?'

'Leaned on whom, precisely? Ms Dundy, we need names. Now.'

Dundy's smile was steely. 'That would be to incriminate myself and them.'

Fran returned smile for smile. 'Your phone will give plenty of evidence. And I can tell you now, we'll be investigating from the chief constable downwards. Let me mention some names. Then you can tell me how you know them — where you met, and so on. We'll start with the chief constable, shall we?'

'Of course I know him. I meet him every day.'

'Of course you do,' Naz said soothingly. 'But when and where did you first meet?'

'I can't recall.'

'How about Mr Webster?'

'Another stupid question. Since he's assistant chief constable we're also in pretty much daily contact.'

'And you first met where?'

'Here. Here at Hindlip.'

'Really? Very well,' Fran continued, her instincts giving a sudden twitch, 'when did you first meet his wife?'

Dundy rolled her eyes. 'Here at Hindlip, of course.'

Fran pounced, 'Why *of course*?'

'Because she's head of Human Resources, isn't she?'

'What do heads of HR do?' Fran wondered aloud. 'They have access to everyone's files, including those of visiting freelance consultants, don't they?'

Dundy's face closed. 'I've had enough of this. I wish to return home.' But she added, perhaps foolishly, 'I won't answer any more questions till I have my lawyer with me.'

'Of course. I'll make sure you can make your phone call and I'll organize some refreshment for you,' said Fran, forgetting she couldn't. She got to her feet, and was already at the door when she turned to ask casually, 'Though it would be really good if you could tell us how long you've known Ann.'

'Ann Sumner? We go back — No, no comment. I told you no more questions!'

CHAPTER TWENTY-SIX

Mark and Dan walked together up the Garbutts' drive, Mark deliberately breaking step so they didn't seem to be marching. Mrs Garbutt must have been caught unawares; she opened the door fully.

Standing, they dominated the already crowded room. Mark would have sat down, but Dan walked over to the fireplace, clearly happy to maintain his authority. 'We've come,' he said, 'to apologize for losing some of the memorabilia you entrusted to us. We hope it'll come to light as we investigate other problems that have arisen in connection with the case, but I'm truly sorry. Some newspaper cuttings — we think that's all.'

Surely Mark caught a puzzled glance flying between the Garbutts? But he'd let Dan press on and come back to the cuttings when everyone thought he'd forgotten them.

'Everything else is safely bagged and logged. We hope to return it within twenty-four hours.' He was a good speaker, eye-contacting each person in turn, pausing longer than many would have dared before the next point. 'But we do have some good news.' Another, longer pause — heavens, had the man been taking lessons from Edwina? Slowly he took from his inside pocket his mobile. 'He who was lost is now found. Here is the latest picture of a very fine young man.' He showed the tiny image to each in turn. And waited for a reaction.

When he got no more than a silence, not delighted or relieved, but stunned, baleful or resentful according to which face he looked at, he returned the phone to his pocket. And looked at Mark, as if expecting him to pull a conversational rabbit from a non-existent hat.

He obliged: 'You all knew, didn't you? Why don't I tell you what we think happened? We believe that for whatever reason, Natalie decided to leave her husband, taking her children with her. But he was a possessive man, and would have fought with every means at his disposal to keep them — not her, perhaps. He sacked you, Anna: perhaps you'll tell us why later. But I suspect that you had already become a close friend of Natalie's, and agreed to help her. Perhaps because of the weather, you didn't make the rendezvous point, and so Natalie decided to come to you, wherever you were parked, leaving her vehicle where it was — even if it meant abandoning her dying son.'

Surely by now he should have had a general response, people murmuring in protest or shock. But they all regarded him impassively. It was surely meant to be unnerving and it was.

'Anna? Am I correct so far?'

'He was already dead,' Anna snapped. 'There's no way she'd have left him if he'd still been alive! She loved him. It broke her heart even doing that. But she had another son to protect.'

'So she gathered him up and ran with him to the pick-up point — one near the A456, I'd imagine. You drove her to an airport? And saw her on a flight to . . . ?'

'Italy. My parents helped her with clothes, money, things for the journey. If she'd wanted, she could have stayed with them. But then she left for Buenos Aires.'

'Why Argentina?' Dan asked.

She gave a snort of laughter. 'Love, of course. For a footballer she'd met through Phil. They're still together. Very rich.

Though she told me she settled all Phil's cash on Adrian.' She pronounced it Aydree-arn. It sounded far more glamorous than the English Adrian, if not as overblown as Hadrian.

Mark wasn't sure how far to trust her. 'But as soon as you knew we wanted to question you, you fled to Italy. Why bother?'

She spread her hands. 'Since you've been here, we've all been — paranoid, I suppose. Perhaps I wanted to pull the wool over your eyes. But I'd have much preferred you not to contact my employers. That was a breach of my privacy.'

Mark bowed, non-committally. 'But all of you have been involved one way or another. Ted, you pulled a certain amount of wool, too, didn't you? And I suspect it'd take a man with your strength to deal with Edwina's floodgate, if not the culvert that someone kindly blocked. Criminal damage, that. As for hitting poor Edwina — I'm downright ashamed of you. Leaving her face down in the water, too. It was only by chance that Fran and Paula turned up. You might have had the death of a good woman on your hands.'

'No good your pointing a finger at me, Mark. That wasn't me. I put my hands up to the culvert: never did like the idea of all these holiday lets when there are decent local folk who can't buy homes. And I thought it'd give that Fran of yours something real to whinge about too.'

That was one thing Mark would try to keep off the record. 'And Edwina deserved to be assaulted?' He turned to Sandra Mould. 'She's a friend of yours! Why be part of a group committing nasty little crimes like that? Against a totally innocent woman who loved Natalie as much as any of you do?'

'I asked you at the meeting: what right do you have to come to our village and poke your nose into things that don't concern you? Things that are best left undisturbed anyway?' In a younger woman her movement would have been a flounce. 'Edwina's such a stupid woman when she's in her cups: so damned indiscreet.'

'I'd like to take that as a denial that you touched her? Very well, if it wasn't Ted, who was it? No?' He looked around feeling for all the world like a teacher about to keep a class in. 'Ah, one person who isn't here today. The woman Iris doesn't like, eh, Ted? Bethan Carter?'

The silence spoke.

'Don't worry, we'll soon run her to earth,' Dan declared, even if he'd never heard of the woman before.

'Was it you who stole the paperwork, then, Ted? Or did you get Iris to do that? But it must have been you who tried to hack into the iPad. Right? After all, you help teach IT. Sorry you won't get full marks for that attempt.'

'Always assuming I made it. I'd say the burden of proof lies with you.' He smiled confidently. 'Or rather, your new puppet master.' He glared at Dan.

'And there's another important issue: who's your mole inside Hindlip? The one who squealed as soon as we tried to access CCTV coverage that would have included any visitors to our corridor?'

Ted narrowed his eyes. 'Reckon that's another job for you IPCC people to find out. Earn your corn for a change.'

Mark left that one to Dan. But the younger man ignored the jibe, turning instead to the Garbutts. 'Mr and Mrs Garbutt, my apology still stands. But I wish, I dearly wish, that you had told someone about this right at the start. I presume you knew all about it.'

'Then you presume wrong,' Mrs Garbutt declared. 'I'd have told her outright, I can see why you don't want any more children, I can see why you don't want him to hit you any more, I can see you don't want your nanny assaulted. But you get yourself a proper divorce. That's what I'd have said. Get yourself some fancy lawyers. Get court orders. Do the thing right.'

'But she never got the chance, see,' Mr Garbutt said quietly. 'We know she's all right, because we get letters she sends via — via a number of people,' he ended lamely. 'When we saw that that bloody PI might ask the postie if he ever delivered letters from abroad to our house.'

Mark's head shot up. 'Fran said she didn't think you knew about the PI, Mrs Garbutt. You became very angry when he was mentioned.'

'Of course I was angry. I was angry anyone knew.'

She wasn't going to tolerate much more, so Mark had to take his chance. 'Just for the record, Mrs Garbutt, so we can deal with whoever was responsible for stealing your property. As a matter of interest, what was in the cuttings you saved with Natalie's other stuff? You saved so very little it seems—'

Mr Garbutt blinked. 'What's all this rubbish you're talking? We saved loads of stuff. It's in the loft.'

'Shut up, you old fool!'

But he continued, 'And we never saved any newspaper cuttings.'

'Nothing about a man faking his death in a canoe accident?'

'No. No. Why should we?'

Before he could ask about the stuff in the loft, even if he'd thought it appropriate to do so, Mrs Garbutt was on her feet. 'Clear out, all of you. Father over there's had enough. Go on. Clear out.'

* * *

What was it about retiring? For more than thirty years her stomach had tolerated only getting food when it was offered some — and often had to do without for long periods of time. Now it was disgracing her by rumbling insistently. Fortunately neither Naz nor Sumner seemed aware of it. Wrong. After five more minutes of stonewalling from Sumner, Naz held up a quietly authoritative hand. 'We're getting nowhere fast, aren't we? I'll ask someone to organize a cup of tea for us. Naturally I'd like to take possession of your mobile, DCI Sumner. Thanks.' He had his hand on the door before he turned. 'All your mobiles, actually, DCI Sumner. Thanks.'

Fran followed him from the room.

'It's like extracting teeth, isn't it?' he said. 'I could do with a breather, couldn't you?' He detailed the uniformed constable sitting outside to stay where he was; if Sumner wanted a toilet break he had to summon one of the women staff who made up the rest of Dan's team to accompany her.

To Fran's surprise, he led the way out of the building. 'Do you know where we can get a sarnie at this time of day? The pubs'll have finished serving long since, won't they?'

'Sainsbury's? Why not the canteen?' But she knew the answer before he gave it.

'Once or twice in your career, you must have walked into a big room where everyone loathed you? Hisses, muffled boos? In my job I certainly have. And you have to choose at random from wrapped sandwiches because someone might have spat in the soup or put crap in a salad? I'm not exposing either of us to that. Of course, it may be Sumner they loathe, and I can't have them doing that to her food on my watch. Can you navigate?'

'I can and I will.' Her phone rang. 'But I have to take this. It's from our best witness yet.'

'I seem to have stirred up quite a hornet's nest,' Marion Roberts declared. 'This morning I've had two separate telephone calls from the police, advising me not to speak to you again. Furthermore, I was asked whether I didn't think it advisable to retract what I said to you last week. After all these years, apparently, my memory might be at fault,' she added.

'And this caller,' Fran asked, almost seeing the glint in Marion's eye, 'was male or female?'

'Female. At first I thought it might be that nice young woman you brought along, but then I wasn't so sure. My memory may still be acute, but my ears are less satisfactory.'

'I shall send Mark round to proselytize: he has a pair of little miracles to help his.'

'Please bring him. I would love to meet you again before you head back to Kent.'

'And I you. Now, because this is germane to something I'm working on right now, could you recall the time of the calls? I'd like to have a few minutes' conversation with the caller.'

'One was at nine fifty-five; the other at eleven forty. Before you go, may I ask you about that colleague of yours? Why was she so distraught? Was it simply the talk of sick and dying children that upset her?'

'I think so,' she said, suddenly quite sure there was more to it than that. She added, not sure if it would convince Marion any more than it convinced herself, 'She's been very much on edge through the whole case.'

They made their goodbyes. But Fran was already planning what question she'd ask Sumner when they resumed.

* * *

But it wasn't Sumner she spoke to first. It was Paula, whom she took to a soft interview room, complete with teddy bears and tissues. 'How long has Sumner been blackmailing you, Paula?'

The young woman put her hands up as if physically to fend off the question.

But Fran persisted. 'You remember how you brought your kids in to work the day you rescued us. They got a bit lively. I presume you'd penned them in your car while you were busy in our office and in the incident room and they'd got bored. The next morning you told me how hard it was not to smack them. You were more upset than I'd have expected. Far more. But not if someone else had already seen you smack them and had mentioned that they could always get social services involved, which might end in your losing your kids and would certainly result in your losing your job — one on which your family depends. Right? And your blackmailer didn't want you to do much — just to keep her informed of our goings on by hacking our iPad and so on. I think you're the victim, here, Paula. Blackmail's a criminal offence.'

'So is hitting your kids.'

'Often?'

'Just the once. In Sainsbury's. They smashed six dozen eggs. Sumner saw me.'

'Of course she did. We certainly didn't see anything more than normal parental anger. But perhaps if you thought it would do you good, HR might arrange some counselling.'

'HR? With the ACC's wife in charge? You've got to be joking. It'd be all round the force in three minutes flat. She's got a good little network of serfs, too.'

Mark would have smiled at the old-fashioned term. Fran just clasped Paula's hand. 'We were going to donate our fee to the Police Benevolent Fund. We still will, most of it. But first there's an officer sitting right here who needs help. We'll pay for as much counselling as you need. Understand? By the way,' she added casually, 'just tell me why Stu came up with that idea about a newspaper cutting?'

'He'd sussed me out. He just came up with the idea of something that would never be found.'

'But why lie? Why not say there was nothing amiss?'

'Because he wanted to warn you that there were security problems without dobbing me in. And because he's just being Stu. I've never fathomed him out — don't suppose I ever will.'

* * *

Dan waited for the others to drive away before starting the car.

'You're very brave,' Mark said. 'I'd have been off like a shot. They're probably waiting round the next bend to ambush you.'

'I'll sit here a bit longer then and let them get bored. My God, won't our friends at the Crown Prosecution Service have a lovely time deciding what to do with that lot!'

'You think some of them will be taken to court?'

'You can't have people going round whacking old ladies on the head and causing criminal damage. Maybe we can get them to accept a caution apiece. However, that really is a job for the local lads, assuming there are any of them left when we've given Hindlip a thorough going over.'

Despite himself, Mark was shocked. 'Ninety-nine point nine per cent of them will be good decent officers, hard-working and conscientious.'

'Point taken. We shall just have to find that nought point one per cent, won't we?' He paused to take a call.

Mark listened intently, even turning up the volume on his aids. And was rewarded. Sumner had undisclosed debts; Dundy's promise of promotion — one which, of course, she wasn't entitled to make — had ensured enthusiastic cooperation.

CHAPTER TWENTY-SEVEN

'The thing about legs,' Dean said helpfully, 'is that the top half is connected to the bottom half by a knee. And they're also connected to hips, which have a pretty close relationship to backs. And via the back to the neck. So while you may think you've just got a stiff neck, I'd point out there's a lot of tension just here—' he paused to let Fran squeak as a point halfway between her shoulder and her spine exploded. 'And so on. So, before we adjourn to Turners Restaurant, and while Mark sleeps, you talk to me to take your mind off what I have to do.'

Fran shifted on Dean's treatment table in the clinic attached to his house. Mark was theoretically watching TV, but she wouldn't argue with Dean's analysis of the situation. Not after Mark's game of tennis earlier in the day. A man his age against a professional sportsman. But he'd enjoyed buying new kit from the club shop.

'Just as Phil Foreman used to do,' she observed.

'Quite. But clearly you have a different viewpoint. And remember, what's said in this room stays in this room. Even twenty years on.'

'First up,' she said, wincing under a probing thumb, 'there's good news. Hadrian is now Adrian.' She attempted the Spanish pronunciation. 'Yes, thanks to your information about his ball skills, we managed to track him down. He plays polo.'

Dean whistled. 'The rich man's sport.'

'Heading for the Argentinian national team, apparently. No doubt his mother pays all the bills. And her husband of the last nineteen years.'

'Ah, she married her footballer, did she? I hoped it would last.'

'You sound like a kindly priest.'

'This muscle says you could do with some kindness.'

'So it does,' she agreed. 'What I can't understand — because unlike you they didn't have to observe professional silence — is why the people we spoke to didn't simply come clean. All Natalie's parents had to do the first time I saw them was to put their hands up and tell me the truth. I'd have said "Well done, Natalie" and legged it back to Kent as soon as the weather would let me.'

'People get locked into their stories. Perhaps they need to rewrite their own stories to make them bearable.' He worked on a knot. 'So many of my patients lie to me about their injuries, you know. They swear blind that they've done the exercises I've suggested, or contrariwise that they've rested when it's clear they've been out jogging.'

Fran acknowledged the temptation with a chuckle. 'But my physios always found out within two minutes: it wasn't worth it. And I did want to get fit quickly — walking up the aisle on crutches was never on my agenda. So, for once in my life, I did as I was told.'

'So if I suggest you try Pilates, you might give it a go?'

'I play tennis regularly,' she bridled.

'But I bet you still play as if it's badminton. Get yourself a coach and use the correct muscles. And give Pilates a try for the sake of all the others. OK?'

'OK.'

'Good. To go back to your question, if Natalie's parents wouldn't come clean, how could the others?'

'Not without damning old friends. You're right, of course.' But if she could accept the community's silence, she found it hard to take the collateral damage. Edwina might be prepared to forgive and forget, but Dan and the Crown Prosecution Service might not be so keen to condone the assault, to which Bethan, perhaps even now ogling the interviewing officers, had confessed. Alex, the letting agent, was apparently pressing for action against Ted; at very least he wanted restitution, as did the property owner and her insurers. And restitution would be better than a criminal record, so he might agree.

'So what happens now?'

'I wish I knew. It's so frustrating not being part of the process. We've got to pack our bags and walk away.' They were taking Marion to lunch before they set off for home the following day. As for Edwina, they were worried about her and her future. But perhaps belonging in the village would trump being a snitch.

'Surely you've always had to do that — to hand decisions to a jury.'

'Of course. But I've always been able to discuss with the Crown Prosecution Service the best way forward. This time it's simply none of my business.' She'd made it her business to help Paula, of course, and had given Stu a bit of an earful, though she'd made it clear she understood his motives. As for Robyn, she'd been back in court again; all she could do was text her to wish her well. She wouldn't search out Iris and talk her into withdrawing her resignation: in her position she'd have felt too compromised. As for Ted, would he lose his job? Not her business. 'Hell's bells! What's that you're doing?'

'That's you getting tense again. Go on, let the tension go. That's better. Now, let's just work on this area here, and then you can have a drink of water and join Mark . . .'

And tomorrow, tomorrow, they could go home.

* * *

'I wanted to thank you, Mrs Roberts, for all the assistance you've given during the course of this enquiry. Ms Harman said it was invaluable, in more ways than you know.' Naz smiled his handsome smile, and looked across to Fran and Mark, who were about to take the old lady to lunch.

'But what a waste of police time and resources, all because one stupid young man couldn't get my statement right twenty years ago.'

'Couldn't or wouldn't?'

Mrs Roberts's smile was one of pure delight. 'What an observant young man you are. Why do you ask? Oh, I suppose that's a question I'm not supposed to ask. After all these years, it's hard to tell. But what I'd like you to do is reach something down from the loft for me. A desk diary. Come with me.'

Naz obeyed; Fran and Mark inspected her books.

Mrs Roberts was carrying the diary when she returned. 'When I retired, I was afraid I'd go gaga if I didn't keep my brain active. So I made myself write down from memory all sorts of trivia. But you may find it less trivial — who knows? I recorded the name of the constable who took my statement. See? If you have any doubts about its authenticity as a contemporary record, I'm sure your forensics team will be able to dismiss them. Now, some people have a good memory for faces.'

'I have myself, actually, Mrs Roberts,' he explained.

She clapped her hands with pleasure. 'Well, I can't pick out villains in crowds, but when two or three weeks after I gave my statement I saw the dim young man who took it canoodling with a young woman I'd seen in TV shots of press conferences, I took enough notice to jot that down too, together with the name of the pub where I saw them. I had it in mind to complain to the police, but thought they'd write me off as a nosy old busybody. I have no doubt, Naz, that if I saw them now I'd be able to identify them. From photographs or in the flesh.' She handed him the diary, open at the page.

Naz nodded seriously. 'You recorded the man's name as Webster. Would this be the same Webster?' He brought up a photo on his laptop.

'It would indeed. He's getting a bit paunchy, isn't he?'

'Thank you. And would you like to look at some images of women and do the same?'

'With pleasure. It so fascinates me that such a small device can hold so much material.' She pointed with a manicured and varnished fingernail. 'That one, Naz. That one. And from some dark corner of my brain, a name is emerging. As it should. She had her name on bylines in local papers for a while. Bettany or Beth something? Well, either they were too wrapped up in each other for him to do his job properly, or she was actively distracting him.'

'May I take this with me? I assure you that I shall take personal responsibility for it.'

She watched him insert it into a plastic bag and write out a receipt.

'Thank you. I trust that you'll use the information both well and wisely. And now I wonder if I might ask you to return the box to the loft before you go. As you can see, Fran and Mark are wearing their best bibs and tuckers; I'd hate them to get dirty before we leave for lunch.'

'Of course. But before I do, would you mind telling me about all those books?' He nodded at the bookshelves.

'Those are for pleasure. And those — well, I celebrated my seventy-fifth birthday by completing a doctorate on the influence of landscape on behaviour.'

EPILOGUE

'Time for a nightcap before we head back to the hotel?' Mark asks. The evening is warm, calm. And tomorrow there's yet another trip to yet another crusader castle. He'd rather not think about that. At least coming with a coach party — a very upmarket coach party — meant he hadn't had to drive up, or even worse, down those terrifying roads.

'Why not?' Fran tucks her hand in his and they set off gently along the Kyrenia sea front, hand in hand. 'Alcohol units on holiday are like calories on holiday: you don't have to count them, do you? And you deserve a reward for going all the way up Saint Hilarion Castle this morning.'

'You know what, I'd rather have stayed behind with the wrinklies with the bad knees or hips. I'm going to have to tackle this damned vertigo — Caffy says she knows a hypnotherapist who might help.'

'That's something to drink to, then. How about that place over there? No, too noisy. And not that Irish bar. How come there are Irish bars all over the world?'

'Because they all show live sport? Bloody hell.' Mark stops dead in his tracks. 'Fran, that guy behind the bar. The one yelling at the other guy.' He moves them closer.

'The tall one about to throttle the shorter one? No, I don't want to be involved in someone else's problems.'

'I think we've been involved in the tall one's problems already, though he doesn't know it. Fran, it's Phil Foreman — got to be, surely. He may have gone to seed a bit, but that's him, isn't it?'

He draws her closer. Shrugging, Fran colonizes a table as far from the bar as possible. He orders them both white wines. The tall guy abandons his victim with a snarl, and reaches for a bottle.

'That's not an Irish accent.' Mark's interrogation skills have completely evaporated, but he gets away with this poor gambit.

'Yorkshire. Mind you, it's probably picked up a few others on the way.' He breaks off to speak to a woman who must once have been startlingly pretty and is still attractive in a sun-baked way. He pulls her to him uxoriously and kisses her, before despatching her with a pat on her bum, though he watches her on her way as she slips into a back room.

'Have one yourself,' Mark suggests as the wine glugs attractively into chilled glasses.

He feels like a PI in a noir movie. No doubt Fran is watching and chuckling.

He returns with the wine, which is unexpectedly good.

'It is him, isn't it?'

'Yes. I pretended I thought I knew him from the TV — I could hardly talk football with my background, could I? The question is, do I — do we — say anything?'

'Two old folk turn up at the bar and on the basis of a glass of nice cold wine tell him his wife and son are still alive?'

'He's got no other children, remember. And there's a handsome, well-turned-out young man the other side of the world. Don't we have some sort of moral duty?'

'Like you'd tell Homer he's got eyesight problems and what he thinks is reddish purple is actually blue so his most quoted line is rubbish? He might not have his son, Mark, but he's got a good marriage — you can see from the body language.'

'Except they're not married. Can't be. Natalie's never been declared dead.'

'And that would stop a man like Phil if he really wanted a wedding? It would have stopped you, but you're a law-abiding goodie, not a guy who half murders an employee in front of a dozen witnesses.'

Mark's not happy. 'It's always been our rule to find out the truth and let other people make of it what they will.'

'Generally speaking, those would be the people who wanted the truth found.'

'Didn't he? He employed that private detective friend of yours.'

'But only for a while. And remember Markwell saw him burn everything connected with Natalie. He's made a new life. A number of new lives. And why not?'

'But he doesn't know he still has a son.' Mark's grief for his daughter was never far away, was it?

'Ask yourself this: if he did find out that Hadrian had been alive all these years, what would he do? Specifically, what would he do to Natalie?'

As one they look to the bar. The argument with the barman has erupted again. Almost unconsciously Mark is on his feet, pushing his way towards the trouble. 'Cool it, Phil, eh?'

The tall man abandons his fight, though he still bunches the barman's T-shirt tight to his throat, to jab a finger at Mark's chest. 'What's it got to do with you, eh? Oi, I was talking to you!'

But Mark is walking back to his table and, leaving the rest of his wine untouched, has taken Fran's hand and is walking back to the hotel.

THE END

ACKNOWLEDGEMENTS

I could not have written this without:

Paul Bethel, ex-Detective Chief Inspector, South Wales Police, who inspired and encouraged me, and provided invaluable information on cold cases.

Ex-Detective Superintendent Mick Turner, now Director of Sancus Solutions, equally inspiring, encouraging and informative.

Lynne Masters, from West Mercia Police Press Office, who provided me with invaluable information about Hindlip Hall and was discretion itself about the people working there.

The staff of West Bromwich Albion Football Club, especially John Simpson, always cheerful and positive however dispiriting the weekend results, and the chair of the Supporters' Club, Alan Cleverley, who is even more charming and knowledgeable than he appears in the novel.

Ivor Higgins, constantly on the watch for typos and other infelicities.

The staff of the Vine pub in Wombourne, who responded to a casual enquiry about their pub sign as if it was as serious as finding the God particle, and also provided lovely food.

All the inhabitants of the Wyre Forest area, none of whom are at all like their fictional counterparts.

THE JOFFE BOOKS STORY

We began in 2014 when Jasper agreed to publish his mum's much-rejected romance novel and it became a bestseller.

Since then we've grown into the largest independent publisher in the UK. We're extremely proud to publish some of the very best writers in the world, including Joy Ellis, Faith Martin, Caro Ramsay, Helen Forrester, Simon Brett and Robert Goddard. Everyone at Joffe Books loves reading and we never forget that it all begins with the magic of an author telling a story.

We are proud to publish talented first-time authors, as well as established writers whose books we love introducing to a new generation of readers.

We won Trade Publisher of the Year at the Independent Publishing Awards in 2023. We have been shortlisted for Independent Publisher of the Year at the British Book Awards for the last four years, and were shortlisted for the Diversity and Inclusivity Award at the 2022 Independent Publishing Awards. In 2023 we were shortlisted for Publisher of the Year at the RNA Industry Awards.

We built this company with your help, and we love to hear from you, so please email us about absolutely anything bookish at feedback@joffebooks.com

If you want to receive free books every Friday and hear about all our new releases, join our mailing list: www.joffebooks.com/contact

And when you tell your friends about us, just remember: it's pronounced Joffe as in coffee or toffee!

ALSO BY JUDITH CUTLER

FRAN HARMAN MYSTERIES

Book 1: COME TO HARM
Book 2: DO NO HARM
Book 3: IN HARM'S WAY
Book 4: NO HARM DONE
Book 5: NO HARM, NO FOUL
Book 6: ROAD TO HARM

DETECTIVE KATE POWER MYSTERIES

Book 1: MURDER THE BOYS
Book 2: MURDER BY THE CANAL
Book 3: MURDER BY ARSON
Book 4: MURDER BY FRAUD
Book 5: MURDER IN DEVON
Book 6: MURDER ON THE JOB

Printed in Dunstable, United Kingdom

81069517R00150